ARSÈNE LUPIN SUPER-SLEUTH

BY MAURICE LEBLANC

Contents

CHAPTER I
... AND THE BLUE-EYED ENGLISH GIRL

Ralph de Limézy was strolling along the boulevards with the careless air of a happy man, who has only to look about him to enjoy the charming sights and the light gaiety which the life of Paris presents to the intelligent observer on certain luminous days in April. Of middle height, he had a figure at once slender and powerful.

As he passed the Gymnase, he had the impression that a man who was walking abreast of him was following a woman, an impression which he was presently able to assure himself was exact.

In the humor he was in nothing appeared more comic and amusing to Ralph than a man who followed a woman.

Only the vast experience of the Baron de Limézy enabled him to divine that this discreet gentleman was following the lady. Ralph de Limézy was no less discreet, and availing himself of the screen afforded by the throng, he quickened his steps in order to make a careful examination of these two persons.

Viewed from behind, the gentleman was distinguished by an impeccable back-parting which divided exactly his black and pomaded hair, and by a coat, no less impeccable, which gave full value to his large shoulders and high waist. Seen from in front, his face was of extreme regularity, furnished with a carefully trimmed beard and a fresh, pink complexion. Thirty years of age perhaps. With a confident walk. Carrying himself with an air of importance. Vulgar in appearance. Rings on his fingers. A gold tip to the cigarette he was smoking.

Ralph again quickened his step. The lady, tall, self-possessed, of noble bearing, set firmly on the pavement an Englishwoman's feet, which were redeemed by well-shaped legs and slim ankles. Her face was uncommonly pretty, lighted by eyes of a wonderful blue, crowned by a heavy mass of fair hair. Those who passed her half stopped and turned to stare after her. She displayed an utter indifference to this homage of the crowd.

"Goodness!" thought Ralph. "What an aristocrat! She deserves something better than that pomaded bounder who is following her. What is he up to? A jealous husband? A jilted lover? Or simply a lady-killer in search of adventure? Yes: that must be it. The fellow wore the air of a man lucky in love who believes himself to be irresistible."

The girl crossed the Place de l'Opera without taking any notice of the vehicles which thronged it. A dray was about to bar her way; she quietly seized the horse's reins and stopped it. The driver jumped down from his seat in a fury and began to abuse her, thrusting his face into hers. She landed a jolting right hook on his nose that sent the blood gushing out of it. A policeman hurried up and demanded an explanation; she turned her back on him and went quietly on her way.

In the Rue Auber two small boys were fighting, she caught them by the scruff of the neck and flung them away from her with such violence that they rolled over and over for a good ten feet. Then she threw a ten-franc note to each of them.

On the Boulevard Haussmann she went into a confectioner's and from a distance Ralph saw her sit down at a table. Since the man who was following her did not enter the shop, he went into it himself and took a seat in a quiet fashion that did not attract her attention to him.

She ordered tea and toast which she ate hungrily with magnificent teeth. The people sitting at the neighboring tables stared at her. She took no notice whatever of them. Presently she ordered more toast.

But another young woman, sitting at a table further off also excited Ralph's curiosity. Fair as the English girl, with wavy hair, dressed less expensively but with a Parisienne's surer taste, she was surrounded by three poorly dressed children, whom she was feeding with cakes and glasses of grenadine.

More of a child than the children themselves, she was amusing herself infinitely as she babbled for the three of them.

"What was it you said to the young lady?"

"Louder ... I did not hear.... No: you shouldn't call me 'Madame'. You should say: 'Thank you, Mademoiselle.' "

Ralph was instantly enslaved by two things: the natural gayety of her expression, and the profound seductiveness of her large green eyes, the color of jade, and streaked with gold, from which one could not tear one's own eyes once one had fixed them on them.

As a rule such eyes are filled with strangeness, thoughtful and melancholy; and that was perhaps the habitual expression of those eyes. But at the moment they diffused the same radiance of intense life as the rest of the face, the mischievous mouth, the dilated nostrils, and the warmly-colored cheeks with smiling dimples.

"Extravagant joys or excessive griefs: there is no mean for creatures of that kind," said Ralph to himself; and he felt spring to sudden birth in him the desire to play a part in those joys and fight those sorrows.

He turned to the English girl again. She was really beautiful, with a powerful beauty compounded of balance, poise, and quietness. But he found the girl with the green eyes, as he called her, far more fascinating. If one admired the former, one desired to know the latter, to discover the secret of her existence.

Nevertheless, when she had paid her bill and left the confectioner's with the three children, he hesitated. Should he follow her? Or should he stay where he was? Which should carry the day? Green eyes? Blue eyes?

He rose hastily, dropped some money on the counter and went out into the street. The green eyes had their way with him.

As he came out his eyes fell on an unexpected sight. The girl with the green eyes stood on the curb talking to the lady-killer who, a little while before, had been following the English girl, with the air of a timid or jealous sweetheart. It was animated, heated talk too, on both sides–more like a dispute than a talk. It was evident that the young girl was trying to pass the lady-killer and that the lady-killer would not let her; and this was so evident that Ralph was, contrary to every convention, on the point of interposing.

He had no time to do so. A taxi stopped in front of the confectioner's; a man sprang out of it who seemed to have already taken in the altercation on the curb, for he stepped up to the squabbling pair, raised his stick and with a hearty whack sent the lady-killer's hat flying off his pomaded head.

Dumfounded, he started back, then, careless of the people hurrying up, sprang forward and howled: "You're mad! Absolutely mad!"

The newcomer, who was smaller and older, threw himself into a posture of defense, and, ready to strike, shouted:

"I've forbidden you to speak to this young lady! I'm her father and I tell you that you're nothing but a rotter—a miserable rotter!"

Both of them were fairly shaking with spasms of hate. The lady-killer, stung by the insult, drew himself up to spring on the newcomer, whom the young girl had gripped by the arm and was trying to drag to the taxi. He had succeeded in separating them and snatching the newcomer's cane, when he found himself glaring into a face which had suddenly interposed between him and his adversary, an unknown, curious face, the right eye of which was winking nervously, and the mouth, curved into an expression of the grimmest irony, holding a cigarette.

It was Ralph who had thus risen before him; and he said in harsh accents:

"Could you oblige me with a light?"

A truly inopportune request. What was this interloper up to? The pomaded one bristled.

"Clear off! I haven't any matches!" he snapped.

"But you have. A minute ago you were smoking," the interloper asserted.

Beside himself, the lady-killer tried to thrust him away. Not succeeding in doing so and being unable even to move his arms, he looked down to see what was paralyzing them. He appeared thunderstruck. The two hands of the interloper gripped his hands in such a manner that it was impossible to move them. An iron band could not have paralyzed them more thoroughly. And the interloper did not cease to repeat in obstinate, worrying accents:

"Please oblige me with a light. It would be most unfortunate if you were to refuse me a light."

The group that had gathered round them began to laugh. The exasperated lady-killer snarled:

"Will you leave me alone? I tell you I haven't got a light!"

The interloper shrugged his shoulders with a melancholy air.

"Most uncivil, I call it," he said mournfully. "I never heard of any one refusing a light when he was asked for it politely. But since you make such a fuss about rendering me this slight service—"

He loosed his grip. The liberated lady-killer turned and ran. But the taxi had gathered speed and was bearing away his adversary and the girl with the green eyes, at a pace that made it quite plain that the most strenuous effort on his part to catch them would prove vain.

"And a lot forwarder I've got," said Ralph watching him run. "I play the Don Quixote to a lovely unknown; and she rushes off without giving me her name and address! There isn't a chance of finding her. Well?"

Well, he decided to return to the English girl. She also was withdrawing, having doubtless been a witness of the row. He followed her.

He found himself at one of those periods at which life is in a way suspended between the past and the future. When one is thirty years old, it is woman who appears to us to hold in her hands the key of our destiny. Since the green eyes had vanished he would guide his wavering steps by the light of the blue.

Then, almost immediately, having pretended to set out in the opposite direction and returned on his steps, he perceived that the pomaded lady-killer had betaken himself once more to the chase, and, rebuffed in one quarter had turned, like himself, to the other. And all three of them resumed their stroll without the English girl perceiving the maneuvers of her followers.

She walked along the crowded pavement, strolling quietly all the while, with a keen eye on the shop windows and careless of the homage lavished on her beauty. Strolling thus, she came to the Place de La Madeleine, and by way of the Rue Royale, reached the Faubourg Saint-Honoré and entered the Grand Hotel Concordia. The lady-killer stopped, walked on about fifty yards, bought a packet of cigarettes, came back, entered the hotel. Three minutes later he came out and went off; and just as Ralph was about to question the clerk about the English girl, she herself came out of the hall and entered a car to which a servant had carried a small trunk. Was she then off on her travels?

Ralph hailed a taxi and said to the driver: "Follow that car."

The English girl did some shopping and at eight o'clock stopped at the Paris-Lyon Station; there she went into the refreshment room and ordered dinner.

Ralph dined at a distant table.

When she had finished her dinner she smoked a couple of cigarettes and then she made her way to the 9.46 express.

Ralph considered for a few moments, then made up his mind. Those blue eyes were certainly worth a journey. Moreover it was in following those blue eyes that he had made the acquaintance of the green eyes; and it might be that by way of the English girl he might find the lady-killer and by way of the lady-killer come to the green eyes again.

He turned quickly and bought a ticket to Monte Carlo and hurried to the platform.

He saw the English girl step into the third compartment of car No. 5, slipped into the middle of a group and saw her, through the window, taking off her cloak.

There were but few passengers. It was some years before the war, the end of April, and this express, without sleeping or restaurant car, was too uncomfortable to carry more than a few first-class passengers to the South. Ralph indeed only saw two, both men, who were in the compartment just in front of the one occupied by the English girl in car No. 5.

He strolled up and down the platform some distance from the car, hired two pillows, provided himself with a traveling library of papers and magazines, and when the whistle blew jumped on to the step, opened the door, and entered the third compartment of car No. 5 in the manner of a man who has caught the train by the skin of his teeth.

The English girl was alone in the corner by the window facing the engine; Ralph settled down, with his back to the engine, in the corner next to the corridor. She raised her eyes and glanced at the intruder, carelessly enough, and went on eating chocolates from the box open on her knee.

A conductor walked down the corridor and punched their tickets. The train rushed towards the outskirts; and the lights of Paris grew farther and farther between. Ralph ran his eye listlessly over the evening papers and since he found nothing to interest him in them, cast them aside.

"Nothing happening," he said to himself. "Not even a sensational crime. How much more interesting is this young lady."

The finding of one's self alone in a small closed compartment with a pretty unknown lady, of passing the night together and sleeping in the same compartment, had always appeared to him a rather diverting anomaly. But he saw no use in wasting time in reading magazines or in meditating or exchanging furtive glances. He moved to the middle of the seat. The English girl could not doubt that her traveling companion was about to speak to her, and, wholly unmoved, she neither seemed to avoid it nor to lend herself to it. The burden therefore of establishing relations fell upon Ralph alone. That did not worry him at all. In an infinitely respectful tone he said:

"However incorrectly I may be acting I should like to ask your permission to inform you of a fact which may be of importance to you. May I say a few words?"

She selected another chocolate and, without turning her head, said quietly: "If it's only a matter of a few words, sir, you may."

"Well, madam—"

"Mademoiselle," she interjected.

"Well, mademoiselle, I happen to know that you've been followed all day in an uncommonly equivocal manner by a well-dressed man, who kept out of your sight, and—"

She interrupted him to say: "Your behavior is of an incorrectness which astonishes me on the part of a Frenchman. It is no business of yours to keep an eye on the people who follow me."

"It was because the fellow appeared to me a suspicious—"

"The gentleman, with whom I am acquainted—he was introduced to me last year—M. Marescal, at least has the delicacy to follow me at a distance and not to invade my compartment."

Ralph, touched on the raw, bowed.

"Good, mademoiselle, a direct hit. I can only say no more," he said mournfully.

"You can only say no more till the next station, where I advise you to get out," she said drily.

"A thousand regrets. But business calls me to Monte Carlo," he protested.

"It called you to Monte Carlo only when you knew that I was going there," she said coldly.

"No, mademoiselle," Ralph contradicted flatly. "Ever since I perceived you–hours ago–in a confectioner's shop on the Boulevard Haussmann."

The retort came swiftly.

"Inaccurate sir. Your admiration for the young person with the green eyes would certainly have drawn you along in her wake, if you had been able to rejoin her after that row in the street. Not being able to do that, you set out on my tracks–at first as far as the Hotel Concordia, like the person you have denounced to me, then to the railway refreshment room."

Ralph was frankly amused,

"I am indeed flattered that so few of my actions and movements have escaped you, mademoiselle," he said smiling.

"Nothing escapes me, sir," she said firmly.

"So I see. I expect that for two pins you would tell me my name."

"Ralph de Limézy, explorer, just returned from Tibet and Central Asia."

He could not hide his astonishment.

"I'm still more flattered. May I ask you as a result of what enquiry–"

"As a result of no enquiry," she said quickly. "But when a lady sees a man come bursting into her compartment at the last minute, without as much as a suit-case, she owes it to herself to observe. You cut two or three pages of your magazine with one of your visiting cards. I read that card and I remembered a recent interview in which Ralph de Limézy gave an account of his last expedition. It's quite simple."

"Quite simple," he agreed. "But one must have wonderful eyes to—"

"My eyes are excellent," she said quickly,

"But they have never left your box of chocolates. And you're already at the eighteenth chocolate," he said.

"I have no need to look to see, nor to think to guess," she retorted.

"To guess what?"

"To guess that your real name is not Ralph de Limézy," she said coolly. "If it were, the initials at the bottom of your hat would not be an H. and a V.... Always supposing that you are not wearing a friend's hat."

Ralph began to lose patience. It annoyed him that in any duel he chanced to be fighting his adversary should constantly get the better of him.

"And what, according to you, does this H. and V. stand for?" he asked with just a touch of warmth in his tone.

She crunched up her nineteenth chocolate and answered in the same careless tone:

"They are initials which you rarely find joined; and when by any chance I do come across them together my mind always makes an involuntary connection between them and the initials of two names that were once brought to my notice."

She stopped and apparently was not going to continue. He said a trifle impatiently:

"And might I ask what they are?"

"If I were to tell you it would not enlighten you. The first is a name you never heard of," she assured him.

"All the same?"

"Well, if you must know, it is Horace Valmont."

"And who is Horace Valmont?"

"Horace Valmont is one of the numerous false names behind which was hidden—"

She paused to yawn.

"Behind which was hidden?" he said yet more impatiently.

"Arsène Lupin."

Ralph burst out laughing.

"Then I must be Arsène Lupin!" he cried.

"What an idea!" she protested quickly. "I only told you the remembrance called up in my mind, quite stupidly, by the letters in your hat. And I say to myself, also quite stupidly, that your pleasing name of Raoul de Limézy is uncommonly like the pleasing name of Ralph d'Andrésy, by which Arsène Lupin was also known."

"An excellent answer, Mademoiselle. But if I had the honor to be Arsène Lupin, believe me I should not be playing the rather simple part I am now playing. With what mastery do you make a joke of the innocent Limézy!"

She held out the box of chocolates to him.

"A chocolate to console you for your defeat," she said. "And now, let me go to sleep."

"But surely our conversation is not going to stop at this point?" he said in pleading accents.

"No. If the innocent Limézy does not interest me, on the other hand people who have some one else's name always excite my curiosity. What are their reasons? Why do they disguise themselves? A rather perverse curiosity...."

"A curiosity which a Bakersfield may permit herself," he said a trifle clumsily. And he added. "As you see, Mademoiselle, I know your name as well as mine."

"And so does Cook's clerk," she said laughing.

"Well," said Ralph, "I'm beaten. I shall take my revenge at the first opportunity."

"Opportunity most often presents itself when one is not seeking it," she said gravely.

For the first time she frankly looked fairly and squarely into his eyes. He quivered.

"As lovely as you are mysterious," he murmured.

"Not the least mysterious," she protested. "My name is Constance Bakersfield. I am joining my father, Lord Bakersfield, at Monte Carlo, and I am going to play golf with him. Besides golf, I am fond of all games, and I contribute to the papers to increase my allowance and feel independent. My profession of reporteress enables me to have first hand information about all celebrities, statesmen, generals, chiefs of industry, and chevaliers d'industrie, great artists and illustrious burglars. I wish you goodnight, sir."

Even as she spoke she was drawing over her face the folds of a shawl. She stretched herself at full length on the seat, drew a rug over herself, and buried her fair head in the pillow.

Ralph who had started at the word "burglar" again spoke to her two or three times. His words did not seem to reach her ears; it was like knocking against a closed door. It was better to keep silent and wait for his revenge. He remained silent therefore in his corner, disconcerted by the way the adventure had turned out, but in his heart of hearts charmed and full of hope. What a delightful creature, original and ravishing, mysterious and so frank! And gifted with what keen powers of observation! What an insight she had shown into his motives! How she had revealed the slight errors which his contempt of danger sometimes allowed him to commit! In the matter of those two initials—

He took his hat from the rack, tore the silk lining out of it, stepped into the corridor, and threw it out of the window. Then he also laid himself at full length on the seat, buried his head in his two pillows and fell into an idle reverie. Life wore a rosy hue. His note-case was full of notes easily gained. Twenty profitable plans that he could certainly carry out jostled one another in his ingenious brain, and next morning he would awake with the pleasing sight of a charming girl in the corner facing him.

He dwelt on this thought with uncommon pleasure; presently in a doze he saw her beautiful blue eyes, the color of heaven. Then a strange thing happened. Slowly, to his surprise, they changed color and became green, the color of the sea. He was no longer quite sure whether it was the eyes of the English girl or of the Parisienne that gazed at him in this half-light. Then the young Parisienne was smiling at him, a charming smile. In the end it was really she who slept on the seat facing him; and with a smile on his lips and an easy conscience he went to sleep himself.

He did not hear the opening of the door of the collapsible passageway, which was the means of communication with the car behind them, nor the stealthy approach of the three masked figures, clothed in long grey blouses, who came to a halt at the door of his compartment.

One of the men, revolver in hand, remained to keep watch in the corridor. The two others chose their quarries by signs and drew blackjacks from their pockets. The one was to strike the nearest passenger, the other the passenger who was sleeping under the rug.

The signal of attack was given in a low voice, but low though it was, the murmur reached Ralph's ear. He awoke and instantly the muscles of his arms and legs contracted. It was too late; the blackjack hit his forehead and stunned him. He scarcely felt his assailant's grip on his throat; he did not see the figure that passed him fall upon Miss Bakersfield.

After that came a night of the blackest darkness into which he sank like a drowning man. Then came incoherent and painful impressions which later rose to the surface of consciousness. Some one bound him and gagged him with feverish energy and wrapped his head in a rough piece of cloth. He was relieved of his bank notes.

"Good business!" murmured a voice. "But this is only the *hors d'oeuvre*. Have you tied up the other one?"

"The blow must have stunned him all right."

On the instant it became clear that the blow had not stunned the other one sufficiently, and that that other one was resolved not to be tied up, for there came suddenly the noise of oaths and blows, of a furious struggle all over the opposite seat, then cries—then cries of a woman.

"Curse it! It's a woman!" growled one of the voices. "She's scratching and biting like hell. Here: do you recognize her?"

"You're the one to recognize her, not me," snapped the other.

"I must make her shut up first!"

The ruffian employed such means that little by little the girl grew quieter. Her cries grew fainter and sank to moans. Nevertheless she went on struggling; and Ralph was aware, as in a nightmare, of all the efforts of the assailant and her efforts to resist him.

Suddenly the struggle came to an end. A third voice from the corridor, evidently that of the man on watch, gave an order in a hushed voice.

"Stop! Leave her alone! I hope to God you haven't killed her!"

"I'm jolly well afraid I have. In any case I may as well search her," said the voice of the ruffian who had been struggling with the girl.

"Stop! Be quiet, dammit!"

Their two assailants left the compartment. There was a discussion, a dispute rather, in the corridor; and Ralph who was recovering more and more of his wits and could now move his limbs, caught the words: "Yes ... further down ... the end compartment ... and be quick about it ... the conductor may come."

One of the three thieves stepped into the compartment and bent down over him and snarled:

"If you move, you're a dead man. Keep quiet!"

The three ruffians went along towards the end compartment in which Ralph had noticed two passengers. Already he was trying to loosen his bonds and working his jaws to get the gag out of his mouth.

Close to him the English girl was moaning more and more feebly in a manner which wrung his heart. He struggled to free himself with all his might, chilled by the fear lest he should be too late to save the unfortunate creature's life. But his bonds were strong and firmly knotted.

However the cloth which blinded him, carelessly tied, suddenly fell to the floor. He saw the young girl on her knees, her elbows on the seat, looking at him with eyes which no longer saw anything.

Then came the sound of shots at a distance. The three masked ruffians and the two passengers must be fighting in the end compartment. Almost on the instant one of the scoundrels came running down the corridor as fast as he could run with a bag in his hand. For two or three minutes the train had been slackening speed. Probably it was compelled to go slower by the fact that the track was being repaired; probably also the thieves had been aware of this and chosen that moment for their attack.

Ralph was at the end of his wits. As he strained against his unbreakable bonds, he succeeded in working his gag loose enough to mutter to the girl:

"For goodness sake hold out.... I shall be able to look after you in a minute.... What's the matter? What have they done to you?"

The brutes must have squeezed the girl's throat inordinately and twisted her neck, for she was black in the face; her features were distorted; she displayed all the symptoms of asphyxiation. Ralph thought that she was on the very point of death. She was gasping and trembling from head to foot.

Her chest was bent over the seat close to him. He could hear the faint harsh sound of her breathing and through what sounded to him the death-rattle he caught a few English words she muttered:

"Monsieur.... Monsieur.... Listen.... I'm done for."

"No!" he cried in anguish. "Try and raise yourself and reach the bell-rope."

She was too feeble to make the effort; and not a chance remained of his being able to free himself, in spite of the superhuman energy with which he strove to do so. Used as he was to make his will prevail, he suffered horribly at being the impotent spectator of this dreadful death. Matters had passed entirely out of his hands; he seemed to turn giddy in a tempestuous whirl of horrible happenings.

The second of the masked scoundrels, revolver in hand, hurried along the corridor. Behind him came the third. Doubtless at the end of the car the two passengers had succumbed to their assault and since the train was moving more and more slowly along the line they were repairing, the murderers were about to escape unhindered.

Then to Ralph's great surprise they stopped short just outside the compartment as if some formidable obstacle barred their way. Ralph guessed that some one had appeared at the entrance of the collapsible passageway—perhaps the conductor making his rounds.

At once there came an outcry of furious voices, then the sound of a struggle. The first thief had no time to use his revolver, which was dashed out of his hand, as a man in the uniform of a railway official grappled with him and tripped him, and the two of them rolled on the floor. While the third scoundrel, a short, slight man whose gray blouse was now red with blood, and whose head was half-hidden by a hat much too large for him, to which was fastened a mask of black sateen, tried to free his comrade from the conductor's grip.

"Good for the conductor!" cried the exasperated Ralph. "Help at last!"

But the conductor was weakening, one of his hands had been put out of action by the ruffian's short, slight accomplice. The ruffian himself got the upper hand and hammered the conductor's face with a shower of blows.

Then the short, slight accomplice rose to his feet and, as he rose, his mask caught in his sleeve and fell, dragging down with it his big hat. With a quick movement he covered his face with the mask and his head with the hat, but not before Ralph saw the fair hair and ravishing face, now livid with terror, of the unknown with green eyes whom he had chanced on that afternoon in the confectioner's on the Boulevard Haussmann.

The tragedy came to an end. The two thieves fled. The astounded Ralph watched without a word the conductor drag himself slowly and painfully up to the communication cord and pull it. The English girl was in her death agony. Almost with her last breath she muttered these incoherent words:

"For God's sake.... Listen to me.... You must take—"

"What? I promise you I will."

"For God's sake take the wallet ... get away the papers to—"

"Where?"

Her head fell back; she was dead.

The train stopped.

CHAPTER II
INVESTIGATIONS

The death of Miss Bakersfield, the savage attack of the three masked ruffians, the probable murder of the two passengers, the loss of his bank-notes, weighed but lightly on Ralph's spirit compared with the incredible vision which had dashed itself as it were against his eyes. The girl with the green eyes! The most charming and ravishing girl he had ever set eyes on rising among the black shadows of a crime! The most radiant image appearing from behind the ignoble mask of a thief and murderer! The girl with the eyes of jade, towards whom his man's instinct had fairly thrust him the very minute he saw her, whom he now found in a blood-stained blouse with panic-stricken face, robbing and murdering along with two horrible assassins!

Although his life of a great adventurer, full as it had been of horrors and ignominy, should have hardened him against the most terrible spectacles, Ralph (let us continue to call him this since it is under this name that Arsène Lupin played his part in this drama) de Limézy remained thunderstruck before a reality in which it was impossible for him to believe or even, in a way, grasp. The actual fact was worse than anything he could imagine.

The conductor opened the window, leaned out, and shouted: "Murder! Murder! Look out for the murderers!"

The workmen within hearing gripped their picks and looked about them. Some way down the line a man shouted and began to run. The others ran after him. The conductor cut Ralph's bonds, listening to his explanations as he did so. Then he bent down over Miss Bakersfield and said:

"This young woman's dead, isn't she?"

"Yes ... strangled. And that isn't all: there are two passengers in the end compartment."

They went quickly to the end of the corridor. In the last compartment were two corpses. There were no signs of a struggle. There was no luggage.

Then some workmen from the line tried to open the door of the corridor facing that compartment. It was stuck. Ralph understood why the three robbers had had to hurry all the way up the corridor to escape by the door at the top of it, which was found to be open.

The workmen came through it; then some passengers came into the car through the collapsible passageway, and they and the workmen were on the point of entering the two compartments, when a loud voice cried in imperious accents:

“Nobody must touch anything! No, my man, leave that revolver where it is. It’s a very important piece of evidence. In fact it would be better that all you people should clear out! The car will be taken off the train at the next station. What do you say, conductor?”

Ralph looked at him and was astounded to recognize the individual who had followed Miss Bakersfield and accosted the girl with the green eyes, the man of whom he had asked a light, in a word the pomaded lady-killer whom Miss Bakersfield had called Monsieur Marescal. Drawn up to his full height at the entry of the compartment in which Miss Bakersfield was lying, he barred the way of the intruders and waved them back towards the open doors.

There he stood till the train ran into the station of Beaucourt and the station master entered the car.

“Ah, there you are, station master,” he cried in a tone of relief. “Will you have the goodness to see to this business at once. Telephone to the nearest police station, send for a doctor and send word to the office of the Public Prosecutor at Romillaud. We are face to face with a crime.”

“With three crimes—murders,” the conductor amended. “Two masked men have escaped, two men who assaulted me.”

“Yes, some of the workmen repairing the line saw them climbing the embankment. There’s a little wood at the top of it; and they’re hunting through it and along the high road. If they catch any one we shall hear about it here," said Marescal.

He uttered the words sternly with an air of authority.

Ralph was growing more and more astonished; then of a sudden his head ceased humming; and he recovered his usual clear-sighted coolness.

The workmen, passengers, and station master trooped out; the car was left empty but for Marescal, the conductor, Ralph, and the dead. Ralph made to return to his seat. Marescal barred his way.

"What do you mean, sir?" cried Ralph indignantly, certain now that Marescal did not recognize him. "I was in this car and I want to go back to it."

"No, sir," replied Marescal. "Every place in which a crime has been committed belongs to justice, and no unauthorized person can enter it."

The conductor intervened.

"This gentleman was one of the victims of the attack. They bound and robbed him."

"I'm sorry," said Marescal. "But the orders are strict."

"What orders?" snapped Ralph.

"Mine."

Ralph crossed his arms.

"That's all very well, but by what right do you give them? It's all very well for you to lay down the law with an insolence that these other people stand. But I am not in the humor to submit to it myself."

The lady-killer held out his visiting card and chanted in pompous accents:

"Rudolph Marescal, Commissary of the International Investigation Department, attached to the Ministry of the Interior."

He had the air of saying: "In the face of such qualifications there is nothing to do but to give way."

He added: "If I have taken charge of the matter it is by agreement with the station master and because my special qualifications authorize me to do so."

Ralph taken aback, controlled himself. The name of Marescal suddenly awoke in his memory the confused remembrance of certain affairs in which it seemed to him that the Commissary had shown cleverness and remarkable clearsightedness. In any case it would be absurd to oppose him.

"It's my fault," he thought. "Instead of acting at once in the matter of the English girl and fulfilling my last promise to her, I wasted time in getting excited about the masked girl. But all the same I'll catch you before I've done with you, my pomaded friend."

In a tone of deference, as if he was quite alive to the prestige conferred by these high qualifications, he said: "Pardon me, Monsieur, little of a Parisian as I am—I spend most of my time out of France—your fame has reached my ears; and I recall among others an affair of earrings."

Marescal seemed to swell slightly.

"Yes, the earrings of Princess Laurentini," he said, pompously. "It wasn't a bad piece of work. I don't mind telling you that before the police, and above all the examining magistrate come on the scene, I should very much like to have carried the inquiry to a point at which——"

"At which," Ralph broke in in a tone of warm approval, "these gentlemen will have nothing to do but draw their conclusions. You are quite right; and I will not continue my journey till to-morrow, if my presence can be of any use to you."

"It would be very useful to me and I'm very much obliged to you for the offer," said Marescal gratefully.

The car was shunted into a siding; the train continued its journey. The conductor had to go with it; but before he went he made his statement

Marescal began his investigations, then evidently with the intention of getting Ralph out off the way, he begged him to go to the station to find some sheets to cover the corpses.

With an air of zeal Ralph bustled off down the corridor and out of the car. Then he slipped back, stepped on to the foot-board and raised his head to the level of the edge of the third window of the corridor.

"Its just as I thought," he said to himself, "my pomaded friend wished to be alone. He had a little preliminary game to play."

Marescal in fact had raised the body of the English girl a little and unbuttoned her coat. Round her waist was a belt to which was fastened a little red leather wallet. He unfastened the clasp and took away the wallet. Then he laid the corpse gently back on the floor and opened the wallet. It contained papers and at once he set about reading them.

Ralph, who could only see his back, could not judge from his expression the effect that the papers had on him. He went off grumbling:

"It's no use your hurrying, comrade, I shall catch you all right before the end of the business. Those papers were bequeathed to me; no one but me has any right to them."

He accomplished the task with which he had been charged and brought back with him the station master's wife and mother who insisted, as was the custom of the country, that they ought to keep watch over the dead. He found one of the workmen from down the line talking to Marescal and learned that two men had been seen hurrying through the wood and that one of them was limping.

"Was that all they found?" asked Ralph.

"Everything," said Marescal. "They did find, on the track these two scoundrels took, a heel stuck between two roots which had gripped it, a heel torn off a shoe, but it was the heel of a woman's shoe."

"Then the workmen had nothing to report," said Ralph in a tone of keen disappointment.

"Nothing," said Marescal a trifle glumly.

They raised the English girl from the floor and laid her on the seat. Ralph gazed at his beautiful and charming traveler for the last time, and murmured beneath his breath: "I shall avenge you, Miss Bakersfield. If I was unable to guard you and save you, I swear that your murderers shall be punished."

He thought of the girl with the green eyes and swore again to take vengeance also on that mysterious creature.

"She was a beautiful creature," he said. "Don't you know her name?"

"How should I know it?" asked Marescal.

"But what about this wallet?"

"It must only be opened in the presence of the public prosecutor," snapped Marescal; then, hastily changing the subject, he added: "The surprising thing is that the scoundrels did not rob her of it."

"It should contain papers," said Ralph, pressing his point.

"We must wait for the public prosecutor," repeated the Commissary firmly. "But in any case it is quite clear that the robbers who stripped you took nothing from her–neither this wrist-watch, nor this brooch, nor this necklace."

His vanity and pretentiousness did not escape Ralph; he said in a tone of awed admiration: "I have an impression, Monsieur Commissary, that you have already made considerable progress towards the discovery of the truth. I feel that you are a master of the detective's art. Would it be possible for you to tell me in a few words what point you have reached?"

"Why not?" said Marescal, taking Ralph's arm and drawing him into the empty compartment next door. "The police won't be long coming, nor will the doctor. In order to make clear my position in the matter and make sure of the reward, I shall be glad to inform you of the preliminary result of my first investigations."

"Go it, old pomade-pot!" said Ralph to himself. "You could not find any one better than me to confide in!"

"Sit down," said Marescal, offering him a cigarette. "I propose to demonstrate two fundamental facts, in my humble opinion, of the greatest importance. The first of them is that the English girl, as you describe her, has been the victim of a mistake. Yes, Monsieur, of a mistake. Don't burst into protests; I can prove it. At the moment fixed by the train's slackening speed, as they knew it would be forced to do, the robbers, who were in the car behind—I remember having noticed them from a distance, and I even believe that there were three of them—attack you and rob you; they attack your traveling companion and try to tie her up. Then of a sudden they leave her and move on—to the end compartment. What was the reason of this right-about turn? It was the fact that they had made a mistake, because the young woman was hidden under her rug, because they thought they were attacking two men and found that what they had attacked was a man and a woman. Hence their consternation.... 'Curse it! It's a woman!' And hence their hasty departure. They explore the car and find the two men they are really seeking—the two men in the end compartment. These two are on their guard and defend themselves. They shoot them and strip them of everything they have—suit-cases, bags, everything has gone. That's the first point clearly established. What?"

Ralph was surprised, not by the hypothesis, for he had formed the same hypothesis himself some time before, but that Marescal should have formed it and set it forth with such a logical astuteness. He expressed his warm admiration.

"The second point," said Marescal, evidently delighted by Ralph's appreciation.

He held out a small silver box, delicately chased.

"I found that at the back of the seat."

"A snuff-box?" said Ralph.

"Yes, an old snuff-box," said Marescal. "But it is used as a cigarette-case." He opened the box. "Seven cigarettes, you see. A mild tobacco—for a woman."

"Or for a man," said Ralph, smiling. "For after all there were only men there."

"For a woman, I tell you."

"Impossible," Ralph protested.

"Just smell the box."

Ralph took it, sniffed at it, and agreed.

"You're right—of course, you're right. The scent of a woman who keeps her cigarette-case in her vanity bag along with her handkerchief and powder-puff and scent-spray. There's no mistaking the smell," he said.

"Well?" said Marescal in a tone of triumph.

"Well, I don't understand anything about it. There are two men here whom we found murdered, and two men who attacked them and murdered them and bolted," said Ralph in a tone of bewilderment.

"Why not a man and a woman?"

"What? A woman? One of these robbers a woman?" cried Ralph in well-feigned amazement.

"What about this box of cigarettes?" asked Marescal, tapping it.

"It's hardly sufficient proof," protested Ralph.

"I've got another," declared Marescal.

"What is it?"

"The heel—this shoe-heel that they picked up in the wood, stuck between two roots. How many more proofs do you want to make you believe in this second fact I'm drumming into your head: the fact that of the two murderers one was a woman?" said Marescal, impatiently.

His clearsightedness irritated Ralph. He was careful, however, to let no vestige of irritation be seen, and muttered in the tone of one from whom a tribute is forced: "By Jove, you're devilishly smart!"

Then, more loudly, he added: "Is that all? Have you made any more discoveries?"

"Goodness!" cried Marescal, laughing triumphantly. "Give me time to get my breath!"

"Do you mean to go on working all night, then?"

"At any rate I'm going on working till they bring in the two fugitives. And that won't take long, if they follow my instructions," said Marescal confidently.

Ralph had followed Marescal's dissertation with the simple air of admiration of a man who is not very clever himself and leaves to others the task of unraveling a tangle of which he understands very little himself.

He shook his head and, yawning, said: "Enjoy yourself in your own way, Monsieur Commissary. For my part I don't mind telling you that all this excitement has upset me a bit, and an hour or two's sleep—"

"Take it," said Marescal readily. "Go to sleep in any of these compartments you fancy. I'll see that no one disturbs you. And when I've finished, I'll come and take a nap as well."

Ralph went into the next compartment, shut the door, drew the curtains, pushed up the shade over the lamp.

"I've got you all right, old pomade-pot," he said to himself. "You're like the crow in the fable: a little flattery will always loosen your tongue. You're all right to look at; but you talk too much. As for your jailing this unknown girl and her accomplice, I shall be jolly well surprised if you bring it off. It's a job I shall have to take in hand myself."

Then he heard the sound of voices from the direction of the station. They grew louder. Then he heard Marescal, who was leaning out of a window of the corridor, cry out:

"Who is it? Ah, excellent! It's the police, isn't it?"

A voice replied: "Yes, Monsieur Commissary. The station master sent us to you."

"Good. Have you made any arrests, inspector?" said Marescal.

"Only one, sir. One of the robbers they were hunting dropped on the turf by the high road, utterly done. We picked him up about a mile away. But the other managed to escape."

"That's a pity. What about the doctor?" said Marescal.

"He was having his horse harnessed as we came by his house. He had just had a night call; but he'll be here in about forty minutes," said the inspector.

Marescal paused; then he asked: "Did you catch the smaller of the two robbers?"

"Yes. A pale-faced lad, wearing a hat much too big for him. He's crying and making promises and whining: "I'll tell the truth, but only to the examining magistrate. Where is the magistrate?" said the inspector.

"Have you left him at the station?"

"Yes—well guarded."

"I'll come along," said Marescal.

"If you don't mind, sir. But first I should like to learn exactly what happened on the train."

"Right," said Marescal

The inspector climbed up into the car, with a policeman. Marescal at once took him to the compartment in which lay the body of the English girl.

"Everything's going all right," Ralph said to himself. "If old pomade-pot starts expounding his theory, it will keep him busy for a while."

The confusion had cleared from his mind; he was aware of quite unexpected intentions which had suddenly risen in his mind, without his knowing it, so to speak, and without his understanding at all the secret motives of his actions.

He opened the window, leaned out, and examined the line on that side of the carriage. Darkness and not a soul!

He jumped down.

CHAPTER III
THE KISS IN THE DARK

The station of Beaucourt is situated in the open country at a considerable distance from the outskirts of the village, with not even a cottage near it. The platform was lighted by all the lamps, lanterns, and candles they had been able to lay hands on, so that Ralph was obliged to approach it with infinite care. The station master, a workman, and a porter were talking to the policeman in charge of the prisoner.

In the shadowy dusk of this room were piles of baskets and crates, intermingled with boxes and trunks of all kinds. As he drew near, Ralph fancied that he saw, sitting on a heap of objects a bent and motionless figure.

"That must be the girl with the green eyes," he said to himself. "No need to lock the door since the jailors, standing in front of it, make it a safe enough prison."

He slipped into the booking-office and looked about him. There was a door on the left of him, a waiting-room on the right, out of which a staircase rose to the story above, and in the right-hand wall of this waiting-room another door. From the position of the rooms that must be what he wanted.

For a man like Ralph a bolt was an obstacle hardly worth taking into account. He always had on him four or five small tools with which he could make sure of opening the most recalcitrant of doors. At the first attempt the bolt yielded. He opened the door an inch or two and found that not a ray of light fell on him. He opened it wider, and, stooping, entered. The men outside had been able neither to see nor hear him, nor had the prisoner, whose dull sobs broke the silence with a rhythmical monotony.

Ralph took advantage of the noise outside to slip his head between two piles of baskets to get a clear view. He found himself just behind the heap of mail-bags on which the prisoner had thrown herself. This time she must have heard the sound he made, for her sobbing ceased. As it ceased he whispered: "Don't be frightened."

"Is it you, William?" she whispered.

Ralph gathered that she was speaking of the other fugitive; he answered:

"No. It's a friend who will save you from the police."

She did not say anything. She must be suspecting a trap.

He went on in a yet more urgent whisper: "You're in the hands of the police. If you don't follow me it means the court and prison."

"No. The magistrate will let me go free."

"He won't let you go free. Two men have been murdered. Your blouse is covered with blood. Come along—a moment's hesitation may destroy you. Come along!" he insisted.

After a few seconds' silence she murmured:

"My hands are bound."

Crawling along and hugging the darkness as he crawled he cut her bonds with his knife and asked in a whisper:

"Can they actually see you?"

"Only the policeman when he turns round," she replied. "And he can't see me very well, for I'm in the shadow. As for the others, they're too far to the left."

"That's all right," he said with a sigh of relief; then: "Wait a moment! Listen!"

They heard the sound of feet coming along the platform; he recognized the voice of Marescal.

"Not a movement!" he said in low, imperative accents. "They're coming sooner than I expected. Lie still."

"Oh! I'm frightened!" the girl muttered. "It seems to me that that voice—Oh, dear! Can it be possible?"

"Yes," he muttered. "It's the voice of your enemy, Marescal. But you mustn't be frightened. Don't you remember this afternoon, on the Boulevard, that a man interposed between you and him. It was me. I beg you not to be frightened."

"But he'll come in here," she quavered.

"We don't know that."

"But if he does come in?"

"Pretend to be asleep, or to have fainted. Bury your head between your crossed arms. Don't stir," he urged.

"But if he tries to get a look at me. Suppose he recognizes me?" she muttered in a harried tone.

"Don't answer him. Whatever happens, don't say a word. Marescal will not act immediately. He will take time to consider what to do. And then—"

But he was not at all easy in mind. He thought it more than likely that Marescal would be anxious to know whether he had made a mistake, or not, and whether the robber was really a woman. He would then start to question her at once, and in any case, considering her insecurely imprisoned, inspect her prison himself.

He was right. At once the Commissary exclaimed in a joyful tone: "Well, station master, this is good news! You've got a prisoner, have you, and an important prisoner too. Beaucourt railway station is going to become celebrated. You seem to me to have selected a very good place to confine him in; indeed, I don't see how you could have done better. But just to make sure, I'm going to take a look myself."

So without the loss of a moment, as Ralph had foreseen, he set about making sure. It was a terrible game for a young girl to be called on to play: a movement or two, a word or two, and she would be irremediably lost.

Ralph nearly beat a retreat; but that would have been to throw up the sponge and draw on his heels a whole horde of adversaries who would prevent him from resuming the enterprise. Therefore he kept still and trusted to luck.

Marescal came into the room, still speaking as he came to the people outside, and in such a fashion as to hide the motionless figure which he wished to be the only person to examine. Ralph remained at a distance, sufficiently hidden by the pile of baskets for Marescal not to see him.

The Commissary stopped short and said loudly: "Asleep, are we? Ah, well, my friend, we ought to be able to manage a little chat."

He drew from his pocket an electric torch, pressed the switch and turned the illuminating ray on to the supine form. Only seeing two crossed arms and a hat, he drew the arms aside and tilted the hat up.

"I was right," he muttered in a low voice. "It is a woman—a fair woman! Come on, baby: let's have a look at your pretty mug."

He took hold of her head rather roughly and turned her face towards him. The sight that met his eyes was so astonishing that he seemed unable to believe the incredible fact.

"No, no! I can't believe it!" he murmured.

He looked towards the door of the room. It would never do for any of the others to join him. Then, feverishly, he tore off the hat. The full light of the lamp fell on the face, revealing every feature.

"You! You!" he muttered. "But I'm mad! This is incredible! You! You a murderess! You, You!" He bent lower. The prisoner did not stir. Her pale face did not even quiver.

"It *is* you!" muttered Marescal in a breathless voice. "By what miracle? So you've murdered a man; and the police have caught you and here you are—you! it's impossible!"

One would have sworn that she was really asleep. Marescal was silent. Was she really asleep?

"That's right, don't stir," he said. "I'm going to get these people away and come back. Then, presently, we'll have a talk. We must go gently indeed, my child."

What did he mean? Was he going to propose some abominable bargain? Ralph guessed that he had not really any fixed plan. This astonishing occurrence had taken him by surprise and he was asking himself what advantage he might expect from it.

Marescal drew the hat back over the fair head, pushed all the curls under it, then, opening the blouse, felt in all the pockets of the jacket. He found nothing in them. Then he stood upright and turned to go out; his mind was in such a state of confusion that he never thought to examine the other door of the room.

"A queer-looking lad," he said, joining the group outside. "He certainly isn't twenty. A young rascal misled by his accomplice."

He went on talking, but in an absent-minded manner which made it clear that his mind was in a whirl and that he needed time to consider the matter.

"I think that my little preliminary inquiry won't be quite lacking in interest to the examining magistrate," he said proudly. "While we wait for him, I'll keep guard here with you, inspector. Or no, I'll keep guard alone. For really I don't need any one else; and if you'd like a little sleep——"

Ralph lost no time. He caught up from among the trunks three rolled-up sacks, of pretty much the same color as the blouse beneath which the prisoner was hiding her boy's clothes. He held out one of the sacks and muttered:

"Slip your legs over towards me so that I can stick this over them into their place. But move them slowly, scarcely moving at all—do you understand? Then draw away your body towards me—and then your head."

He squeezed her hand which was icy cold and repeated these instructions, for the girl did not stir.

"I beg you to do as I say," he whispered yet more urgently. "Marescal will stick at nothing. You have humiliated him; and he will take revenge on you in some way or other, since you are entirely in his hands. Move your legs towards me."

She began to obey him, moving with the tiniest movements which changed her position almost insensibly and took three or four minutes. When the movement was completed there was in front of her and a little higher than she, a gray form huddled together, presenting the same contour as she had presented, which produced a sufficient illusion of her presence to bring it about that the policeman and Marescal, if they cast a glance at her, would believe that she was still there.

"Come on. Take advantage of their being turned away from you and talking, and slide towards me," whispered Ralph.

She did as he bade her; he picked her up and keeping her crouching, slipped with her noiselessly through the door. Only in the waiting room did they rise to their full height. He shot the bolt; they went out through the booking office. But scarcely were they outside the station when she half-swooned and almost sank to her knees.

"I shall never be able to! Never!" she moaned.

Without the least effort he hoisted her on to his shoulder and started to run towards the line of trees which marked the road to Romillaud and Auxerre. He was filled with a deep satisfaction by the knowledge that he had gripped his prey, that the murderess of Miss Bakersfield could no longer escape him, that his action had substituted itself for that of society. What would he do? At the moment he was convinced, or at any rate he assured himself that he was actuated by a keen craving for justice, and that the punishment would take the form that circumstances should dictate.

Two hundred yards further on he stopped. Not because he was out of breath, but to listen and question the deep silence which was hardly broken by the rustling of the leaves and the stealthy passage of the little creatures of the night.

"What is it?" asked the girl in a tone of anguish.

"Nothing–nothing to worry about," he said in a reassuring tone. "On the contrary–the trotting of a horse a long way off. It's just what I wanted, and I'm delighted. It means safety for you."

He lowered her from his shoulder and carried her in his arms as if she were a small child. He went at a jog-trot for another three or four hundred yards, and came to the cross-roads, at which the main road crossed the road from Romillaud.

The grass was so damp that as he sat down on the embankment he said: "Stay where you are on my knee and listen to me carefully. That carriage you hear is that of the doctor they have sent for. I will get rid of the good fellow by tying him very gently to a tree. Then we'll get into the carriage and drive all night to some station on another line."

She did not answer. He suspected that she did not hear what he was saying. Her hand was burning.

She stammered in a kind of delirium: "I did not murder them! I did not!"

"Be quiet," said Ralph roughly. "We'll talk about that later on."

They were both silent. The immense peace of the sleeping plain seemed to spread around them stretches of silence and safety. Only the trotting of the horse now and again struck on their ears in the darkness; two or three times, how far away they could not guess, they saw the lamps of the carriage like wide open eyes. There came no noise, no menace from the direction of the station.

Ralph reflected on this strange situation and beside the form of this mysterious murderess, whose heart was beating so strongly that he could feel its distracted rhythm, he summoned up the figure of the Parisienne, which he had seen eight or nine hours previously, happy and to all seeming without a care in the world. The two images, so different from one another, grew confused in his mind. The memory of the ravishing vision was lessening his hatred against this girl who had murdered the English girl. But did he hate her?

He dwelt on the word and said to himself savagely: "I do hate her. Whatever she may say, she *is* a murderess. It is her fault and that of her accomplices that the English girl is dead. I do hate her. Miss Bakersfield *shall* be avenged!"

However, he let none of these thoughts find utterance. On the contrary, he was aware that he was uttering the gentlest of words.

"Misfortune falls on people when they're not even dreaming of it, doesn't it? One is happy—full of life—then the crime occurs. But it will be all right. You shall tell me all about it, and we'll smooth things out."

He had the impression that slowly a deep calm was stealing over her. She was no longer shaken by those feverish shudders which shook her from head to foot. Her troubled spirit was growing quieter; the nightmares, the anguish, the terror, all the hideous creatures of night and death, were growing fainter. He enjoyed fiercely this manifestation of his influence and power, magnetic to a degree, over creatures whom circumstances had thrust from their ordinary round and to whom he restored balance and for a while gave forgetfulness of the horrible reality.

Moreover he was withdrawing himself also from the tragedy. The dead English girl grew faint in his memory, and it was no longer a girl in a blood-stained blouse whom he was clasping, but the girl of Paris, elegant and radiant. It was useless for him to say to himself: "I will punish her. She shall pay the penalty." How could he fail to be aware of the fresh breath breathed out through lips so near to him?

The eyes of the carriage lamps were growing larger. The doctor would reach them in a few minutes.

"And then," said Ralph to himself, "I shall have to leave her and act– all this will be over. Never again shall I be able to spend moments like this with her–moments of such intimacy."

He bent down over her and divined that she was lying with her eyes closed, trusting herself wholly to his protecting care. Plainly she was thinking that in his arms all was well, that the danger was lessening.

Quickly he bent lower and kissed her lips. She tried weakly to thrust him away, sighed and said nothing. He had the impression that she accepted the caress, and that, in spite of a slight recoil, she yielded to the sweetness of that kiss. That lasted a few moments. Then a wave of revolt surged through her. She stiffened her arms and thrust him away with a sudden energy, crying:

"This is hateful! Shameful! Leave me alone. You're behaving disgracefully!"

He tried to laugh, and furious with her could well have abused her. But he could not find the words; and as she fled from him through the darkness, he murmured under his breath:

"What does this mean? But what modesty! And what next? What! You might think I had committed sacrilege."

He turned and sprang up the embankment and searched for her. Where? Thick bushes hid her in her flight. There was no hope of catching her.

He cursed and swore; once again he was full of hate for the murderess, a hate whetted keener by the rancor of a man rebuffed; he was even considering the horrible plan of returning to the station and giving an alarm, when he heard an outcry some way off. It came from higher up the road and from a hollow in it which probably hid the carriage from his eyes. The noise of its wheels had suddenly ceased. He ran towards it, came to the top of the slope, and saw the two lamps. But even as he caught sight of them he saw them swing right round. The carriage went off; there was no longer the quiet sound of a horse's trotting but the clatter of a galloping horse, lashed to its utmost speed. Two minutes later Ralph, guided by his cries, discovered the figure of a man lying among the brambles by the side of the road.

"What's the matter? Who are you?" cried Ralph.

"A doctor from Romillaud. The police told me to come to the railway station."

"What's the matter. Has some one attacked you?"

"Yes; a man on foot who asked me the way. I pulled up, and he sprang up on to the box, got me by the throat, half-strangled me, tied me up, and threw me among the bushes!"

"And did he go off with your carriage?" asked Ralph.

"Yes."

"Alone?"

"No, with some one else, who came running up the road—just as I was able to cry out a bit," said the doctor.

"Was it a man, or a woman?" questioned Ralph, though he was very sure which it was.

"I could not see. They only said a few words, and those in a whisper. Directly they went off I started shouting."

Ralph set about dragging him out of the brambles. Then he said: "So he didn't gag you?"

"Oh, yes; he did, but not successfully."

"What with?"

"With my silk scarf.

"There is a right way of gagging, but very few people know it," said Ralph.

He snatched the scarf from the doctor and set about showing him that right way of gagging people.

That lesson was followed by another operation, that of a much more effective tying up, with the horse-rug and halter that William had employed for the purpose. It was impossible to doubt that William had been the doctor's assailant and that the girl had stumbled across him in her flight.

"I'm not hurting you, am I, doctor? I should be frightfully sorry if I was," said Ralph. "At any rate I'll find you a more comfortable place than among these brambles and nettles," he added, picking his prisoner up and carrying him deeper among the bushes. "Look, here's a place you won't find too uncomfortable to spend the night in. The moss is thick and dry here. No, no: don't thank me–not a word. Believe me that if I could have helped it——"

His intention, at the moment, was to run after the two fugitives and catch them at any cost. He was furious at having been so balked. He must have been a fool! What! He had her in his claws and instead of wringing her neck he had amused himself by kissing her! How can one keep one's mind clear under such conditions?

But it seemed inevitable that that night his intentions should always result in actions contrary to them. As soon as he had quitted the doctor, without abandoning his plan, he returned towards the station as hard as he could run with the new plan of getting astride the horse of one of the policemen and so making sure of catching the car.

As he hurried from his compartment to the station he had observed the three horses of the policemen in a shed with one of the porters looking after them. He made his way to that shed, to see, by the light of a lantern which lit it, that the porter was asleep. Instead of slipping the bridle of one of the horses off the hook and leading it away, he set about cutting quietly and with every conceivable precaution the girths of the three horses and the straps of their bridles. So when the police or Marescal did discover the disappearance of the girl with green eyes it would be impossible to pursue her.

"I really don't know what I'm doing," Ralph said to himself as he regained the compartment in which Marescal had left him. "I've a perfect horror of this little devil; nothing would please me better than to hand her over to the police and keep my oath of vengeance. But all the efforts I do make help her to get away. Why?"

He knew quite well the answer to this question. If he had been interested in the girl because she had eyes the color of jade, how should he not be protecting her now that he had held her clasped to him, half-fainting and with his lips on hers? Does one hand a girl whose lips one has kissed over to the police? Murderess she might be; but she had quivered to his lips; and he knew well that henceforth nothing in the world would prevent him from defending her against every one and everything. For him that burning kiss in the darkness was the central point of the drama and swept away all the resolutions which his instinct rather than his reason had brought him to make.

That was why he felt obliged to resume contact with Marescal, in order to learn the result of his inquiries about her; and he was almost as eager to get into touch with him again about the business of the English girl and the wallet which she had begged him to carry away.

Two hours later Marescal staggered into the compartment, harassed and exhausted, and dropped on to the opposite seat of the compartment in the detached railway car, in which the slumbering Ralph quietly waited for him. Ralph started up from his sleep, pulled down the lampshade, and seeing the distressed face, the parting all ruffled, the drooping mustache of the Commissary, cried out:

"What on earth's the matter, Monsieur Commissary? I hardly recognized you."

Marescal stammered: "Don't you know? Didn't you hear?"

"I know nothing. I've heard nothing since you shut that door on me," said Ralph.

"Escaped!" groaned the Commissary.

"Who?"

"The murderer!"

"So you caught one?"

"Yes."

"Which of them? The man or the woman?"

"The woman."

"It was really a woman, then?"

"Yes."

"And you weren't able to keep her?"

"Yes. Only—" said the Commissary, and paused.

"Only what?"

"Well, she left some rolled-up sacks in her place."

In abandoning the pursuit of the fugitives Ralph had followed, among other motives, the wish for immediate revenge. Baffled, he wished to baffle in his turn and to score off some one else as he had been scored off. Marescal was to hand, the appointed victim; Marescal from whom he hoped to tear other confidences, Marescal whose distress was almost on the instant giving him a keen pleasure.

"It's a catastrophe!" he cried in the most sympathetic accents.

"You may well say so," the Commissary groaned.

"And you have no clew?" asked Ralph eagerly.

"Not the slightest."

"No fresh trace of her accomplice?"

"What accomplice?"

"The accomplice who was sharing her flight," said Ralph impatiently.

"But he played no part in her escape. We know his footprints, scattered about all over the place, along the line and especially in the wood. But, just outside the entrance to the railway station, in a patch of mud, side by side with the print of the shoe without a heel, we found quite different footprints—a smaller foot—with a more pointed toe."

Ralph pushed his muddy boots as far as possible under the seat.

With an air of the liveliest interest he asked: "Then was there some one waiting outside the station?"

"Undoubtedly. And it's my opinion that that person must have got away with the murderer by making use of the doctor's carriage," the Commissary explained.

"The doctor's carriage?"

"Well, if he didn't we should have seen the doctor; and since we haven't seen the doctor, it must be that he was pulled out of his carriage and thrown into some hole."

"But you can always overtake a carriage," said Ralph.

"How?"

"The horses of the police," said Ralph.

"I ran straight to the shed in which they were standing and mounted one of them. But the saddle turned right round and I came a cropper," said the Commissary glumly.

"What do you mean?"

"The man who was looking after the horses had fallen asleep and this brute had taken advantage of it to cut the girths and bridle straps. Under those circumstances it was impossible to go after the carriage," said the Commissary.

He spoke in such a tone, with such an air of misery that Ralph could not help laughing gently; then he said: "By Jove! This *is* a foeman worthy of your steel."

"A master," said the Commissary. "I once had occasion to follow in detail an affair in which Arsène Lupin was pitted against Ganimard. To-night's coup was brought off with the same mastery."

Ralph had no pity for him; he said; "It really is a catastrophe, for I take it that you looked to find this arrest of great advantage to your future career?"

"Of the greatest," Marescal admitted, for his defeat made him more and more inclined to grow confidential. "I've powerful enemies in the Ministry; and the so to speak instantaneous capture of this woman would have been of the greatest use to me. Just think! The noise the affair would have made!—The fuss there would have been about a criminal like this, a young girl disguised and so pretty! Day after day the limelight would have been full on me. And besides——"

He appeared to check himself and paused.

"And besides?" said Ralph softly.

Marescal still hesitated. But there are hours during which no effort of the reason will prevent you from speaking and revealing the very bottom of your soul at the risk of regretting it bitterly. He could not keep his secret.

"Besides it would have doubled, it would have tripled the value of the victory I had won in another field," he said in an even gloomier tone.

"Another victory?" cried Ralph in a tone of warm admiration.

"Yes; and a decisive victory too."

"Decisive?"

"Undoubtedly. No one could have snatched it from me since it was a victory over the dead."

"Not the English girl?" cried Ralph.

"The English girl."

Still keeping his simple air and plainly showing that he could not refrain from giving way to his desire to enjoy the fullest admiration of his companion's skill, Ralph said: "You couldn't, I suppose, explain to me how?"

"Why not? After all you will only get the information two hours before the examining magistrate."

Marescal was started, and in his weariness and confusion, contrary as it was to his usual habit, he could not stop babbling.

Bending towards Ralph, he said: "Do you know who that English girl is?"

"You knew her then?" said Ralph.

"I should think I did know her! We were even on excellent terms. For six months I have been her shadow. I watched her always, seeking for proofs against her I could not collect."

"Proofs? Against her?" cried Ralph in astounded accents.

"Yes, indeed: Against her–against Miss Bakersfield, on the one hand the daughter of Lord Bakersfield, an English peer and multi-millionaire, but on the other an international crook, hotel thief, and chief of a gang–entirely to amuse herself, a veritable dilettante of crime. And she had penetrated my disguise as I had penetrated hers; and when I spoke to her I found her quite sure of herself and ready to jeer at me. A thief? Yes. And I've warned my chiefs of it. But how to catch her? Then, ever since yesterday, I held her in my grip. I had been warned by a person in our service at her hotel that she had received from Nice yesterday, the plan of a villa to be burgled—Villa B. it was named in the letter which accompanied the plan—and that she had put the plan and the letter along with a packet of compromising papers, in a little red leather wallet, and was taking the train to the South. Hence my leaving Paris. 'Down there,' I thought, 'either I shall catch her in the very act, or I shall get hold of those papers.' I had not even to wait till I got to the South. The train-robbers handed her over to me."

"And the wallet?" asked Ralph.

"She carried it under her clothes, fastened to a belt; and now it's here," said Marescal patting the breast-pocket of his overcoat. "I've just had time to cast a glance over it, from which I gathered that there was no explaining away some of the papers, such as the plan of Villa B, to which she has added with a blue pencil in her own handwriting the date of the twenty-eighth of April. The twenty-eighth of April is the day after to-morrow—Wednesday."

Ralph could not help feeling shocked. His pretty traveling companion a thief! He had indeed been deceived; and his deception had been the greater since he could not protest against an accusation justified by so many details and which explained so completely the insight of the English girl with regard to himself. A member of a gang of international crooks, she possessed such a knowledge of the world of crime that she had been able to see the figure of Arsène Lupin behind the mask of Ralph de Limézy; and he was forced to believe that the words which she had forced herself so vainly to utter, were a confession and a prayer, addressed directly to Arsène Lupin himself. "Defend my memory—Let my father know nothing—Destroy my papers."

"Then this means a terrible scandal for the noble family of Bakersfield, Monsieur Commissary?" said Ralph gravely.

"Of course it does," Marescal replied.

"Isn't the idea a bit painful to you? And the idea too of handing over to justice a young girl like the one who has just escaped you. Isn't that a bit painful to you? For she is quite young, isn't she?" said Ralph even more gravely.

"Quite young and very pretty."

"But in spite of that—"

"In spite of that and in spite of any consideration whatever, nothing shall ever prevent me from doing my duty," said Marescal firmly.

He uttered these words in the tone of a man who manifestly desires his worth to be recognized, a man whose professional conscience governs his every thought.

"Well said, Monsieur Commissary," said Ralph in approving accents, considering the while that Marescal appeared to mix up his duty with a good many other things among which in particular were rancor and ambition.

Marescal looked at his watch, then seeing that he had plenty of time to get some rest before the coming of the examining magistrate and his clerk, he drew his legs up on to the seat and scribbled a few notes in a little note-book. Presently the note-book came to rest on his knee; his hand loosed its hold on it; the Commissary yielded to his weariness and slept.

Ralph sat watching him for two or three minutes. Since their meeting in the train his memory had been busy with the good gentleman, presenting him little by little with a more precise remembrance of his doings and his character. It had summoned up the figure of a rather interesting detective, or rather of a rich amateur who had taken up the detection of crime from a taste for it and to amuse himself, but also to serve his interests and his passions. A man fortunate in love, as Ralph now remembered, a woman-hunter, by no means always scrupulous, a man who was on occasion helped by women in his rather too rapid career. Did not people say that he had the entry into the house of the Minister himself, and that the Minister's wife knew a good deal about certain undeserved favors he had received?

Ralph took the note-book, and with one eye on the detective wrote:

Notes regarding Rudolph Marescal.

"A remarkable policeman. Clearsighted and full of initiative. But too fond of talking. He confides in the first comer, without asking his name or examining the state of his boots, or even looking closely at him and observing carefully his physiognomy.

"Badly brought up. If he meets a young girl of his acquaintance leaving a confectioner's on the Boulevard Haussmann, he accosts her and talks to her, though she does not wish it. If he finds her some hours later disguised, covered with blood, and guarded by the police, does not make sure that the bolt is in its proper place and that the gentleman whom he left in the railway car is not crouching behind the mail-bags.

"He ought not therefore to be astonished if that gentleman, taking advantage of such gross carelessness, decides to preserve a precious anonymity, to reject the rôle of witness and base informer, to take a hand in this strange affair, and to defend energetically, with the help of the papers in the wallet, the memory of the unfortunate Constance Bakersfield and the honor of the Bakersfields, and to concentrate all his energy on punishing the unknown with green eyes, without permitting any one else to touch a single one of her fair hairs or to demand a reckoning for the blood which stained her adorable hands."

By way of signature Ralph sketched the head of a man in spectacles with a cigarette between his lips and wrote beneath it:

“*Could you oblige me with a light?*”

The Commissary snored. Ralph set his note-book back on his knee, then drew a little bottle from his pocket, uncorked it, and held it under Marescal’s nose. A strong scent of chloroform filled the carriage. The head of Marescal drooped lower and lower.

Then, very gently, Ralph opened his overcoat, drew from its pocket the belt and wallet, and fastened the belt round his own waist, under his waistcoat.

He had scarcely done this when a train, moving very slowly, came past, a freight train. He opened the door of the car, sprang lightly and without being seen on to the buffers of a truck full of apples, and installed himself comfortably under the tarpaulin that covered them.

“A dead girl crook and a murderess of whom I have a horror, such are the worthy persons to whom I afford my protection,” he said to himself. “Why, in the devil’s name, have I plunged into this adventure?”

CHAPTER IV
THE VILLA B. IS BURGLED

"If there is one principle to which I always cling," said Arsène Lupin to me, when, many years later, he told me the story of the girl with the green eyes, "it is never to attempt the solution of a problem before the proper hour for doing so has arrived. To get to the bottom of certain enigmas, you must wait till luck, or your own cleverness, has brought you a sufficient number of the actual facts. You must only advance along the road to the truth, with the greatest care, step by step, following the course of events."

This reasoning applies to such an affair as this, in which there was nothing but contradictions, absurdities, isolated acts, apparently linked to one another by no connection of any kind; without a scrap of unity in it; without a directing thought; every one playing a lone hand. Never had Ralph felt so strongly how deeply he ought to distrust any kind of precipitousness in any adventure of this kind. Deductions, intuitions, analyses, explorations were just so many snares you must be careful not to fall into.

All day therefore he remained under the tarpaulin of the truck while the freight train rolled southwards through sunny landscapes. He dreamed pleasantly, eating the apples to appease his hunger, without wasting his time on building fragile hypotheses about the pretty girl, about her crimes and her dark soul. He enjoyed the pleasure of the memory of her lips, the tenderest and most exquisite lips he had ever kissed. That was the unique fact which he chose to bear in mind. To avenge the English girl and punish the guilty one, to catch the third murderer and regain possession of his stolen notes would undoubtedly have been interesting; but to find again the green eyes and the lips which yielded to his, what a joy!

The examination of the red leather wallet did not give him much information. There was a list of names and addresses, of confederates doubtless, some letters from associates in different parts of Europe. They were written with a certain discretion, though a more careful person would have destroyed one or two of them; but in view of what Marescal had told him, they proved beyond doubt that Miss

Bakersfield was indeed a thief. Among them were letters from Lord Bakersfield full of a father's frank affection. But there was nothing which gave a clue to the part played by the girl in this affair of the express, nothing which showed any connection between the adventure in which the English girl was engaged and the crime of the three train-robbers; that is to say between Miss Bakersfield and the murderess with the green eyes.

A single document, the document of which Marescal had spoken, the letter addressed to the English girl touching the matter of burgling Villa B., was of real value. It ran:

"You will find Villa B. on the right hand side of the road from Nice to Cimiez, just above the Roman arena. It's a massive building in a large, walled garden.

"On the fourth Wednesday in every month the old Comte de B. settles himself on the back seat of his carriage and goes down to Nice with his man, his two maids, and some baskets for provisions. Therefore the house is empty from three o'clock till five.

"Go round the garden walls to the wall which looks down upon the valley of Paillon. You will come to a small, worm-eaten, wooden door, of which I send you the key by the same messenger.

"It is certain that the Comte de B. who has quarrelled with his wife, has not found the packet of deeds which she hid. But a letter written by the dead lady to a friend, speaks of a broken violin case which is lying in a kind of little tower used as a lumber room. Why this allusion which seems to mean nothing? The friend died on the very day on which she received the letter, which was mislaid and only fell into my hands two years later.

"Enclosed herein is the plan of the house and garden. The turret is situated at the top of the staircase and is in a tumble-down condition. Two persons are necessary for the expedition, one to keep watch, for you have to look out for the laundress, who often comes by another garden door fastened by a padlock of which she has the key.

"Fix the date (a note in blue pencil on the margin fixes it as the 28th of April) and let me know that we may meet at the same hotel.

G.

"P.S. My information with regard to the great enigma of which I spoke to you is still uncommonly vague. Is it a matter of a considerable treasure, or of a scientific secret? I do not yet know. The journey for which I am getting ready will therefore settle the matter. How useful your help will be then!"

For the time being Ralph paid little attention to this somewhat strange postscript. He saw in it, according to a phrase he affected, one of those jungles into which one can only penetrate by means of dangerous suppositions. But the burgling of Villa B.—

This burglary little by little excited his keen interest. He considered it at length. A kickshaw perhaps; but there are kickshaws as nourishing as a substantial dish. And since he was rolling towards the South, it would be rather foolish to neglect such a good opportunity. That night he slipped out of his truck at the railway station at Marseilles and took an ordinary train to Nice, where he arrived on the morning of Wednesday the 28th of April, after having relieved a good gentleman of some bank notes, which permitted him to buy a suit-case, clothes, and linen, and to establish himself in one of the best hotels on the front.

There he breakfasted, and over his breakfast he read in the local papers more or less fantastic accounts of the murders in the express. At two o'clock in the afternoon he left the hotel, so changed in dress and countenance that it would have been almost impossible for Marescal to recognize him. But how should Marescal suspect that the man who had tricked him would have the audacity to substitute himself for Miss Bakersfield in the burglary at the Villa?

"When a fruit is ripe, one gathers it," Ralph said to himself. "And this one seems to me quite ripe and I should certainly be too stupid for anything if I let it rot. And I'm sure that that unfortunate Miss Bakersfield would never forgive me if I did so."

The Villa Faradoni stands on the edge of the road and looks over a vast stretch of mountainous country covered with olive trees. Stony paths, almost always empty, run beside the other three walls which surround it. Ralph made a careful inspection of them, observed the small, worm-eaten, wooden door and further on a padlocked door. He perceived also in a neighboring field the cottage which must be that of the laundress, and came back to the high road in time to see a rackety old carriage on its way to Nice. The Count Faradoni and his staff were going shopping. It was three o'clock.

"The house is empty," thought Ralph. "It's hardly probable that Miss Bakersfield's correspondent, who cannot be ignorant of the murder of his accomplice, is likely to try to do the job himself. The broken violin-case therefore belongs to me."

He retraced his steps nearly to the little worm-eaten door, to a spot at which he had observed that some projections in the wall would make it easy to climb. Forthwith he climbed over it easily enough and took his way towards the house along little-used paths. All the long windows of the ground floor were open. That of the hall led him to the staircase at the top of which rose the turret. But even as he set foot on the first step of it an electric bell rang.

"Confound it!" he said to himself. "Is the house full of burglar alarms? Can the Count be on his guard against something?"

The bell which was ringing in the hall, with a sustained and disquieting ring, stopped, without Ralph's having stirred. Wishing to make sure, he examined the bell which was fixed near the ceiling, followed the wire which ran along the moulding, and ascertained that it went through the outside wall of the house. The ringing therefore was not the result of any action of his; but someone outside had set it going.

He went out of the house. The wire ran through the air at a good height, fastened to branches of trees, and in the very direction from which he himself had come. It did not take him long to understand what had happened.

"When one opens the little worm-eaten door, the bell is set in action. Consequently some one was on the point of entering and stopped on hearing the bell ring."

He went quickly and quietly to the top of a hillock on his left, covered with shrubs, from which one had a view of the house, most of the garden, and some parts of the wall. The part in which the little door was set was one of them.

He waited. There would soon be a second attempt if any one were trying, like himself, to get into the Villa and take advantage of the Count's absence. He was right; but the attempt was made in a manner he had not expected. A man came on to the top of the wall, as he had done himself and at the same place, straddled it, unhooked the end of the bell-wire, and dropped to the ground.

Then the door was pushed open from outside; the bell did not ring; another person entered, a woman.

In the lives of great adventurers and above all at the beginning of their enterprises, chance plays the part of a veritable collaborator. Ralph who knew this, never missed the opportunity of making use of it, and the instant he saw who this woman was he attributed her presence to this obliging collaborator. But, astonishing as it was, was it really by chance that the girl with the green eyes was there and that she was there in the company of a man who could only be the good William? The rapidity of their flight, their sudden intrusion into this garden on this day, the 28th of April, and at this hour of the afternoon, surely made it clear that they also knew all about the Villa and that they were going straight to the same goal with the same sureness as himself. Was it not even allowable to see here what he was seeking? A certain connection between the enterprises of the English girl, the victim, and of the French girl her murderess? Provided with their tickets, their luggage registered at Paris, the confederates had quite naturally gone on with their expedition.

They came, together, along the little-used path, the man rather thin, clean-shaven, with the appearance of an actor, and an unpleasant actor at that, held a plan in his hand and advanced with an anxious air and watchful eye.

As for the young woman, though he did not doubt for a moment that it was she, Ralph recognized her with difficulty. How changed it was, that pretty face, smiling and happy, which he had so admired a day or two before in the confectioner's on the Boulevard Haussmann! It was no longer the tragic countenance he had seen in the corridor of the express but a poor little shrunken face, miserable, fearful, which hurt him to look upon.

She was wearing a very simple gray frock, without ornaments, and a close-fitting straw hat which hid her fair hair. Then, as they came along the bottom of the hillock, from which, crouching among the shrubs he was watching, Ralph had a sudden vision, as brief as a flash of light, of a head which rose above the wall, at a place where he had climbed it, a man's head, hatless, the black hair sticking up above a face of the vulgarest.

Was it the third confederate posted on the path, or was it an enemy spying on the two of them?

Ralph accepted this second explanation when he saw the couple halt a little way beyond the hillock, at the fork of the road to the door of the house, and the path to the padlocked door, and William hand a whistle to the girl, post her on guard behind a screen of shrubs, pointing to the padlocked door as to a place on which she was to keep watch. It was plain therefore that to William there was only one peril to guard against and that was the coming of the laundress; it was evident that at the door there was an enemy, some agent of Marescal perhaps, laying a trap for them.

Having given his instructions, William set out at a run towards the house. He left the girl, alone, exposed to a danger of which he was ignorant and which she did not suspect.

Ralph, who was at a distance of about fifty yards from her, gazed at her greedily, and reflected that another gaze, that of the hidden man must also be fixed on her through the cracks of the worm-eaten door. What was he to do? Warn her? Carry her off, as at Beaucourt, and protect her against unknown dangers?

But stronger than his perplexity was his curiosity. He wished to know. In the midst of this imbroglio in which was a very entanglement of opposing actions in which attacks came from opposing quarters, without its being possible to see from which quarter one would come first, he hoped some guiding thread would present itself and allow him, at a given moment, to choose one path rather than another and no longer act haphazardly from an impulse of pity or the lust to avenge.

The girl remained leaning against a tree and played idly with the whistle which she was to use in case of surprise. The youngness of her face, almost a child's face, though she was certainly not less than twenty, surprised Ralph. At that distance he could not see the color of her strange eyes, but her hair beneath her hat, which she had pushed back a little, shone like curls of gold and formed a halo of light and gaiety.

The moments slipped by. All at once Ralph heard the hinges of the padlocked door creak, and saw, on the other side of the hillock, a country-woman who came up the path, singing, and took her way towards the house, a basket of linen on her arm. The girl with the green eyes had also heard her. She tottered, sank to the ground under the tree, and raised the whistle to her lips. She was so overcome with terror that she had not the strength to blow it; the laundress went on up the path without having perceived that figure, hidden behind the trunks of the shrubs which stood at the fork of the path.

Terrible minutes slipped away. There is nothing more terrifying than to wait for an event which every circumstance foretells will be dramatic. What would William do, disturbed in the very middle of his burglary and confronted with this intruder? Did not the thief's actions during the attack in the express enable one to guess the dénouement?

Ralph made ready to intervene, when there came an unexpected happening: the laundress entered the house by a side door; and the moment she disappeared, William came out of the front door, carrying a newspaper parcel of the shape of a violin case. He and the laundress did not meet.

The girl, hidden among the trees did not at once see this, and during the stealthy approach of her confederate, who was walking noiselessly on the turf, she wore the mask of terror she had worn at Beaucourt, after the murder of Miss Bakersfield and the two men. Ralph filled with detestation of her.

William, if William it was, rejoined the girl, and Ralph saw her tell him of the coming of the laundress. He caught her roughly by the arm and hurried her along into the cover of the path to the worm-eaten door. As they passed the hillock Ralph saw that they were both shaken by this narrow escape and he felt an immense contempt for them.

"All right," he said to himself. "If it is Marescal or his agents who are in ambush behind that door all the better. Let them collar the two of them and stick them into prison! That girl isn't worth taking any trouble about."

It may be that he might yet have yielded to a sudden impulse, to an irresistible need to impose his will on these puppets and force an affair he had started to the end he desired. It may be. But this was a day of surprises, on which the events falsified all his predictions, so that he was driven to act almost in spite of himself and at any rate without a moment's reflection.

Some twenty yards from the door, that is to say some twenty yards from the spot at which he supposed the agents of Marescal to be lurking, the man whose head Ralph had seen rise above the wall, sprang out of the bushes which hung over the path, knocked William out with a swing to the jaw, gripped the young girl and tucked her under his arm as if she had been a parcel, snatched up the violin-case, and started to run, not in the direction of the wooden door, but through the plantation of olive trees at the bottom of the garden, and away from the house. Ralph at once grasped the fact that the man had made a circuit round the walls and entered the garden through some breach in the wall, or some accident of the ground. He dashed off in pursuit. His quarry was at once swift and powerful; he ran at a good pace, without looking behind him, as if he had no doubt whatever that no one would be able to prevent him from reaching his goal.

He came out of the olive plantation and plunged into a plantation of lemon trees. The ground on which they were planted sloped gently upwards nearly to the top of the wall so that not more than three feet of it rose above the top of the slope. He set the young girl on the top of the wall, gripped her wrists, lowered her over it to the full length of his arms, and let her drop; then he dropped the violin-case over the wall and let himself drop from it.

"Splendid!" said Ralph to himself. "He must have hidden a car at the end of the lane which runs along this side of the wall. Then, having spied upon the girl and then captured her, he is returning to the point from which he started and will drop her, inert and helpless, on to the seat of the car."

Running on, Ralph learned that he had been right. He saw a large open car at the end of the lane. The abductor of the girl lost no time: he laid her on the seat, cranked up the car, jumped in beside her, and started.

The lane was ploughed up in deep ruts. The car bumped along, needing all the driver's attention. Ralph caught up to it, sprang on to the back, slipped over the hood and crouched down under a rug which was hanging over the back of the driver's seat. The driver, all his attention given to getting the car over this awkward piece of ground, had heard nothing.

Three minutes brought them to the end of the garden wall on to the high road. Before accelerating, the man took hold of the girl's neck with a sinewy and powerful hand and growled:

"If you stir, you're lost. I'll wring your neck as I wrung the other girl's–you know what that means." He laughed a sinister laugh and added: "Besides, you've no more desire to call for help than I have. What?"

Country folk were walking along the footpath; they saw a man and a girl taking a joy-ride in a car. It skirted Nice and turned off towards the mountains.

Ralph had no difficulty in piecing together the facts, or in understanding the meaning of the ruffian's words. In the midst of this confusion of events, none of which seemed connected with any other, he grasped the fact that the man was the third of the train-robbers on the express, the man who had wrung the neck of the other girl, that is to say of Constance Bakersfield.

"That's as clear as paint," he said to himself, "it doesn't require any more thinking out. And here's another proof that there is a connection between this burglary at the Villa and the coup of the three train-robbers. Undoubtedly Marescal was right in maintaining that the English girl was killed by mistake. But all the same all these different people were on their way to Nice with the same object in view; the burgling of the Villa B. It was William, the obvious writer of the letter signed 'G,' who planned the burglary, William who was a member of both gangs, William who was the confederate of the English girl in the burglary and was at the same time seeking the solution of the enigma of which he speaks in his postscript. As clear as paint it is. Consequently when the English girl was murdered William had to execute alone the burglary he had planned. He brings with him his friend with the green eyes since the burglary demanded a confederate; and he would have brought off his coup if the third train robber who was keeping an eye on the pair of them, had not snatched the spoil from him and seized the opportunity also to carry off little Green Eyes. With what object? Are he and William rivals in love? But for the moment we won't ask any more questions."

Some miles further on the car turned to the right. Ralph knew this country well. It scaled the slopes which lead to the curious village of Falicon, descended by a steep, abruptly zigzagging road, then turned on to the Levens Road, by which one can reach the gorges of the Var, or the region of the high mountains. And then?

"Yes; and then?" he said to himself. "What am I to do if the journey ends in some robbers' lair? Ought I to wait to find myself facing alone half a dozen jail-birds whom I shall have to fight for the girl? Or had I better get to work now?"

A sudden movement of the young girl forced a decision. In an access of despair she tried to spring from the car at the risk of killing herself. The man caught her and held her with a grip of steel.

"No foolishness!" he cried. "If you've got to die, you'll die by my hand and at the appointed hour. Have you forgotten what I told you on the express, before you and William did in the two brothers? So I advise——"

He did not finish. There suddenly appeared a head and bust separating him from the girl. A grinning head and a shoving bust which pressed him into his corner.

"And how are you, old friend?" snarled a voice.

The ruffian was dumfounded. A wrong turn of the wheel must throw all three of them into a ravine.

"Cristi de Cristi!" he stammered. "Who on earth is this blighter? Where did he come from?"

"What?" said Ralph. "You don't remember me? But since you were speaking of the express, you must remember me—the first gentleman you knocked on the head—the unfortunate chap from whom you collared twenty-three notes and two rings. The lady recognizes me perfectly, don't you, mademoiselle? You recognize the kind gentleman who carried you away in his arms that night and whom you quitted without a word of thanks."

The girl said nothing; she crouched lower, shrinking away from him. The dumfounded driver babbled on: "Who the devil is the blighter? Where the hell did he come from?"

"From the Villa Faradoni, where I was keeping an eye on you. And now it's time to stop and let Mademoiselle get down."

The ruffian did not answer. He accelerated.

"Are you going to be naughty? You're wrong, my friend," said Ralph. "You must have seen in the papers the care I took of you. I never whispered a word about you; and the consequence is that everybody is accusing me of being the leader of the gang. Me! An inoffensive passenger who only did his best to save everybody. Come, comrade, take a pull at the reins and slow down."

The road was winding down a defile, on one side the walls of the cliff, on the other a parapet which ran along the top of another cliff which dropped sheer to a torrent beneath. Very narrow, it was made narrower still by a street-car line. Ralph decided that the situation was reversible. Standing nearly upright he had a better view of the road than the driver as they came round each turn. Of a sudden he raised himself to his full height, bent down, opened his arms, passed them to the right and left of his enemy, dropped down heavily on him and over his shoulder seized the wheel with both hands.

The startled ruffian yielded a little as he stammered: "Cristi! The blighter's mad! Damnation! He's going to pitch us into the ravine. Loose me, you fool!"

He tried to free himself but the two arms gripped him like a sheath.

Ralph laughed and said: “You’ve got to choose, my dear sir, the ravine or getting smashed up by the car. Look! There it comes bucketting along to meet you. You must stop, my friend. If you don’t—”

In truth the heavy car came round a corner sixty yards away. At the pace at which they were moving the stop must be instantaneous. The driver grasped this and put on the brakes, while Ralph bent down over the wheel and brought the auto to a standstill on the two rails of the car line. The two vehicles came to a stop nose to nose.

The driver was still raging; he cried: “Cristi de Cristi! Who the hell is this blighter? Ah, you shall pay for this!”

“Make out your bill. Have you got a fountain pen? No? Then, if you don’t mean to spend the night in front of the car let’s get out of the way.”

He held out his hand to the girl, who refused his help and sprang down and stood waiting by the side of the road. The passengers on the car began to grow impatient. The driver and conductor shouted. Ralph and the ruffian started to get the auto out of the way; and as soon as it was clear the car went on.

Ralph stepped away from the car and said to the driver in imperious accents: “You’ve seen how I operate, comrade. Well, if you venture to molest the young lady any more, I’ll hand you over to the police. It was you who planned the coup on the express and strangled the English girl.”

The driver turned, paling. In his hairy face, its skin already riddled with wrinkles, the lips were twitching. He stammered: “It’s a lie! I never t-t-t-touched her!”

“It was you all right. I’ve got the proofs,” snarled Ralph. “If you’re caught, it’s the scaffold. So clear out. You can leave me your car. I’ll take it back to Nice with the girl. Come, get!”

He cleared him out of the way with a savage thrust of his shoulder, sprang into the car and picked up the wrapped-up violin case. Then he swore and cried: "She's bolted!"

In truth the girl with the green eyes was no longer by the roadside. The street car was disappearing round the corner. Taking advantage of their being busy clearing the auto out of the way, she must have jumped on to it.

Ralph's fury turned on the driver.

"Who are you? Eh? You know that girl? What's her name? And what's your name?"

The driver no less furious sprang at him and tried to snatch the violin-case from his hands. There was a fierce struggle and in the middle of it a second street car came by. Ralph staggered his opponent with a left hook to the temple, sprang away from him and sprang on to the car. The ruffian recovered as it went round the corner and started to stagger after it. It left him behind.

Ralph returned to his hotel in the worst of tempers. Fortunately he had by way of compensation the deeds of the Countess Faradoni.

He unwrapped the newspaper. Although it had lost its neck and bridge and strings, the violin was much heavier than it should have been.

On examining it Ralph discovered that the chest had been deftly sawn through all the way round then replaced and glued on. He unglued it.

The violin only contained a bundle of old newspapers. They made it clear that either the Countess had hidden her fortunes somewhere else or that the Count, having discovered its hiding-place, was peaceably enjoying the income of which she had wished to rob him.

"Defeated all along the line!" growled Ralph. "This girl with the green eyes is beginning to get on my nerves! And she refused to touch my hand, confound her! What? Is she really furious with me for having stolen a kiss? To the devil with the little prude!"

CHAPTER V
THE ST. BERNARD

For the rest of the week, not knowing where to renew the struggle, Ralph read very carefully the reports in the newspapers describing the triple murder on the express. There is no point in treating at full length events which have become stale in the public mind, or the theories that were advanced, or the mistakes that were made, or the clues that were followed. This affair, which has remained such a profound mystery and which at the time excited the extravagant interest of the whole world, is of no interest to-day except by reason of the part that Arsène Lupin played in it and of the degree in which he helped to bring about the discovery of the truth which we are at last able to establish with absolute certainty. There is no point therefore in bothering about trivial details and in throwing light on facts of secondary importance.

Moreover Ralph perceived quickly enough the limits within which the results of the enquiry were confined and he made a careful note of them in order to classify the facts, to select those of importance, and to eliminate those of no importance.

These notes ran:

"1. The third confederate, that is to say the brute from whom I delivered the girl with the green eyes, keeping in the shadow and no one even guessing at his existence, it came about that, in the eyes of the police, it was the unknown passenger, that is to say myself, who was the instigator of the affair. At the evident suggestion of Marescal, whom my detestable maneuvers with regard to myself must have strongly prejudiced against me, I am transformed into a diabolical and omnipotent personage, who planned the coup and dominated the whole of the drama. Apparently a victim of my confederates, bound and gagged, I direct their actions, watch over their safety, and vanish into the darkness without leaving my trace except my footprints.

2. With regard to the other confederates, it is admitted, in accordance with the doctor's story, that they took to flight in his carriage. But whither did they fly? Early in the morning the horse brought back the

carriage across country. In any case Marescal does not hesitate: he tears the mask from the youngest of the train-robbers and without pity denounces a young and pretty girl. All the same he does not give a description of her, thus reserving to himself the credit for an early and sensational arrest.

3. The two murdered men have been identified. They were two brothers, Arthur and Gaston Loubeaux, in partnership in placing a brand of champagne and living at Neuilly on the banks of the Seine.

4. An important point: the revolver with which these two brothers were shot, which was found in the corridor of the express, furnishes some definite information. It was bought a fortnight before the crime by a tall and slender man whom his companion, a young woman in a veil, called William.

5. Finally there is Miss Bakersfield. No charge is brought against her. Marescal, deprived of his proofs does not dare to chance it and keeps prudently silent. An ordinary passenger, a lady well-known in society in London and on the Riviera, she is traveling to join her father at Monte Carlo; and that is all that can be said about her. Was she murdered by mistake? That is possible. But why were the two Loubeaux murdered? That and the rest of the business is shrouded in darkness.

"And since I'm not in the humor to bother my head about it any longer, I'll stop thinking about it; let the police go pottering about at their own sweet will, and act," said Ralph to himself.

If Ralph talked about acting in so determined a fashion, it was because he knew at last how to make a beginning. The local papers published a paragraph which ran:

"Our distinguished guest, Lord Bakersfield, after having attended the funeral of his unfortunate daughter, has returned to the Riviera and will pass the end of the season, as is his custom, at the Bellevue Palace Hotel, at Monte Carlo."

That very evening Ralph took a room at the Bellevue Palace next to the suite of three rooms occupied by the Englishman. All these rooms, like the rest of the rooms on the ground floor, looked out on to a large garden, which extended the whole length of the back of the hotel. From the long window of each of them a short flight of steps led down into the garden.

The next day he caught sight of the Englishman as he went down the steps from his room into the garden. He was a man still young, with a rather heavy face, rendered the heavier by the expression of deep sadness at the loss of his daughter.

Two days later as Ralph was thinking of sending in his card to him with the request for a private interview, he saw in the corridor a man who was knocking at the door of the room next his. It was Marescal.

The sight did not cause him any surprise. Since he himself was on the point of seeking some information from Miss Bakersfield's father, what was more natural than that Marescal should also be trying to learn all he could from him?

Accordingly he made haste to open one of the double doors between his room and the next. But he was unable to catch a word of the conversation.

Thinking it unlikely that this would be the only conversation they would have, he took the precaution of slipping into Lord Bakersfield's room when he was out and drawing the bolt of the other door between their two rooms. He watched for the arrival of Marescal and when he went into Lord Bakersfield's suite, he opened the second door two or three inches, only to meet with another check: Marescal and Lord Bakersfield were talking in such low voices that he could not hear a word they said.

In this way he wasted three days which Lord Bakersfield and the detective spent in long confabulations, for the most part walking up and down the garden, which excited his liveliest curiosity. At what was Marescal aiming? Was he paving the way for the revelation that Miss

Bakersfield was a crook? It was practically certain that he was not even thinking of doing so. Must one then suppose that he expected to get from these interviews some unexpected piece of information?

Then the idea that the two men were planning something in the nature of a trap presented itself several times to Ralph's mind; and this idea was presently strengthened by the sight of William and the girl with the green eyes strolling in the neighborhood of the hotel, drawn to it, like himself and Marescal, by the fact that Lord Bakersfield was staying there. It was a quite admissible hypothesis, and events suddenly invested it with even greater credibility.

One morning Ralph who had hitherto been unable to hear several conversations of Lord Bakersfield over the telephone which was in the further room, succeeded in catching the end of one of them.

"It is settled, Monsieur. Come to the hotel garden at three o'clock this afternoon. The money will be ready and my secretary will hand it over to you in exchange for the four letters of which you told me."

"Four letters?... Money?" said Ralph to himself. "This looks to me uncommonly like an attempt at blackmail. And in that case the blackmailer can be no one but the good William. Miss Bakersfield's confederate, he must be trying to-day to turn his correspondence with her into money."

These considerations confirmed Ralph's belief in his hypothesis of a trap; he was sure that it explained the relations between Lord Bakersfield and Marescal. Doubtless William had threatened Lord Bakersfield with the exposure of his daughter's nefarious activities, and the Englishman had called on the Commissary to help him. The Commissary had set a trap into which the young crook would inevitably fall. Well and good: Ralph could not but be delighted that he should. But what about the girl with the green eyes? Was she also taking part in this blackmailing scheme? How in that event was he himself going to act? Was he going to rescue her again? The thought was repugnant to him, considering the baseness of their enterprise. Was he going to let Marescal capture her?

That day Lord Bakersfield kept Marescal to lunch. After the meal they went into the garden and walked round it several times, talking with considerable animation. At a quarter to three the detective came back into Lord Bakersfield's sitting-room; Lord Bakersfield sat down on a bench in sight of the windows of his suite, not far from the gate of the garden which opened into the street.

Ralph kept watch from his window.

"If she comes, all the worse for her," he murmured to himself. "I won't move a finger to help her."

Nevertheless a great weight lifted from his spirit when he saw William appear alone, advancing cautiously, looking about him anxiously, at the gate of the garden. He went straight to Lord Bakersfield, and they talked. Their conversation was brief, doubtless they settled the terms of the transaction. Then Lord Bakersfield rose, and the two of them came towards his suite. They came in silence, William ill at ease and suspicious, Lord Bakersfield thoughtful and frowning.

At the foot of the steps he said coldly: "Go in, Monsieur, I don't want to be mixed up in this dirty business myself. My secretary knows all about it and will pay you the money for the letters, if their contents are what you say they are."

He turned on his heel and went along the path back to his bench.

William hesitated, then went up the steps. Ralph hurried to the doors between the two rooms. The door on his side was already opened, he opened the other an inch or two and listened, awaiting the explosion. It was clear that William did not know Marescal, but believed him to be Lord Bakersfield's secretary. Ralph found that he could see the Commissary in a mirror on the opposite wall of the room.

"Here are the fifty thousand-franc notes and a cheque on a London bank for the same amount. Have you the letters?" said Marescal in sharp, staccato accents.

"No," said William.

"What do you mean by 'no?' In that case there's nothing doing. My instructions are strict. The money for the letters only," snapped Marescal.

"I will mail them on to you."

"You're mad, my man; or rather you're trying to trick us!"

William hesitated; then he made up his mind: "I've got the letters all right," he said quickly. "What I mean to say is, they're not on me."

"Where are they?"

"A friend of mine is taking care of them for me," said William.

"Where is he?" snapped Marescal.

"In the hotel. I'll go and find him."

"There's no need to do that," said Marescal, guessing the identity of his friend.

He rang the bell. The chambermaid answered it.

"You'll find a young lady waiting in the corridor," said Marescal. "Tell her that Mr. William wants her and bring her here."

William started.

"What does this mean?" he cried. "It's contrary to my agreement with Lord Bakersfield, the young lady who is waiting for me has nothing to do with the matter."

He tried to go through the door. But Marescal smartly blocked the way. There came a knock; he opened the door, keeping out of sight behind it; and the girl with the green eyes entered on hesitating feet.

She uttered a faint cry of terror when the door was banged behind her and the key turned sharply in the lock.

On the instant a hand gripped her shoulder.

She turned, saw the Commissary, and groaned: "Marescal!"

As the name passed her lips, William saw that the Commissary only had eyes for her, seized his chance and bolted through the window and across the garden. Marescal swore; then turned on the girl, who tottering and overwhelmed, staggered to the middle of the room.

He snatched her bag from her and cried: "Nothing can save you this time, you little crook! You've run straight into the trap!"

He rummaged in her hand-bag and growled: "Where are those letters? Blackmail now! You've sunk to that, have you? Shameful!"

The girl dropped on to a chair.

Not finding the letters in her hand-bag, he stormed at her savagely: "The letters! The letters! Where are they? Have you got them on you?"

He caught the front of her dress and tore it open, abusing her furiously, and felt for the letters. He stopped short, stupefied, with his eyes starting out of his head as they stared into the face of a man with one eye closed in a protracted wink and a cigarette hanging from the corner of his lips, set in a jeering snarl.

"Could you oblige me with a light, Rudolph?" said the intruder.

"Could you oblige me with a light!" That disconcerting phrase, already heard in Paris, already read in his private note-book! What did it mean! And this familiarity! That wink?

"Who are you? T-T-The m-m-man on the express? The third confederate? Impossible!" stammered Marescal.

He was no coward; on more than one occasion he had faced two or three adversaries with uncommon courage. But this was an adversary such as he had never met before, who employed unheard-of means, and with whom he found himself in a condition of permanent inferiority. Shaken and speechless, he stood on the defensive, almost, for the moment, paralyzed.

Ralph seized the advantage surprise had given him. He said imperiously to the girl: "Put the four letters on the corner of the mantelpiece."

Like an automaton she took an envelope from her bosom and set it on the mantelpiece.

"Are the four letters in it?" he snapped.

Staring at him, she nodded.

"Right! Now slip out quickly by the corridor, and goodbye. I don't think that we're likely to meet again. Goodbye. Good luck!"

Without a word, she hurried across the room, unlocked the door, slipped through it, and was gone.

Ralph turned to Marescal and said in a jeering tone: "As you see, Comrade Rudolph, I am slightly acquainted with this young lady. But I am neither her confederate nor the murderer who inspires you with such salutary dread. I'm merely a noble-hearted traveler who took a dislike to your pomaded wig the moment I set eyes on it and thought it would be rather a joke to snatch your victim from you. For my part, she no longer interests me and I propose to leave her severely alone. But I also propose that you shall leave her severely alone too. We're all of us going separate ways: she to the right, you to the left, I straight on. Do you get me, Rudolph?"

Marescal's hand darted towards his hip-pocket; Ralph quicker on the draw, had him covered before his fingers closed on the butt of his revolver; and there was so sinister an expression on his face that the Commissary kept quite still.

"Come into the next room. We're less likely to be interrupted while we talk things over," said Ralph quietly.

Marescal led the way; Ralph taking the letters from the mantelpiece, followed, still keeping him covered, and shut the door. Then, on the instant he caught up the cloth from the table and threw it over the Commissary's head. Marescal did not resist. This fantastic adversary had him paralyzed. He did not dream of shouting for help, or trying to ring the bell; he was sure that counterstroke would be smashing. He therefore allowed himself to be rolled up in the bed-clothes, in a fashion that half smothered him and held him helpless.

"That's all right," said Ralph cheerfully when he had completed his task. "Now we know where we are. I should think that you'll be set free about nine to-morrow morning, which will give you time to think things over properly, and give the lady, William, and me time to remove ourselves, in different directions, to a place of safety."

He packed his suit-case in a leisurely manner. Then he struck a match and burnt the four letters of the English girl.

Then he said: "Just a last word, Rudolph: don't go on bothering Lord Bakersfield. On the contrary, since you have no proofs against her and never will have, play the kind gentleman and give him his daughter's diary, which I found in the red leather wallet and will leave you. That will convince him that she was the most honest and noble of women. You will do a kind action; and that is always something gained. As for William and his confederate, tell him that you made a mistake, that it was just ordinary blackmail and had nothing to do with the murders on the express, and you let them go. And finally, just on general principles, leave this business of the murders on the express alone. It's much too complicated for you and you'll only get more kicks than ha'pence out of it."

He went out of the room, locked the door of it, and went to the hotel office and paid his bill.

Then he said: "Please keep my room for me till to-morrow. I'll pay in advance in case I'm prevented from coming back."

He left the hotel, congratulating himself on the way the business had turned out. His part in it was at an end. Let the young woman get clear of it herself. She would doubtless find a way. It no longer mattered to him.

His resolution was so definite that when he caught sight of her at the station, as he was taking the 3:50 express to Paris, he made no effort to join her but kept out of sight.

At Marseilles she changed her route and took the train to Toulouse, in company with some people, whose acquaintance she seemed to have made and who seemed to be actors. William, suddenly turning up, joined the group.

"A pleasant journey," said Ralph to himself. "I'm delighted to have severed my relations with this charming couple. They may go and get hanged in somebody else's society!"

However, at the last minute, he jumped out of the train and took the same train as the girl. Like her, he left it the following morning at Toulouse.

Following the murders on the express, the burglary at the Villa Faradoni and the attempted blackmail at the Bellevue Palace Hotel, two episodes, sudden, violent, furious and unexpected, like scenes in a badly constructed play which give the audience no time to understand what is happening and to connect the incidents with one another; a third episode was about to take place which Arsène Lupin was wont to describe later, as the last scene of his triptych as rescuer, an episode of the same rough and brutal character as the others. This episode also came to its crisis in a few hours and can only be presented after the manner of a scene devoid of psychology and apparently of any logic.

At Toulouse Ralph made discreet enquiries of the porter at the hotel to which the girl with the green eyes accompanied her companions. He learned that these travelers were part of the touring company of Leonide Balli, a singer in light opera, who that very evening was playing the part of Veronique at the Municipal Theater.

He kept watching the hotel. At three o'clock the girl came out of it, wearing an air of considerable agitation and kept looking behind her as if she was afraid lest some one should come out immediately after her and spy upon her. Was it her confederate, William, whom she distrusted? She hurried, still looking behind her to the post office where she scribbled a telegram, which she had to begin three times, with feverish haste.

After she had left the post office Ralph entered it and managed to possess himself of one of the crumpled up forms. He read:

Hotel Miramare, Luz, Hautes-Pyrenees. Shall arrive to-morrow first train. Tell them All.

"What the devil is she going to do among the mountains at this time of year?" he murmured to himself. "'Tell them all'—Does that mean that her people live at Luz?"

He resumed his cautious watch on her and saw her enter the stage door of the Municipal Theater, doubtless to take part in a rehearsal of the company.

For the rest of the day he watched the exits from the theater. But she did not stir out of it. As for her confederate William, he remained invisible.

In the evening Ralph slipped into the back of a box at the theater: and the moment the girl with the green eyes appeared on the stage he could hardly repress a cry of surprise: she was taking the part of Veronique.

"Leonide Balli. So that's her name?" he said to himself. "She sings in light opera in the provinces?"

He could not get over it. The fact was so different from everything he had imagined about the girl with the green eyes.

Provincial or Parisienne, she showed herself an uncommonly clever comedienne and a most adorable singer, simple, with no straining for effect, moving, full of tenderness and gayety, of modesty and charm. She had all the gifts and all the graces, plenty of cleverness; and a lack of experience of the stage which was a further charm. He recalled his first impression on the Boulevard Haussmann and his fancy that the young girl, whose mask was at the same time so tragic and so childlike, had a double destiny.

Ralph passed three delightful hours. He could not tire of admiring the strange creature whom he had only seen, since the charming initial vision, by flashes, in crises of fear and horror. This was another woman in whom everything seemed lightness and harmony. Yet it was indeed she who had murdered and played a part in infamies and crimes. It was indeed the confederate of William!

Of these two so different images which was he to consider the true one? He watched her in the hope to learn, and watched in vain, for a third woman overlay the other two and united them in an intense and moving life, the life of Veronique. Only a few gestures a little too nervous, a few phrases badly delivered, displayed to the eyes of the man who knew the truth, the woman under the heroine, and revealed a state of mind which insensibly weakened her rendering of the part.

"Something fresh must have happened," Ralph thought. "Sometime between noon and three o'clock there has been some serious incident, which drove her suddenly to the post office, the consequences of which sometimes spoil her artistic efforts. She is thinking about it; it makes her anxious. And if I were to make a guess, I should say that this incident is connected with William, with William who has suddenly disappeared."

When the girl appeared at the fall of the curtain she received an ovation; and a curious crowd thronged the approach to the stage door. Before the door itself was standing a closed landau, drawn by a pair of horses. Since the only train by which it was possible to arrive at Pierrefitte-Nestales, the station nearest to Luz, in the morning, left Toulouse at 12:50, there was no doubt that the girl was going straight to the station, having already sent her luggage there. Ralph had already left his suit case in the cloak-room.

At a quarter past twelve she entered the carriage which drove slowly off. William had not appeared; and it looked as if she was taking this journey without his knowing anything about it.

Little more than twenty seconds later Ralph, who was going to the station on foot, was struck by a sudden idea, started to run, caught the landau halfway down the old boulevard and clung on to the back of it as best he could.

Presently what he had foreseen happened. At the turning of the road to the station, the driver turned suddenly to the right, lashed the horses savagely with his whip, and drove the carriage along dark and deserted side-streets which brought it out at the Jardin des Plantes. At the pace at which it was going it was impossible for the girl to get out of the carriage.

The horses had not far to gallop. They galloped into the deserted square and came to a sudden stop at the corner of it. The driver jumped down from his seat, opened the door of the carriage and stepped into it.

Ralph heard the girl scream, but did not hurry himself. Certain that her assailant was no other than William he wished to learn what it was all about and get the meaning of events in the middle of their quarreling. But, almost on the instant, the attack seemed to him to assume such a dangerous complexion that he interfered at once.

"Speak, will you!" the girl's confederate cried. "So you thought that you were going to decamp and leave me in the lurch? Well it's true that I meant to let you down, but it's just because you know it that I'm not going to leave you now. Come, speak—tell me—if you don't—"

Ralph was frightened. He remembered the groans of Miss Bakersfield. A sharp turn of the wrist and the victim died. He opened the door, caught the confederate by the leg, flung him to the ground, and dragged him roughly to one side. The ruffian tried to put up a fight. With a sharp twist Ralph broke his arm.

"Six weeks' rest," he said. "And if you start annoying the lady again I'll break your spine for you."

He went back to the carriage. The girl was already nearly out of sight in the darkness.

"Run, little one," he said. "I know where you're going and you shan't escape me, I've had enough of playing the St. Bernard without even getting a lump of sugar for my pains. When Lupin sets out on a path, he goes to the end of it and never fails to reach his goal. You are his goal to-day, you and your green eyes and warm lips!"

He left William with his carriage and hurried to the station. The train came in. He got into a compartment without being seen by the girl. Two compartments, full of passengers, separated them. An hour afterwards he stole down the corridor to take a look at her. She was asleep with her head wrapped in a shawl.

At Lourdes the train left the main line; an hour later it arrived at Pierrefitte-Nestales, the terminal.

Ralph hung back; scarcely had the girl reached the platform than a band of young girls, all dressed alike in chestnut frocks and cloaks bordered with a broad blue ribbon, rushed at her, followed by a nun wearing an immense white cap.

"Aurelie! Aurelie! You've come at last!" they cried.

The girl with the green eyes passed from the arms of one to the arms of another. Last of all the nun hugged her affectionately and said joyfully: "How pleased I am to see you again, Aurelie dear! And you're going to stay a good month with us, aren't you?"

CHAPTER VI
BETWEEN THE BRANCHES

With her arm through the arm of the nun and surrounded by her young companions carrying her luggage, the girl with the green eyes walked, smiling happily, towards a brake drawn by three mules. They climbed into it; and it set off up the steep road to Luz, with a tinkling of the mules' bells. Ralph, who had kept out of sight, hired a Victoria to carry him to Luz.

"Ah, my pretty lady with the green eyes, henceforth you are my prisoner," murmured Ralph. "An accomplice of a murderer, a burglar, and a blackmailer, murderess yourself, daughter of the polite world, prima donna of light opera, boarder at a convent—whatever you may be, you shall not slip between my fingers again. Trust is a prison from which one cannot escape; and however angry you may be with me for stealing those kisses, in the bottom of your heart you trust the man who never tires of saving you and is always on the spot when you stand on the edge of the abyss. One grows attached to one's St. Bernard, even if he has bitten you once.

"Lady with the green eyes, who takes refuge in a convent to escape all those who persecute you, till something fresh happens, you shall not be to me a criminal or formidable adventuress, or even a singer of light opera, and I shall not call you Leonide Balli. I shall call you Aurelie. It's a name I love because it's old-fashioned and honest and suits a little sister of the poor.

"Lady with the green eyes, I know now what it is you possess, a secret your old confederates do not know, a secret they wish to tear from you and which you keep fiercely. That secret shall belong to me some day because secrets are my strong point; and I shall learn that one, even as I shall scatter the darkness in which you hide yourself, mysterious and fascinating Aurelie."

This apostrophe satisfied Ralph, and he went to sleep to think no more of the disturbing enigma of the girl with the green eyes.

The little town of Luz and the neighboring town of Saint-Sauveur are famous for their baths which at that season few invalids were taking. Ralph chose a hotel that was nearly empty and gave out that he was a student of botany and mineralogy. He devoted all the afternoon to a careful examination of the country.

A very bad and narrow road, nearly a mile in length and steep, led up to the Maison des Soeurs Sainte-Marie, an old convent which had been turned into a boarding-school. In the midst of a bare and rocky stretch of ground the buildings and gardens of the convent stretch along the point of a projecting cliff, on terraces which rise above one another and support strong walls, along the foot of which Sainte-Marie's brook formerly boiled. To-day, along this part of its course, it runs under the earth. A pine forest covers the other slope, traversed by two roads, that cross one another, for the use of the wood-cutters. There are grottoes and rocks of strange shapes to which excursions run on Sundays.

It was on this side that Ralph kept watch. It was a deserted spot, the silence of which was only broken by the sound of the axes of the wood-cutters in the distance. From the point he had chosen he looked over the smooth lawns of the garden and an avenue of carefully clipped limes which sheltered the path along which the boarders took the air. In the course of a few days he knew the customs of the convent and the hours of recreation. After the mid-day meal the walk which ran along the edge of the gorge was reserved for the big girls.

It was not till the fourth day that the girl with the green eyes—doubtless she had been so worn out by what she had gone through that it had kept her indoors—appeared on this walk. Thereupon each of the big girls seemed to have no other object in life but to monopolize her, and they quarrelled jealously with one another for the privilege of enjoying her society.

Ralph perceived at once that she was changed like a child who is recovering from an illness and expands in the sunshine and keen air of the mountains. She flitted about among her young companions, dressed as they were, alert and full of life, charming with all, the leader of their games, and enjoyed herself so thoroughly that her silvery laugh was forever echoing among the walls of the gorge.

"She laughs!" murmured the astonished Ralph. "And not with her artificial and almost dolorous stage laugh, but with the care-free laugh of one who has no crimes to remember, a laugh in which her true nature finds expression. She laughs—what a miracle!"

Then the others went back to their lessons and Aurelie remained alone. She did not appear any the more melancholy for that; her gayety did not leave her. She busied herself with trifles such as gathering the pine cones and filling a basket with them, or plucking flowers and laying them on the steps of a neighboring chapel.

Her actions were all gracious. She often talked in a low voice to a little dog who was always with her, or to a cat who was always rubbing itself against her calves. Once she twined herself a garland of roses and laughing, looked at herself in a pocket mirror. Furtively she powdered her cheeks and put a little rouge on them and at once rubbed it roughly off. It must have been forbidden.

On the eighth day she made her way along the wall to the last and highest of the terraces, along the edge of which ran a hedge of shrubs. On the ninth day she returned to it, bringing a book. On the tenth day before the hour of recreation Ralph made up his mind.

First of all he had to force his way through the thick underwood on the edge of the pine forest, then cross a large sheet of water. The brook of Sainte-Marie flows into a basin, as into a large reservoir, and then sinks under the earth. A worm-eaten boat was moored to a stake, and by means of it he was able, in spite of some fairly strong eddies, to reach a little creek at the very foot of the high terrace which rose like the rampart of a fortress.

The walls of it were made of flat stones set, without mortar, on the top of one another, and wild plants grew between them. The rain had worn runnels full of sand along the face of the wall and paths, which the boys of the neighborhood would on occasion climb. Ralph climbed to the top without difficulty. The terrace formed a kind of summer drawing-room, surrounded by shrubs and set with stone benches; its center was adorned with a fine terra cotta bowl.

He heard the murmur of the girls at play below. Then there came silence and a few minutes later the sound of a light footfall coming towards him. A voice was humming an air from an opera. His heart began to beat quickly. What would she say when she saw him?

The branches rustled; the foliage was parted like curtains that hang before the door of a room; Aurelie entered.

She stopped short on the threshold of the terrace with an air of stupefaction; the song died on her lips. Her book and her straw hat, which she had filled with flowers and hung by the ribbons from her arm, fell to the ground. She did not stir, an engaging and delicate figure in her simple dress of chestnut cloth.

For a few seconds she failed to recognize Ralph. Then she blushed deeply and stepped back.

"Go away," she murmured. "Go away."

Not for a second had he any intention of obeying her; one might almost have believed that he had not heard her command. He gazed at her with indescribable pleasure such as he had never before felt in the presence of any woman.

She repeated in more imperious accents: "Go away!"

"No," he said.

"Then I shall go away myself."

"If you go away I shall follow you," he declared. "We will go back to the convent together."

She turned as if to fly. He caught her arm.

"Don't touch me!" she said indignantly, freeing herself. "I forbid you to touch me. I forbid you to come near me!"

Surprised by her vehemence, he said: "But why?"

In a low voice she replied: "I have a horror of you."

The answer was so astonishing that he could not refrain from smiling.

"Do you detest me as much as that?"

"Yes."

"More than you detest Marescal?"

"Yes."

"More than you detest William and that ruffian at the Villa Faradoni?"

"Yes, yes, yes."

"But they were harming you and without me who protected you—"

She was silent; she had picked up her hat and was holding it across the lower part of her face so that he could not see her lips. Her attitude was explained by that concealment; Ralph had not a doubt of it. If she detested him, it was not because he had been the witness of all the crimes and infamies that had been committed, but because he had held her in his arms and kissed her lips. A strange modesty in a girl like her; yet it was so sincere and threw such a light on the very recesses of her soul and her instincts that, in spite of himself, he murmured:

"I beg you to forget it."

Then drawing back a few steps to show her that she was free to depart, he continued in a tone of involuntary respect:

"That night was a night of observation of which neither you nor I must cherish the remembrance. Forget the way in which I acted. Besides it is not to recall that to you that I am here, but to continue my work of helping you. Chance threw me across your path and chance willed it that from the beginning I should be useful to you. Do not reject my help. The threat of danger, far from being ended, is growing graver. Your enemies are exasperated. What will you do, if I am not there?"

"Go away," she said stubbornly.

She remained on the threshold of the terrace as if she were on the threshold of an open door. She avoided Ralph's eyes and hid her lips. However she did not go. As he had thought, one *is* the captive of one who indefatigably saves you. Her look was fearful. But the memory of the kisses he had stolen was giving way to the infinitely more terrible memory of the trials she had undergone.

"Go away," she said again. "I was at peace here. You are mixed up with all those things—with all those—*hellish* things."

"Fortunately," he said gravely. "And also I must be mixed up with all the things that are about to happen. Do you think they are not searching for you? Do you think that Marescal has given you up? At this moment he is on your trail. He will follow it to Marseilles, to Toulouse, to this convent of Sainte-Marie. If you lived here happily during some years of your childhood, as I suppose, he must know and he will come."

He spoke gently with a conviction which impressed the girl deeply; and he hardly heard her as she murmured once again: "Go away."

"Yes: I will go," he said. "But I shall be here again to-morrow at the same hour; I shall be waiting for you here every day. We have to talk. Not of anything which might be painful to you and not about the nightmare of that horrible night. We will not speak about it. I have no need to know; the truth will emerge little by little from the darkness. But there are other points—questions I shall put to you and which you will have to answer. That is what I wanted to say to you to-day, no more. Now you can go. But you will think it over, won't you? And do not worry any longer. Get used to the idea that I am always here and that you must never despair because I shall always be here—in the hour of peril."

She went without a word, without a nod of adieu. He watched her descend the terraces and enter the avenue of limes. When he saw her no longer he picked up some of the flowers she had dropped and becoming aware of this unconscious action, he laughed.

"Heavens! This is growing serious," he murmured in a jeering tone. "Can it be that—come, come Lupin old chap, take a pull."

He took his way back down the wall, once more traversed the pool, and walked through the forest, throwing away the flowers one by one as if he had lost interest in them. But the image of the girl with the green eyes still hovered before his own.

Next day he climbed up again to the terrace. Aurelie did not come; and she did not come the two following days. But on the fourth day she parted the branches without his having heard the sound of her coming.

"Oh, it's you—it's you at last!" he said.

He gathered from her attitude that he was not to advance a step or say a word which might ruffle her sensibilities. She stood as on the first day like an opponent who revolts against being dominated and is angry with an enemy for the service he is rendering.

However her tone was less hard when, with half averted head, she said: "I ought not to have come. It is not fair to my benefactors, the Sisters of Sainte-Marie. But I thought that I ought to thank you—and help you." She paused, then added: "Besides, I'm frightened, really frightened—frightened by what you said to me. Question me—I will answer."

"Question you about everything?" he asked.

"No, no!" she said in a tone of anguish. "Not about the night at Beaucourt. But about the other things. As shortly as you can, please. What is it you want to know?"

Ralph reflected. The questions were not easy to put since all of them must tend to throw light on the matter of which she refused to speak.

He began: "First of all what is your name?"

"Aurelie—Aurelie d'Asteux."

"Then why that name of Leonide Balli? Was it a pseudonym?"

"Leonide Balli exists. She was ill and remained at Nice. Among the actors of her company, with whom I traveled from Nice to Marseilles, there was one I knew because I played *Veronique* last winter in some private theatricals. So they all begged me to take the place of Leonide Balli for one evening. They were so troubled and upset that I felt obliged to render them this service. We told the manager of the Toulouse theatre, who, at the last moment, decided to make no announcement of the change and let it be believed that I was Leonide Balli."

"Then you're not an actress," said Ralph in a tone of relief. "I am glad you're not. I prefer that you should be simply the pretty boarder at Sainte-Marie."

She frowned and said coldly: "Continue."

"Well, the gentleman who knocked Marescal's hat off when you came out of the confectioner's on the Boulevard Haussmann, was he your father?"

"My step-father."

"And his name?"

"Bregeac."

"Bregeac?"

"Yes, Director of Judicial Affairs at the Ministry of the Interior."

"And consequently Marescal's chief?"

"Yes. And they've always disliked one another. Marescal, who is strongly supported by the Minister himself, is trying to supplant my step-father, and my step-father is trying to get rid of him."

"And Marescal is in love with you?"

"He asked my hand in marriage. I rejected him, and my step-father forbade him the house. He hates us and he has sworn to avenge himself."

"To pass from one to another, what is the name of the man of the Villa Faradoni?" Ralph asked.

"Jodot."

"What's his profession?"

"I don't know. He used to come to the house occasionally to see my step-father."

"And the third?"

"William Ancivel. He used to come to the house too. He is on the stock exchange and engaged in other business."

"More or less doubtful?"

"I don't know–perhaps."

Ralph summed up the results of the conversation so far.

"These then are your three enemies–for there aren't any more, are there?"

"Yes. My step-father," she said sadly,

"What? Your mother's husband?"

"My poor mother is dead."

"And are all these people persecuting you for the same reason—on account of the secret you know and they do not?" said Ralph thoughtfully.

"Yes; except Marescal, who knows nothing about the secret and is only trying to take vengeance."

"Is it possible for you to give me any information, not about the secret itself, but about the circumstances connected with it?" he asked.

She thought for a few moments and then said: "Yes, I can. I can tell you what the others know, the reason of their fury against me."

Up to then she had answered the questions briefly and dryly. Now she appeared to be really interested in what she was saying.

"This is the story, briefly," she began. "My father, who was my mother's cousin, died before my birth, leaving my mother a fair income to which was added an allowance which came from my grandfather d'Asteux. My mother's father, an excellent man, an artist and inventor, was always in search of discoveries and great secrets, always traveling on miraculous business which was to bring us an immense fortune. I knew him very well. I can see myself sitting on his knee and hear him staying to me: 'My little Aurelie will be very rich. It is for her I am working.' Then, when I was just six years old, he wrote to my mother and begged her to join him, bringing me with her, without letting any one know anything about it. One night we took the train and went to him and stayed two days. At the moment of starting on our return journey, my mother said to me in his presence:

"'Aurelie, never tell any one where you have been the last two days, neither what you have done nor what you have seen. It is a secret which henceforth belongs to you as well as to us, a secret which will give you a great fortune when you are twenty.'

"'A very great fortune,' said my grandfather. 'Therefore swear to us never to speak of these things to any one, whatever happens.'

"'To no one, except the man you love and of whom you are as sure as you are of yourself,' my mother amended.

"I made the promise they demanded of me. I was very much moved by their earnestness, and I cried.

"A few months later my mother married Bregeac. It was an unhappy marriage and did not last long. During the course of the next year she died of pneumonia after having secretly given me a sheet of paper on which was set out all the information about the district we had visited and what I was to do when I was twenty. A little while later my grandfather also died, and I remained alone with my step-father, Bregeac, who got rid of me as soon as he could by sending me to this convent at Sainte-Marie. I came to it very unhappy and sad, but I was upheld by the importance this keeping a secret gave me in my own eyes. Then one Sunday I looked for an out-of-the-way place and came here, up to this terrace, to carry out a plan my childish brain had formed. I knew by heart the information given me by my mother. What good was it to keep a document which all the world would know if I did not get rid of it. I burnt it in this vase."

Ralph nodded his head and said: "And you have forgotten all the information it contained?"

"Yes," she said. "As the days passed, without my perceiving it, all that information was effaced from my mind by my absorption in the friendships, the work, and the play I found here. I have forgotten the name of the district, what part of the country it is in, the line which took us to it, and things I was to do–everything."

"Absolutely everything?" he asked.

"Everything except some views of the country and some impressions which engraved themselves more deeply on my childish eyes and ears–pictures that I have never ceased to see since–noises, the chiming of bells which I still hear as if they were chiming still."

"And it is these impressions and images that your enemies wish to know, hoping to get at the truth by means of what you can tell them?" he asked.

"Yes."

"But how did they know?"

"Because my mother was so imprudent as not to destroy certain letters in which my grandfather alluded to the secret which had been intrusted to me. Bregeac, who found those letters, later, never spoke to me of them during my ten years here, ten delightful years, the best years of my life. But the very day I returned to Paris, two years ago, he questioned me about them. I told him what I told you, as I had the right to do, but refused to disclose any of the vague memories which might have put him on the track. After that it was a constant persecution—reproaches, abuse, terrible rages—up to the very moment I resolved to fly."

"Alone?"

She flushed and replied: "No. But under conditions you may believe. William Ancivel was paying court to me, with great discretion, pretending to be a friend who wished to be useful to me without any hope of being rewarded for it. So he won, if not my sympathy, at least my confidence, and I made the great mistake of informing him of my intention of flying."

"And no doubt he approved of it?"

"He approved of it warmly, and helped me in my preparations by selling some jewels and securities left me by my mother. On the eve of my flight, since I was uncertain exactly where to take refuge, he said to me: 'I have just come from Nice and I have to return there to-morrow. Would you like me to escort you there? At this time of year you will not find a quieter place of retreat than the Riviera.' What motive could I have had for refusing his offer? It is true that I did not love him; but he appeared to be entirely devoted to me. I accepted it."

"How imprudent!" said Ralph.

"Yes," she said. "And the more imprudent since we were not on those terms of friendship which would excuse such behavior. But what would you? I was alone in the world, unhappy and persecuted. A helping hand was stretched out to me—for a few hours as I thought. We started."

Aurelie hesitated for a few moments; then she went on with her story more quickly.

"The journey was terrible—for reasons which you know. When William lifted me into the carriage he had stolen from the doctor, I was utterly done. He dragged me wherever he wanted, towards another station and from there, since we had our tickets, to Nice, where I got my luggage. I was in a fever, almost delirious. I acted without knowing what I was doing. He took advantage of it next day to make me accompany him to an estate where he had to recover, during the absence of the owner, some securities of which he had been robbed. I went there, as I should have gone anywhere. I had lost the power to think. I obeyed him passively. It was at that villa that I was attacked and carried off by Jodot—"

"And saved, for the second time, by me—whom you rewarded a second time by flying as soon as you were rescued. But no matter. Jodot also demanded revelations, didn't he?"

"Yes."

"And then?"

"Then I went back to the hotel to which William had begged me to follow him."

"But by this time you knew the kind of man he was!" protested Ralph.

"How? One sees clearly enough when one definitely looks; but for two days I had been living in a kind of madness that had been aggravated by Jodot's attack. I followed William therefore without even asking him the object of the journey. I was alone, ashamed of my cowardice, and harassed by the presence of this man who was becoming more and more a stranger to me. What part did I play at Monte Carlo? It is not very clear to me. William had intrusted some letters to me, which I was to hand over to him in the corridor of the hotel that he might himself hand them over to a gentleman. What letters? What gentleman? Why was Marescal there? How did you snatch me from him? All that is quite obscure. However, my instincts had awakened; I felt a growing hostility to William. I detested him. And I left Monte Carlo resolved to break the agreement which united us and come and hide myself here. He pursued me as far as Toulouse and when I told him my decision to leave him, and he was convinced that nothing would make me return to him, coldly and harshly, with a fury that made him look hideous, he said: 'Well and good, let us separate. It's really all the same to me. But I make one condition.'"

"A condition?"

"'Yes. One day I heard your step-father speaking of a secret which had been bequeathed to you. Tell me that secret and you are free.'"

"Then I understood everything. All his protestations and devotion were so many lies. His sole object was to get from me some day, either by winning my love, or by threats, the revelations which I had refused my step-father and which Jodot had tried to tear from me."

She was silent. Ralph studied her closely. He had the strongest impression that she had told the whole truth.

He said gravely: "Would you like to know exactly the character of this brute?"

She shook her head.

"Is it really necessary?" she asked.

"It would be better that you should know it. Listen. At Nice the securities which he was seeking at the Villa Faradoni did not belong to him. He had merely come to steal them. At Monte Carlo he demanded a hundred thousand francs for the return of some compromising letters. The fellow is just a crook and a thief, perhaps worse; that's what he is."

Aurelie did not protest. She must have had some notion of the real facts, and this brutal enumeration of them did not surprise her.

"You have saved me from him. I thank you," she said gently.

"Alas, you ought to have confided in me instead of flying from me," he said. "What a lot of time we have lost!"

She turned to go but paused to say: "Why should I confide in you? Who are you? I don't know you. Marescal, who accuses you, does not even know your name. You saved me from every danger–for what reason? With what object?"

He laughed gently and said: "With the object of tearing your secret from you, like the others: is that what you mean?"

"I don't mean anything," she murmured despondently. "I know nothing, I understand nothing. For two or three weeks I have been dashing myself against walls of darkness on every side. Do not ask more trust from me than I can give. I distrust everything and everybody."

He took pity on her and let her go.

As he went away himself, he thought: "She has not said a word about that terrible night. Miss Bakersfield was murdered; two men were murdered. And I saw her disguised and masked."

While waiting for her on the topmost terrace he had seen a little door in the wall of the terrace below it. That terrace also was empty. Keeping under cover, he went down to the little door and easily opened it. It gave him a much easier way of access to the topmost terrace.

He descended to the pool, very thoughtful. For him also everything was mysterious and inexplicable. Round him, as round her, rose those same walls of darkness, through the tiniest cracks in which here and there filtered a dim light. In the presence of the girl herself, moreover—and it had been so since the beginning of the adventure—he never thought for a moment of the oath of vengeance that he had sworn above the body of Miss Bakersfield, or of anything else which could disfigure the gracious image of the girl with the green eyes.

During the next two days he did not see her. Then she came three days in succession without a word of explanation of her return, but as if she was seeking a protection she could not do without.

The first day she stayed for ten minutes, the second for fifteen, the third for thirty. They talked little. Whether she wished it or not confidence in him was slowly taking possession of her. Gentler and less distant with him, she came as far as the breach in the wall and looked down on the eddying waters of the pool. Several times he tried to question her. At once she fled, trembling, terrified by anything which might be an allusion to the terrible hours at Beaucourt. However she talked more, but of events in her distant past, of the life which she formerly led at Sainte-Marie, and of the peace she was again enjoying in its kindly and serene atmosphere.

Once, when her hand lay palm upwards on the rim of the vase, he bent down and, without touching it, examined the lines.

"It is exactly as I guessed the first day I saw you—a double destiny, one dark and tragic, the other happy and quite simple. They cross, are entangled and mixed, and it is not yet possible to say which will win in the long run. Which of them is your true destiny, the destiny that corresponds to your true nature?" he said slowly.

"The happy destiny," she said. "There is in me something that rises quickly to the surface, which brings me, as it does here, cheerfulness and forgetfulness, whatever be the perils."

"The danger is passing," Ralph declared, and he continued to study her hand and added: "Distrust water. Water may be fatal to you—ship-wrecks—floods—what perils! But they are passing. Yes; things are settling down in your life. Already your happier destiny is prevailing over the unhappy one."

He lied in order to soothe her, out of the constant desire that a smile should sometimes wreathe her delightful lips, at which he dared hardly look. For his part, indeed, he wished to forget, to be deluded. So he lived for a fortnight in a profound lightness of spirit which he forced himself to hide. He was afflicted by the dizziness of those hours in which love casts you into an intoxication and renders you insensible to everything but the joy of contemplating the beloved and listening to her voice. He refused to call up the threatening image of Marescal, of William, or of Jodot. If none of these three enemies appeared, it was because they had certainly lost track of their victim. Why then should he not abandon himself to the delightful ease which he enjoyed in the presence of the girl? Why should he not, since he loved her and confessed to himself that he loved her, abandon himself to this love which was little by little becoming, almost without his knowing it, the very principle of his life and all his actions?

The awakening was rude. One afternoon, leaning over the wall which ran along the edge of the gorge, they were looking down into the mirror of the pool below them, almost still in the middle, its edges ruffled by little waves hurrying towards the narrow outlet through which the brook sank into the earth, when a distant voice called out in the garden below:

"Aurelie! Aurelie! Where are you? Aurelie!"

"Gracious!" cried the girl in troubled accents. "Why are they calling me?"

She ran to the end of the terrace and saw one of the nuns in the avenue of limes.

"Here I am! What is it, sister?"

"A telegram," cried the sister.

"A telegram? Don't take the trouble to come up here, sister. I'll come down to you."

A few minutes later when she came back to the topmost terrace with a telegram in her hand, she looked distracted.

"It's from my step-father," she said.

"Bregeac?"

"Yes."

"He is summoning you back to Paris?" Ralph said gravely.

"He will be here at any moment."

"What for?"

"To take me away!" she gasped.

"Impossible!"

"Look!"

He read the two lines of the telegram, which had been dispatched from Bordeaux.

"*Shall arrive four o'clock be ready to leave at once. Bregeac.*"

Ralph considered the message and asked: "Have you written to tell him that you are here?"

"No: he must have come to the conclusion that I would come here."

"And what are you going to do?" he asked.

"What can I do?"

"Refuse to go with him."

"The Mother-superior would never consent to keep me."

"Then leave here at once," Ralph suggested.

"How?"

He pointed to the door in the wall of the next terrace and waved towards the forest.

"Go? Run away from the convent as though I were guilty?" she cried in protesting accents. "No. It would cause these poor women, who love me as a daughter too much sorrow. Never will I do that!"

Feebly she sank down on a stone bench under the opposite parapet. Ralph crossed the terrace to her and said gravely:

"I have made a bad mistake in letting myself be distracted from the task I have set myself of protecting you. I ought to have remained as distrustful as I was at the beginning and advised you, urged you rather, to go away from here. From the very first I was sure that it was necessary. But the pleasure of being here, of seeing you every day—no, no: don't run away. I'm not going to say anything that will upset you; I'm not going to tell you how I feel towards you, or the reasons which make me treat you as I do. But all the same you must quite understand that I am devoted to you as a man is devoted to a woman whom—who is so much to him—and it is necessary that my devotion should give you absolute confidence in me and that you should be ready to obey me blindly. It is the one condition of safety for you. Do you understand?"

"Yes," she said, wholly dominated.

"Then listen. These are my instructions—my orders—yes: my orders. Welcome your step-father peaceably. Don't quarrel with him. Don't even talk to him—not a word. It's the best way of avoiding mistakes. Go with him. Return to Paris. On the very evening of your arrival get out of the house on some pretext or other. A gray-haired old lady will be waiting for you in a car, twenty yards from your door. I will drive both of you away into the country to a hiding-place in which no one will find you. And I will go away at once, I give you my word, and stay away from you till you tell me to come back. Do you agree?"

"Yes," she said and bowed her head.

"In that case till to-morrow evening. And remember what I tell you: whatever happens, you understand—whatever happens, nothing shall prevail against my will to protect you and against the success of my enterprise. If everything seems to be against you, do not lose heart. Do not even worry. Tell yourself confidently, fiercely, that when the danger is greatest no danger threatens you. At the very second at which it is necessary I shall be there. I shall always be there. Good-by mademoiselle."

He bent down and lightly kissed the border of her cloak. Then, pushing aside a piece of old trellis-work he stepped into the bushes and took the hardly visible path which brought him to the door in the wall.

Aurelie did not stir from her seat on the bench of stone.

Barely half a minute had passed when she heard a rustling of branches near the breach in the wall. She raised her head and looked towards it. The shrubs were moving. There was some one there. Yes, beyond a doubt some one was hidden there.

She wanted to call out, to shout for help, but could not. Her voice died in her throat.

The bushes were moving more quickly as some one forced their way through them. Who was going to appear? She hoped that it would be William or Jodot. She feared the two ruffians less than Marescal.

A face appeared among the foliage. Marescal came out of his hiding-place.

From below, on the right, came the sound of the closing of the door in the wall.

CHAPTER VII
ONE OF THE MOUTHS OF HELL

If the situation of the terrace at the top of the large garden, a spot where no one ever came and walled in by thick screens of trees, had afforded Aurelie and Ralph some weeks of absolute security, must it not be supposed that Marescal was going to get a few minutes he needed, and that Aurelie could hope for no help? Inevitably the scene would follow its course to the end willed by her enemy and the dénouement would be in accordance with his implacable will.

He was so sure of it that he did not hurry. He advanced slowly and stopped. The certainty of victory spoiled the harmony of his regular features and disturbed their usual immobility. A grin raised the left corner of his mouth and drew up the left half of his square beard. His teeth were shining; his eyes were hard and cruel.

He said in a jeering tone: "Well, mademoiselle, I think that things have turned out rather favorably for me. There is no way of escaping me, as at Beaucourt station, no means of driving me away, as in Paris. You will have to submit to the law of the stronger."

Straight upright, with stiff arms, her fists clenched on the stone bench, Aurelie gazed at him with an expression of wild anguish. Without a groan, she waited.

"How delightful it is to see you here, charming creature! When one loves in the rather excessive fashion in which I love you, it is not disagreeable to find one's self confronted by revolt and terror. It makes one all the more eager to seize one's prey. Magnificent prey," he added in a low voice, "for you really are magnificently beautiful."

Then he saw the open telegram and jeered again.

"That good fellow Bregeac, isn't it, announcing his imminent arrival and your departure? I know, I know. For the last fortnight I've been keeping an eye on my beloved chief and I'm fully acquainted with his most secret plans. I have men devoted to me in his office. That is how I discovered your hiding-place and have been able to get here an hour or two ahead of him. I just had the time to study the ground, the forest, and the gorge, to catch sight of you in the distance and see you hurry up to this terrace. And I was able to climb up here and catch a glimpse of a figure leaving you. Some lover, wasn't it?"

He made a few steps forward. She shrank away from him, and her back touched the lattice-work which ran round the bench. He lost his temper and cried: "That's nice. I don't suppose you shrank away like that just now when this lover was busy caressing you. Who is the happy man? A fiancé? More likely a lover. I see that I have come just in time to look after my property and prevent the innocent boarder at Sainte-Marie from playing the fool! Ah, if ever I had suspected it!"

He curbed his anger and, bending over her, went on: "After all, all the better; it simplifies matters. The game I was playing was already excellent since I had all the trumps in my hands. But this is an extra piece of luck. Aurelie is not of an uncompromising virtue. One can rob and murder and escape the ditch—and now behold Aurelie quite ready to jump over all obstacles. Then why not in company? What, Aurelie, it may just as well be me as any one else, mayn't it? If he has his advantages there are reasons in my favor which are not to be despised. What do you say, Aurelie?"

She kept silent stubbornly.

The anger of her enemy was inflamed by this terrified silence. And he went on, dwelling on each word: "We have no time for trifles, have we Aurelie, or to touch on one subject after another? It is necessary to speak clearly without mincing matters, in order that there may be no misunderstanding. To come straight to the point then—silence about the past and the humiliations I have suffered. Those no longer count. What does count is the present—the present is all important. Now, the present is the murder on the express, your flight through the woods, your capture by the police; twenty proofs, every one of which is fatal to you. And the present is to-day, when I hold you in my grip and all I have to do is to take you and conduct you to your step-father and shout in his face, before witnesses: 'The murderess, whom they are seeking everywhere, is here! The warrant for her arrest is in my pocket. Send for the police!'"

He stretched out his arm, ready, as he had said, to grasp the criminal, and with this threat hanging over her, he ended in yet harsher accents: "On the one hand, then, this: a public denunciation, the court, and a terrible punishment; on the other hand the alternative I offer to your choice: an alliance, an immediate alliance, on conditions I lay down. It is more than a promise I demand; it is an oath, taken on your knees. The oath that, once you have returned to Paris, you will come to see me, alone, at my flat. And more than that an immediate proof that the alliance is honest, signed by your lips on mine—and not with kiss of disgust and hatred, but with a voluntary kiss, like the kisses other women, as prettier and more difficult to win than you, Aurelie, have given me—a lover's kiss. Answer, curse you!" he shouted in a sudden outburst of fury. "Answer that you accept! I've had enough of your airs of a lost soul! Answer, or I'll jolly well arrest you and it will not only be the kiss but prison as well!"

His left hand fell heavily on her shoulder, while with his right, seizing her by the throat, he pressed back her head against the lattice-work and bent down. But his head stopped short, midway to her lips. He felt her collapse; she had fainted.

This unexpected swoon took him aback. He had come without any very definite plan beyond that of speaking to her, and during the hour before the coming of Bregeac, of obtaining from her a solemn promise and the recognition of the fact that she was in his power. Now chance offered him an inert and helpless victim.

He remained some moments bending over her, gazing at her with greedy eyes. He looked round this sylvan retreat, enclosed and discreet. No witness; no interference possible.

But another idea brought him to the wall, and from among the trees he looked down on the deserted valley, the forest with its dark trees, black and mysterious, in which he had noticed as he paused the mouths of the grottos. Aurelie thrown into one of them, a prisoner, and held under the terrible threat of the police, Aurelie a prisoner for two days, three days, a week if necessary, was not that an unexpected, triumphant dénouement, the beginning and the end of the adventure?

He whistled sharply. Opposite him on the further bank of the pool two arms were waved above two bushes on the edge of the forest. The signal agreed on: two men were there, posted by him to help him carry out his plans. On this side of the pool, a boat was rocking.

He hesitated no longer. He knew that opportunity is fleeting and that, if one does not seize it in its passing, it vanishes like a shadow. He crossed the terrace again and perceived that the girl seemed ready to come to.

"Let us act," he said, "if not—"

He threw a handkerchief round her head and knotted it across her mouth to form a gag. Then he took her up in his arms and carried her away.

She was slight and hardly weighed anything at all. He was a strong man. His burden seemed light. Nevertheless as he came to the breach in the wall and perceived the almost vertical descent worn by storms in the lower part of it, he studied it carefully and decided that it was necessary to take precautions. Therefore he set Aurelie down at the edge of the breach.

Was she waiting for him to make this mistake? Was it a sudden inspiration? In any case his carelessness was at once punished. With an unexpected movement and with a swiftness and decision which took him aback, she tore the handkerchief from her mouth, and without caring what happened, let herself slide from the top to the bottom, like a loosened stone which rolls with an avalanche of pebbles and sand from which rises a cloud of dust.

Recovering from his surprise he dashed after her at the risk of falling, and perceived that she was running at haphazard in a zigzag course from the cliff to the bank of the pool, like a hunted beast that does not know which way to fly.

"You're lost, my dear," he muttered. "There's nothing for you to do but bend the knee."

He had almost caught her, and she was tottering and staggering with fear, when he had an impression that something fell from the top of the terrace and struck the ground near him. He turned, saw a man coming at full speed, the lower part of his face masked by a handkerchief. It must be the man he had called Aurelie's lover. He had time to grip his revolver, but not time to use it. A kick from this adversary, the kick of an expert savage fighter, caught him full in the chest and sent him flying into the sticky swamp on the edge of the pool. He sank, then rose, spluttering, to his feet, up to his knees in the mud. Furious and staggering, he aimed at Ralph, who, no more than twenty yards away, was lifting the girl into the boat.

"Stop! Or I'll fire!" shouted Marescal.

Ralph did not answer. He caught up a rotting plank, rested it on a thwart like a protecting shield between Aurelie and himself and the revolver, then pushed off the boat with a vigorous shove which sent it dancing over the waves. Marescal fired. He fired six times, raging and furious. But, slipping about as he was in the ooze, the bullets went wild. Then, he whistled more shrilly than before. The two men on the other shore sprang up from their lairs, like jacks-in-the-box.

Ralph found himself in the middle of the pool, about thirty yards, that is, from the opposite bank.

"Don't shoot!" yelled Marescal.

Why shoot, indeed? The fugitive had no other course, to escape being dragged by the current towards the gulf in which the brook disappeared, than to row straight across and come to shore at the very spot at which Marescal's men were waiting for him, revolver in hand.

He must have perceived this, for suddenly he brought the boat sharply round and rowed back to the shore on which he had to fight only one adversary with an empty revolver.

"Shoot! Shoot!" shouted Marescal, who perceived what Ralph would be at. "You must shoot now! He's coming back! Shoot, damn you!"

One of the men fired.

There was a cry from the boat. Ralph let go the oars and fell back, and with a cry of despair the girl threw herself upon him. The oars floated away on the surface of the water. The boat remained still for a few moments, as it could not make up its mind, then slowly turned, with its prow pointing towards the current, and began to move backwards, slowly at first then more quickly.

"G-G-Good Heavens!" stammered Marescal, horrified. "They're done for!"

What could he do? There was no doubt what the end would be. The boat was caught by two bubbling torrents which were hurrying along both sides of the pool to a central point; once it turned completely round, then, taking a straight course, with the two bodies lying in the bottom of it, it rushed to the gaping cave and was engulfed!

All this happened in less than three minutes after the two fugitives had left the bank.

Marescal did not stir, his legs in the water, his features contorted with horror, he gazed at the accursed spot as if he were gazing at the mouth of Hell. His hat was floating towards it; mud and water dripped from his hair and beard.

"Is it p-p-possible–is it p-p-possible?" he stammered. "Aurelie! Aurelie! Aurelie!"

A shout from his men awoke him from his stupor. They made a long circuit and reached him ten minutes later. They found him drying himself.

"Is it true?" he asked.

"What?" said one of the men.

"The boat? The gulf?"

He no longer knew. In this way in nightmares abominable visions pass, leaving an impression of terrible realities. The three of them made their way above the mouth of the cavern which opened in a rock crowned with brambles, its surface covered with water-plants. The water flowed into it in narrow rapids from which rose the rounded and shining tops of large boulders. They bent over the edge of the rock and listened. Nothing. Nothing but the murmur of hurrying waters—nothing but a cold blast, which rose white with flecks of foam.

"It's hell!" murmured Marescal. "It's one of the mouths of hell."

Then he went on: "She is dead—she is drowned. How stupid! What a terrible death! If that damned fool had only left her alone—I should have—I should have——"

They went away through the woods. Marescal jogged along in a kind of stupor. Several times his companions questioned him. They were shady loafers whom he had picked up for this expedition and not regular men in his service; and he had only informed them roughly of his plans. He did not answer them. He thought of Aurelie, so gracious and so full of life, whom he loved so passionately. He was harassed by memories of her, by remorse and terror.

He was indeed uneasy in mind. The coming inquiry might very well involve him and throw part of the blame for this tragic accident on him. In that case it meant a scandal and ruin. Bregeac would be pitiless; he would be indefatigable in his efforts to avenge his step-daughter.

Presently he could think of nothing but getting out of that part of the country as quietly as possible. He frightened his two assistants by telling them that a common danger menaced them and that it was imperative, if they would escape it, that each should go his own way and look after himself before the alarm was given and their presence marked. He gave them twice the money he had promised them, made a circuit round Luz, and took the road to Pierrefitte-Nestales in the hope of finding some conveyance which would bring him to the railway station in time for the seven o'clock train that evening.

It was not till he had walked three kilometers from Luz that a small two-wheeled cart, covered with a tarpaulin and driven by a countryman wrapped in a large cloak and wearing a Basque cap, overtook him.

He stopped the cart with an air of authority and said imperiously: "Five francs if you get me to Pierrefitte-Nestales in time to catch the train."

The peasant did not appear to be greatly excited by this generous offer and did not even whip up the wretched animal which ambled along between shafts that were much too large for it.

It was a long journey. They crawled along. It almost looked as if the peasant was holding his beast back, instead of urging it on.

Marescal lost his temper. He seemed, indeed, to have lost all control whatever over himself and whined: "We shall never get there–never. What a jade your horse is! Look here: I'll give you ten francs if we catch that train. What about it?"

The country appeared to him hideous, peopled with phantoms and teaming with detectives on the trail of the detective Marescal. He could not endure the thought of passing the night in this district in which the body of the girl he had sent to her death was lying.

"Twenty francs!" he said.

And all at once, losing his head wholly, he shouted: "Fifty francs! I'll give you fifty francs! It isn't further than a mile and a quarter. A mile and a quarter in seven minutes, dammit! It can be done! Get on, curse you, thrash that nanny-goat of a horse! Fifty francs!"

On the instant the peasant became furiously energetic, and, as if he had only been waiting for this magnificent offer, set himself to lash the nanny-goat with such ardor that it set off at a gallop.

"Look out! Mind what you're doing! You'll have us in the ditch!" cried Marescal.

The countryman seemed not to care a hang whether they went into the ditch or not. Fifty francs! He beat his horse as hard as he could with a stick fitted with a large copper ferule. The maddened beast galloped faster and faster. The cart leaped from one side of the road to the other, Marescal grew more and more terrified.

"But it's idiotic!" he shouted. "You're going to upset us! Go slower, confound you! You're mad, I tell you—mad! That's it, you fool! Here we go!"

They went, indeed. The countryman clumsily pulled the wrong rein; the cart made a wilder jump and the whole outfit, cart, driver, passenger and load, plunged into the ditch in such a disastrous fashion that the countryman and Marescal found themselves on their stomachs with the cart on the top of them while the horse, entangled in the harness, with its heels in the air, beat a tattoo on the foot-board. Marescal presently discovered that none of his bones were broken. But the countryman was crushing him with his full weight. He tried to push him off. He could not.

Then he heard a kindly voice murmur in his ear: "Could you oblige me with a light, Rudolph?"

Marescal felt his body chill from head to foot. Death and only death could produce that impression of limbs already stiff and cold that nothing would ever warm again.

He muttered through chattering teeth: "The man of the express!"

"The man of the express, the very man," echoed the voice at his ear-hole.

"The man of the terrace!" moaned Marescal.

"Quite right—the man of the express, the man of the terrace—and also the man of Monte Carlo and the man of Boulevard Haussmann and the murderer of the two brothers Loubeaux and the accomplice of Aurelie, and the navigator of the boat and the driver of the cart. That gives you plenty of warriors to fight, old chap; and I venture to say that they can all hold their own."

The horse had finished its drumming on the foot-board and scrambled to its feet and dragged the cart off them. Ralph sat up, on the small of the detective's back, quietly drew off his big cloak, and wrapped it round the detective, so paralyzing his legs and arms. He caught the reins, pulled the cart towards him and, keeping a foot painfully on the detective's back, stripped the horse of the traces and reins and bound Marescal with excessive tightness. Then he picked him up and carried him to the top of the high embankment into a thicket. He went down again, came back with a couple of straps from the harness, and fastened the detective by the neck and chest to the trunk of a birch.

"I don't seem to bring you any luck, poor old Rudolph. This is the second time I've tied you up like a mummy. Ah, don't let me forget to use Aurelie's handkerchief as a gag. The perfect prisoner should neither be seen nor heard. But you can see everything with your eyes and also listen with all your ears. Hark! Do you hear the whistle of the train? There it goes: puff, puff, puff! It has started for the North and it's carrying away Aurelie and her step-father. I really must set your mind at rest. Aurelie's as much alive as you or I. A little tired, perhaps, after so many emotions. But a good night's rest, and she won't show a trace of them."

He went away and tied the horse to a tree and cleared the fragments of the cart off the road. Then he came back and sat down by the Commissary.

"A queer business that shipwreck, wasn't it?" he said amiably. "But there was no miracle about it, I assure you. And there was no luck about it either. That you may know better how to act in the future, you must know that I never rely on miracles or on luck, but solely on myself. So—but I hope that my little sermon is not boring you? Perhaps you'd rather go to sleep. No? Well, to continue—I had scarcely left Aurelie on the terrace when I turned anxious. Was it quite prudent to leave her like that? Can one ever be sure that some blackguard is not prowling about—that some pomade-pot of a lady-killer is not sneaking about the neighborhood? Intuitions like that form part of my system. I always act on them. So I went back. And what do I see? Rudolph, the infamous ravisher and faithless policeman, plunging into the valley on the track of his prey. Thereupon I fall from Heaven, I kick you into a cold bath, I carry off Aurelie, and there we are! The pool, the forest, the grottoes, that way lay liberty. Off we go! Then you whistle and two ugly-looking customers spring up at your call! What to do? An insoluble problem, if ever there was one. No: A pleasing thought. Suppose I let myself be swallowed up by the gulf? At that very moment a revolver spits a bullet at me. I howl; I let go the oars; I pretend to be dead at the bottom of the boat. I explain my action to Aurelie, and bang we go headfirst into the abyss!"

Ralph tapped Marescal's thigh.

"Don't shudder, old chap, I beg you: we did not run any risk at all. All the countryside knows that, if you make use of that tunnel which the stream has cut through the chalk, you land two hundred yards lower down on a nice little sandy beach from which you mount by a short staircase cut in the cliff. On Sundays dozens of boys make the journey and drag their skiff back and make it again. There is no fear of as much as a scratch. And in that way we were able to observe from a distance your flabbergastedness and see you go off, with bowed head, crushed by remorse. Then I took Aurelie back to the convent garden. Her step-father came to fetch her in a carriage in time to catch the train. As for me, I went to look for my suit-case, bought the cart and cloak and cap from a peasant and started off, gently, with no other object in view than to cover the retreat of Aurelie."

Ralph rested his head on Marescal's shoulder.

"I needn't tell you that this business has tired me a little and that a short nap seems to be in order. Watch over my dreams, Rudolph darling, and do not worry. Everything is for the best in the best of worlds. Every one in it occupies the place he deserves; and blockheads serve as pillows for intelligent people like me." He went to sleep.

Twilight came and then the night fell. Now and again Ralph awoke and said a few words about the shining stars or the clear light of the moon. Then he went to sleep again.

Towards midnight he grew hungry. He had some food in his suit-case. He removed Marescal's gag, and offered him some.

"Eat, darling," he said affectionately, putting a piece of cheese into his mouth.

But once again Marescal lost his temper; he spat out the cheese and growled:

"Imbecile! Idiot! You're the blockhead! Do you know what you've done?"

"Certainly. I've rescued Aurelie. Her step-father is taking her back to Paris; and I'm going to join her there."

"Her step-father!" cried Marescal. "You don't know then?"

"What?"

"That's he's in love with her, her precious step-father!"

Ralph, of a sudden beside himself, buried his hands in Marescal's hair, and tried to shake his strapped-up head.

"Imbecile! Idiot! Why didn't you tell me so, instead of hanging on my sermonizing lips? He's in love with her, is he? The swine! Then everybody's in love with that girl! A lot of silly brutes! Have you *never* looked at yourself in the glass? You, with your pomaded wig!"

He bent forward and added: "Listen to me, Marescal. I'm going to tear that little girl from her step-father. But leave her in peace. Don't bother about us any more."

"It's impossible," growled the Commissary savagely.

"Why?"

"She has murdered."

"So that is your plan?"

"To hand her over to justice; and I shall carry it out, for I hate her."

He spoke these words in an access of so savage a rancor that Ralph could not fail to understand that henceforth hate would have the better of love in Marescal's heart.

"All the worse for you, Rudolph. I was going to propose a trifle of promotion to you, something in the way of the post of Commissioner of Police. But you prefer war. Have your own way. Begin with a night in the open air. Nothing is better for the health. As for me, I shall ride to Lourdes on the main line. Twenty kilometers–about three hours' trot for my fiery steed. And to-night I shall be in Paris, where I shall begin by putting Aurelie into a place of safety. Good-by, Rudolph."

He mounted, fixed his suit-case in front of him as comfortably as he could, and without a saddle or spurs, whistling a hunting song, kicked his horse into a trot, and disappeared in the darkness.

That night in Paris an old lady of the name of Victorine, who had been his nurse, was waiting in a car, outside the house in which Bregeac lived. Ralph was at the wheel.

He kept watch there all night. In the early morning he saw a rag-picker, who was hunting with his hook through the orderly boxes that stood along the curb. Immediately with that sixth sense which enabled him to recognize people by their carriage and bearing, rather than by their faces, he recognized, under the rags and dirty cap, in spite of the fact that he had seen such a very little of him in the garden of the Villa Faradoni and on the road to Nice, the murderer Jodot.

"The devil!" murmured Ralph. "That gentleman's at work already, is he?"

At a few minutes to eight a maid came out of the front door of the house and hurried across to a chemist's shop lower down the street. Ralph hurried after her with a bank-note ready and accosted her. He learned that Aurelie, who had returned the night before with her step-father, had been struck down by fever and was delirious.

In the middle of the afternoon Marescal was prowling about the house.

CHAPTER VIII
PLANS AND STRATAGEMS

Events had taken a course uncommonly favorable to Marescal. Aurelie's confinement to her room meant checkmate to the plan that Ralph had had in mind; it rendered it impossible to fly; it kept her awaiting denunciation in a terrible suspense. Marescal took immediate precautions not to lose these advantages; the nurse they had to put in charge of her, was one of his creatures and, as Ralph was able to ascertain, let him have word every day of the condition of the sick girl. In the event of a sudden improvement, he would have acted.

"Yes," said Ralph to himself. "But if he has not acted already, it must be that he has motives which prevent him still from laying information against her and prefer to await the end of her illness. He is making his preparations. Let us make our preparations too."

Though he was opposed to too logical hypotheses which the event always upsets, Ralph had drawn from the facts of the affair some, so to speak, involuntary, conclusions. The strange truth of which no one in the world had dreamt for an instant, but which was so simple, he saw in a confused fashion, rather owing to the weight of the facts than to any effort of his intelligence, and he understood that the moment had come to attack the problem with the utmost determination.

"In an enterprise," he often said to himself, "the first step is often the most difficult of all."

If certain actions were clear enough to him, the motives of them remained obscure. To him characters in the drama presented the appearance of people struggling in stress and storm. If he meant to win, it was no longer enough to go on defending Aurelie day after day, but he must ransack the past and discover what profound reasons had moved these people and influenced them in the course of that tragic night.

"To sum up," he said to himself, "besides me, there are four leading actors who circle round Aurelie and who, all four of them, persecute her: William, Jodot, Marescal and Bregeac. Of these four, some are drawn to her by love, others by the desire of tearing her secret from her. The combination of these two elements, love and greed, are the determining factors in the affair. Now William is, for the time being, out of action. Bregeac and Jodot do not worry me much, as long as Aurelie is ill. There remains Marescal. That is the enemy to be watched."

There were opposite Bregeac's house, some empty rooms. Ralph established himself in them. Moreover, since the nurse was in Marescal's pay, he renewed his acquaintance with the maid and bribed her. Thrice, during the absence of the nurse, this maid took him into Aurelie's bedroom.

Aurelie did not appear to recognize him. She was still so enfeebled by the fever that she could only utter a few incoherent words and close her eyes again. But he had no doubt that she heard him and that she knew who it was who spoke to her in that gentle voice which comforted and soothed her like the passes of an hypnotist.

"It is I, Aurelie," he said. "You see that I am true to my promise and that you may have complete confidence in me. I swear to you that your enemies are not capable of fighting me and that I will set you free. How should it be otherwise? I think of nothing but you. I reconstitute your life, and little by little it grows clearer and clearer to me exactly as it is, simple and honest. I know that you are innocent. I've always known it, even when I accused you. The most irrefutable proof seemed false to me: the lady with the green eyes could not be a criminal."

He did not fear to go further in his avowals and say the tenderest words to her, to which she was compelled to listen, for he mixed with his advice:

"You are all my life. I have never found so much grace and charm in a woman. Trust yourself to me, Aurelie. I only ask one thing of you, you know, trust. If any one questions you, do not answer. If any one writes to you, do not reply, if any one wishes to take you away from here refuse to go. Trust in me to the very last minute of the cruelest hour. I shall be there. I shall always be there because I live only for you and by you."

The girl's face filled slowly with a restful quietness. She fell asleep, as if lulled by a happy dream.

Then he slipped into the room reserved for the use of Bregeac and sought, vainly enough, papers and information which might guide his actions.

He also made domiciliary visits to the flat which Marescal occupied in the Rue de Rivoli and searched them with extraordinary minuteness.

Finally he made the most careful inquiries in the offices of the Minister of the Interior in which the two men worked. Their rivalry and hatred of one another were known to all. Both of them, supported by people in high places, were the objects of a struggle both at the Ministry and at the Prefecture of Police, waged by powerful personages who battled above their heads. The service suffered from it. Either of them accused the other openly of serious derelictions from duty. There was talk of calling on them to resign. Which of them would be sacrificed?

One day, hidden behind the window curtain, Ralph watched Bregeac at Aurelie's bedside. He was a bilious-looking person with a thin and yellow face. Of rather more than middle height, he carried himself with something of an air, and at any rate he was a man of greater elegance and distinction than the vulgar Marescal.

Awaking suddenly, Aurelie caught sight of him bending over her, and said in harsh enough accents: "Leave me! Go away!"

"How you detest me and how you would love to injure me!" he murmured sadly.

"I should never injure the man that my mother married," she said.

He gazed upon her with eyes full of suffering.

"You are very beautiful, my poor child," he said. "But, alas, why have you always rejected my affection? Yes, I know that I was in the wrong. For a very long while I was only drawn to you by that secret you kept from me for no reason whatever. But if you had not been so stubborn in that absurd silence, I should never have dreamt of the love which now tortures me, for you will never love me—it is not possible that you should ever love me."

She did not wish to listen to him and turned away her head.

However, he went on: "During your delirium you often spoke of revelations you wanted to make to me. Were they revelations about the secret, or about your senseless flight with that fellow William? Where did that outsider take you? What became of you before you took refuge in your convent?"

She did not answer—either because she was too exhausted to answer, or because she disliked him too heartily.

He said no more and went away. When he had gone, Ralph, slipping away in his turn, saw that she was weeping.

Finally, at the end of a fortnight's investigation any one but Ralph would have been discouraged. Speaking generally, apart from certain tendencies, which he had interpreted in his own way, the chief problems remained insoluble, or, at any rate, were incapable of any apparent solution.

"But I am not wasting my time," he said to himself; "and that is the essential thing. Action often consists of inactivity. The atmosphere is less thick. My vision of the characters and events in this affair is growing stronger and more precise. If the fact which is the key to the problem is still missing, I am in the very heart of the enemy's camp. On the eve of a combat which promises to be so violent, when all these mortal enemies confront one another, the needs of the fight itself and of finding effective weapons will certainly give me the unexpected jolt which will strike out the sparks which will show me the truth."

One of those sparks was struck out sooner than he expected, a spark which lighted one quarter of the darkness, a quarter from which he did not think that anything important would come. One morning he was gazing out of his window, with his eyes fixed on the windows of Bregeac's house, when he saw, still disguised as a rag-picker, the murderer Jodot. This time Jodot was carrying on his shoulder a canvas bag into which he dropped his loot. He set it down in front of the house itself, sat down and began to eat his *dejeuner*, poking about in the orderly box which the cook had carried out. The action seemed mechanical, but in a minute or two Ralph perceived that the man was only hooking out of the box crumpled envelopes and torn-up letters. He cast a glance over each scrap and then continued his sorting. There was no doubt that he was interested in Bregeac's correspondence.

A quarter of an hour later he hoisted his bag on to his back and went off. Ralph followed him to Montmartre, to discover that Jodot had a junk shop there. He came three days in succession and on each occasion he repeated the same equivocal operation. But on the third day, which was a Sunday, Ralph surprised Bregeac watching him out of his window. When Jodot went off, Bregeac, in his turn, followed him with infinite precaution. Ralph followed both of them at a distance. Was he going to discover the tie which connected Bregeac and Jodot?

In this order, following one another, they went through the Monceau district, crossed over the fortifications, and came to the banks of the Seine at the end of the Boulevard Bineau. A few modest villas stood between patches of waste land. Jodot set down his bag in front of one of these villas and sat down on the curb and began to eat.

He remained there four or five hours, watched by Bregeac, who had his lunch in the arbor of a small restaurant about thirty yards away, and by Ralph, who, stretched at full length on the river bank, smoked cigarettes.

When Jodot went away, Bregeac went off in the opposite direction as if he had lost all interest in the matter. Ralph went into the restaurant and over a meal, for which he was more than ready, chatted to the proprietor. He learned that the villa in front of which Jodot had been sitting, had belonged a few weeks before to the two brothers Loubeaux, who had been murdered by three ruffians in the Marseilles express. The police had sealed it up and left it in charge of a neighbor who went for a walk every Sunday afternoon.

Ralph had started at hearing the name of the brothers Loubeaux. The maneuvers of Jodot began to assume significance.

He went deeper into the matter and learned that at the time of their death the brothers Loubeaux lived very little at their villa, which they only used as an office for their champagne business. They had separated from their partner and were traveling on their own account.

"Their partner?" said Ralph.

"Yes. You'll still see his name engraved on the brass plate on the door, 'Loubeaux Frères, et Jodot'," said the proprietor of the restaurant.

Ralph started again.

"Jodot?" he said in incredulous accents.

"Yes—a big, red-faced man who looks like a strong man at a fair. No one has seen him about here for more than a year."

Most important information, as Ralph told himself, when the proprietor hurried to welcome a regular customer.

So Jodot had formerly been the partner of the two brothers whom he was to murder later. There was nothing astonishing in the fact that the police had not gone carefully into this matter, for they had never suspected that there had been any Jodot concerned in the crime, since Marescal had made up his mind that Ralph was the third confederate of the murderers. But why did Jodot return to the very place where his victims had formerly lived? And why did Bregeac spy upon his coming?

The week passed uneventfully. Jodot did not appear again in front of Bregeac's house. But on the Saturday Ralph, convinced that he would return to the villa on the Sunday, climbed over the wall of its garden from the piece of waste land which ran along it and made his way into the villa itself through a window on the first floor.

Two of the rooms on this floor were still furnished; and there were signs that they had been carefully searched. Who had searched them? The Police? Bregeac? Jodot? With what object?

Ralph did not search them himself. That which some one else had sought, was either not to be found there, or was to found there no longer. He settled down to spend the night in an easy chair. He found a book lying on the table and began to read it by the light of his electric torch. It sent him to sleep.

The truth is only revealed to those who compel it to emerge from the darkness; and it often happens that, when one believes it to be a long way off, chance comes and sets it in the very place one has prepared for it. One's merit consists in the quality of that preparation. On awaking, Ralph's eyes fell on the book he had been reading. Its cover had been again covered with a piece of cloth cut out of one of those squares of black cloth which photographers use to cover their cameras.

Ralph hunted about. In a corner of a cupboard, devoted apparently to odds and ends, he found one of those very squares of cloth. Three round pieces of about the size of a plate had been cut out of it.

"Here we are!" he said to himself in some excitement. "I *am* in luck! The three masks of the train-robbers came from this house! Here is the irrefutable proof of it. It does throw a lot of light on the affair."

The truth now appeared to him so natural, so exactly in keeping with the unexpressed intuitions he had had, and to a certain extent so entertaining in its simplicity, that he laughed aloud in that silent house.

"Perfect—perfect," he said to himself. "Fortune itself will supply me with the missing facts. Henceforward she will enter my service, and all the details of the affair are going to come at my call and range themselves in order before me in the full light of day."

At eight o'clock in the morning the caretaker of the villa made his Sunday round of the ground floor and satisfied himself that the seals were unbroken. At nine Ralph went down into the dining-room, and opened a window, leaving the shutters closed, just above the spot on which Jodot was accustomed to sit.

Jodot arrived punctually. He came with his sack, which he set against the wall. Then he sat down and began his meal. Over it he talked to himself, but in so low a voice that Ralph could not catch his words. His meal consisted of sausages and cheese washed down by a jug of red wine; and after it he lit a pipe, the smoke of which rose to Ralph's nostrils.

This first pipe was followed by a second, then by a third. So two hours passed, without Ralph's being able to understand the reason of this long stay. Through a hole in the shutter he could see Jodot's ragged trouser-legs and his boots down at heel. Beyond them flowed the river. Passers-by came and went. Bregeac must be on the watch in one of the arbors of the restaurant.

At last, a few minutes before noon, Jodot uttered these words:

"Hang it all! Nothing fresh? But it's pretty stiff, dammit!"

He seemed to be speaking not to himself, but to some one close at hand. But no one had joined him: there was no one near him.

"Hell and blazes!" he growled on. "I tell you the bottle's there! I've had it in my hand and seen it with my own eyes not once but a hundred times. Have you done exactly what I told you? The whole of the right side of the cellar, as you went over the left the other day? Well, well—you ought to have found it."

He was silent for a little while; then he went on.

"It might be as well to try somewhere else and move on to the waste ground at the back of the house, in case they threw the bottle there, before the coup on the express. It's an open-air hiding-place, and just as good as any other. If Bregeac has searched the cellar, he mayn't have thought of outside. Go there and look. I'll wait for you."

Ralph did not wait to hear any more. He began to understand as soon as Jodot spoke of the cellar. That cellar must run from the front to the back of the house, with an air-hole into the street and another at the back. Access to it through the air-hole at the back would be easy.

Quickly he ran upstairs to the first floor and into a back bedroom from which he could look down on the waste ground, to find that he had guessed right. In the middle of the unused building plot, in which stood a board with "For Sale" on it, among a heap of old iron, empty barrels, and broken bottles, a small boy of seven or eight, tiny, incredibly thin in his tightly fitting gray jersey, was searching hard, darting about with the agility of a squirrel. The circle he was searching with the object of finding a bottle, was of very small circumference. If Jodot had been right, the search should not take him long. It did not. In about ten minutes after moving the broken barrels and boxes, the small boy rose and, without wasting time, ran towards the villa, carrying a bottle gray with dust.

Ralph ran down the stairs to the ground floor with the intention of relieving the small boy of his prize. But he could not get the door at the head of the stairs to the basement open, and he hurried to his peep-hole at the dining-room window.

He was just in time to hear Jodot say: "That's it! You've got it! Splendid! Now I'm 'armed'. Bregeac's friend won't be able to give me any more trouble. Hurry up! Get out of sight!"

The small boy got out of sight. He squeezed himself through the opening made by a broken bar in the grating and the air-hole and slipped like a ferret into the sack.

Jodot at once rose, hoisted the sack on to his shoulder, and went off.

Ralph gave him a minute or two's grace, then drew the bolts of the front door, opened it, breaking the seals, and started in pursuit.

Jodot was walking briskly along two hundred yards ahead, carrying the confederate who had first explored for him the basement of Bregeac's house, and then the cellar of the villa of the brothers Loubeaux.

Fifty yards behind him Bregeac was winding in and out among the trees which bordered the road.

Fifty yards behind him an angler was rowing along under the bank of the Seine in pursuit of Bregeac. It was Marescal. So Jodot was followed by Bregeac, Bregeac and Jodot by Marescal, and all three of them by Ralph.

And the stake for which all four of them were playing was the possession of a bottle.

"This is growing exciting," said Ralph to himself. "Jodot is in possession of the bottle it is true. But he does not know that other people are after it. Who will be cleverest of the other three? If there was no Lupin in it, I should back Marescal. But Lupin is in it."

Jodot stopped. Bregeac stopped also, so did Marescal in his boat. Ralph stopped too.

Jodot laid his sack on the ground, stretched out so that the small boy should be comfortable, and sitting on a bench, he began to examine the bottle, shaking it and holding it up to the light.

The time had come for Bregeac to act; at any rate that was his opinion; and he came up very quietly.

He had opened a large parasol and held it before him like a shield behind which he hid his face. On his boat Marescal disappeared beneath a very large straw hat.

When Bregeac was three yards from the bench, he shut his parasol, sprang forward, without bothering about the people strolling along the path, snatched the bottle, and took to flight along a lane in the direction of the fortifications.

He did this with uncommon skill and admirable swiftness. Taken aback, Jodot hesitated, cried out, caught up the sack, set it down again as if he was afraid of not being able to run quickly enough with such a burden, lost time and went out of action.

But Marescal, foreseeing the attack, had landed, and at once dashed in pursuit. Ralph did the same. There were only three competitors left.

Bregeac, like a good runner, gave his mind to nothing but his running and did not turn round. Marescal gave his mind only to Bregeac, and he did not turn round either, so that Ralph was able to pursue them quite openly. Why not?

In ten minutes the first of the three runners reached the Ternes Gate. Bregeac was so hot that he took off his jacket. Near the Custom House a street car had stopped and a number of travelers were waiting at the ticket office to get aboard it and return to Paris.

Bregeac mingled with this crowd. Marescal did the same.

The conductor called out the numbers of the tickets. But the jostling was so violent that Marescal had scarcely any difficulty in pulling the bottle out of Bregeac's pocket without Bregeac's being any the wiser. At once Marescal slipped through the Custom House and set off at full speed.

"My good friends eliminate themselves one after the other," chuckled Ralph. "And each of them is working for me."

When, in his turn, Ralph went through the Custom House, he saw Bregeac making desperate efforts to get out of the car through the crowd which blockaded his way, in order to pursue the man who had robbed him.

Marescal plunged into the streets which run parallel to the Avenue des Ternes. They are narrow and winding. He ran like a madman. When he came to a stop at the Avenue Wagram, he was out of breath. His face was shining with sweat, his eyes were bloodshot, his veins were swollen. He mopped his face and forehead, utterly done.

He bought a newspaper and, after having taken a look at it, wrapped the bottle up in it. Then he stuck it under his arm and went tottering on like a man who only keeps upright by a miracle. In fact, the handsome Marescal could not hold himself upright. His collar was as limp and crumpled as if it had been dipped in water; his beard ended in two points from which dripped drops of sweat.

It was just before he reached the Place de L'Etoile that a gentleman in large dark spectacles, coming from the opposite direction with a lighted cigarette in his mouth, appeared in front of him. This gentleman barred his way, and since his cigarette was already burning, did not ask him for a light, but, without a word puffed a cloud of smoke into his face, and smiled a smile that bared his teeth, nearly all of them pointed like canines.

The Commissary's eyes started out of their sockets; he stammered: "Who are you? What do you want?"

What was the use of asking? He knew quite well that the man who always mystified him stood before him, the man whom he called the third confederate, Aurelie's lover, and his, Marescal's, eternal enemy.

And this man, who appeared to him the devil in person, pointed a finger at the bottle and said in affectionately genial accents:

"Come, hand it over—be nice to the kind gentleman—hand it over. A Commissary of your rank can't go dancing along the streets with a bottle. Come, Rudolph—hand it over."

Marescal gave way at once. Cry out, call for help, set passers-by on this murderer—he could not do it. He was under a spell. This infernal creature robbed him of all his vigor, and, stupidly, without dreaming for a moment of resisting, like a thief who finds it quite natural to restore the thing he has stolen, he allowed the bottle to be taken from under the arm which could not longer hold it.

At that moment Bregeac came up, also breathless, also powerless to spring on the third thief, or to question Marescal. Both of them stood, stunned, on the edge of the gutter and watched the gentleman in dark spectacles hail a taxi, get into it, and wave his hat in farewell out of the window.

As soon as he reached his lodgings Ralph unwrapped the bottle. It was a quart bottle such as is used for mineral water, an old quart bottle of thick black glass. On the dusty, dirty label, which all the same must have been protected against the damp, an inscription in large printed letters could be easily read:

EAU DE JOUVENCE.

Below were several lines hard to decipher which evidently gave the formula of this Eau de Jouvence.

Bi-carbonate de soude 1349 grammes

– de potasse 6439 –

– de chaux 1000 –

....

....mille cures.........................

....

etc.......................

But the bottle was not empty. In the inside something moved, something light, which rustled like paper. He turned the bottle upside down and shook it; nothing came out. Then he let down into the bottle a piece of string ending in a big knot and by means of it, after the exercise of a good deal of patience, drew out a small sheet of paper, rolled up into a cylinder and tied with red thread. Having unrolled it, he saw that it was rather less than a half of an ordinary sheet of paper and that the lower part of it had been cut, or rather torn, irregularly. Some words were written on it in ink, of which many were missing, but which were sufficient for him to form several sentences:

"*The accusation is true. This is my formal confession. I alone am responsible for the crime that has been committed and neither Jodot nor the Loubeaux are to be blamed for it. Bregeac.*"

At the first glance Ralph had recognized Bregeac's handwriting, but written in an ink faded by time, which permitted him, along with the state of the paper, to reckon the document to be fifteen or twenty years old.

What was this crime, and against whom had it been committed?

He reflected for some time before he arrived at this conclusion. Then he said to himself: "All the obscurity of this affair comes from the fact that it is not one affair but two; two enterprises are mingled in it, two dramas of which the first dominates the second. First the drama of the express in which the characters are the two Loubeaux, William Jodot, and Aurelie. The second is a drama which took place years ago and of which to-day the two actors, Jodot and Bregeac, are at loggerheads.

"The situation which grows more and more complicated for any one who does not know the key-word, is becoming clearer and clearer to me. The hour of battle draws near, and the stake is Aurelie, or rather the secret which flutters in the depths of her beautiful green eyes. Whoever shall be for a few minutes, by force, by trickery, or by love, master of her thoughts, will be master of that secret, for which so many victims have already died.

"And to this whirlwind of hate and vengeance and greed, Marescal with his passion, his ambition, and his rancor, brings that terrible instrument of war, Justice.

"Opposing him, myself."

He made his preparations with the most minute care and with all the more vigor because each of his adversaries was redoubling his precautions. Bregeac, without any definite proof against the nurse who gave information to Marescal or against the maid whom Ralph had bribed, discharged them both. The shutters of the windows in the front of his house were shut. On the other hand, the agents of Marescal began to show themselves in the street. Jodot only no longer showed himself. Disarmed doubtless by the loss of the document in which Bregeac had written his confession, he must have buried himself in some safe retreat.

This period lasted for a fortnight. Ralph obtained an introduction, under a false name, to the wife of the Minister who openly protected Marescal, and succeeded in becoming uncommonly intimate with this rather mature lady, who was exceedingly jealous, and from whom her husband kept nothing secret. She was transported with joy by Ralph's attentions. Without being aware of the part she was playing and ignorant moreover of Marescal's passion for Aurelie, from hour to hour she kept Ralph informed of the Commissary's intentions, of his plans with regard to Aurelie, and of the method by which he sought, with the Minister's help, to smash Bregeac and those who supported him.

Ralph was frightened: the attack was so well planned that he asked himself if he ought not to anticipate it, to carry off Aurelie, and so bring it to nothing before it was put into execution.

"And what then?" he said to himself. "What should we gain by flight? The conflict would remain the same and everything would begin all over again."

He was able to resist the temptation.

Returning home one evening, he found a note awaiting him. The Minister's wife informed him that the final decisions had been made, among others that the arrest of Aurelie had been fixed for the next day, July the 12th, at three o'clock in the afternoon.

"Poor little girl with the green eyes," thought Ralph. "Will she have confidence in me in everything and in spite of everything, as I asked her? Will there not again be tears and anguish for her?"

He slept peacefully, like a great commander on the eve of battle. He rose at eight o'clock. The decisive day had begun.

Then, towards noon, as his maid, his old nurse Victoire, returned by the servants' entrance with her basket of provisions, six men posted on the staircase, forced their way into the kitchen.

"Is your master here?" said one of them roughly. "Come, hurry up! There's no point in lying. I am the Commissary Marescal and I have a warrant for his arrest."

Pale and trembling she muttered: "He's in his study."

"Take us to it!"

He set his hand over her mouth, that she might not warn her master, and made her walk along the passage at the end of which she pointed to a door.

Their adversary had not time to throw himself on guard. He was seized and tied up and dispatched almost as if he had been a trunk.

Marescal said simply: "You are the chief of the robbers of the express. Your name is Ralph de Limézy." Turning to his men he added: "Take him to the police station. Here's the warrant. And keep your mouths shut, do you hear? Not a word about the personality of our 'client'. You're responsible for him, Tony. You, too, Labonce. Take him off, And at three o'clock meet me in front of Bregeac's house. It will be the young lady's turn then and the smashing up of her step-father."

Four men took away the prisoner. Marescal kept the fifth, Sauvinoux, with him.

Forthwith he searched the study and took possession of some papers and other unimportant things. But neither he, nor Sauvinoux, found what they were looking for, the bottle on the label of which he had had time to read, when he came to a stop in the Avenue Wagram: "Eau de Jouvence."

They went away to lunch in a neighboring restaurant. They came back and Marescal searched furiously.

At last, at a quarter past two, Sauvinoux discovered the famous bottle behind the marble slab under the mantelpiece. It was corked and carefully sealed with red sealing-wax.

Marescal shook it and held it up against the light of an electric light bulb. It contained a roll of paper.

He hesitated–should he read that paper?

"No, no! Not yet!–Later in the presence of Bregeac! Bravo, Sauvinoux! You've worked splendidly, my lad!"

His joy was overflowing. He went away, murmuring:

"This time I am near my goal. I hold Bregeac in my hands and I've only to tighten my grip. As for the girl, there is no longer any one to defend her. Her lover is in prison. There are just you and I, darling!"

CHAPTER IX
SISTER ANN, SISTER ANN, DO YOU SEE ANYTHING?

At two o'clock the same day Aurelie was dressing feebly. An old servant of the house of Valentine, who was now the only servant they had, had brought up her lunch to her room and had told her that Bregeac wished to speak to her.

She had not fully recovered from her illness. Pale and very feeble, she put some rouge on her lips and cheeks and forced herself to appear before the man she detested, carrying her head high.

Bregeac was waiting for her in his study on the first floor, a large room with closed shutters, lighted by an electric light.

"Sit down," he said.

"No."

"Sit down. You're tired."

"Tell me at once what you want to say and let me go back to my room," she said coldly.

Bregeac walked up and down the room with an harassed and anxious air. He watched her furtively, with as much hostility as passion, as a man who finds himself balked by an indomitable will. Also he was full of pity for her.

He came to her and putting his hand on her shoulder forced her to sit down and sat down himself.

"You're right," he said. "It will not take long. What I have to tell you can be said in a few words. You can then decide."

They were near one another, yet further apart than two bitter enemies. Bregeac was aware of it. The words he was trying to speak would only widen the abyss between them.

He clenched his fists and said: "So you still do not understand that we are surrounded by enemies and that the situation cannot last?"

"What enemies?" she muttered.

"You know quite well," he said. "Marescal, who detests you and is burning to avenge himself."

He looked at her; but as she said nothing, he went on in a lower voice and yet more serious accents. "Listen, Aurelie. For some time we have been under observation. In the Ministry they search my drawers. Superiors and inferiors, all the world is in league against me. Why? Because they are all more or less in the pay of Marescal, and because they all know he is more powerful than I with the Minister. Now, you and I are linked to one another if only because he hates us both. And we are linked to one another by our past, which, whether you like it or not, is the same. I have brought you up. I am your guardian. My ruin is yours. And I even ask myself if it is not you they are really about to attack for reasons of which I am ignorant. Yes; I have got the impression from certain facts that they will leave me strictly alone, but that you are directly threatened."

She looked as if she were about to faint and asked: "What facts?"

He answered: "It's worse than that. I have received an anonymous letter, written on the paper of the Ministry–an absurd and incoherent letter in which I am warned that a prosecution is going to be started against you."

She had the strength to say: "A prosecution? You're mad. And it's because an anonymous letter—"

"Yes, I know what you're going to say," he said quickly. "Some idle official who has heard some stupid rumor. But all the same Marescal is capable of every abomination."

"If you're afraid, keep out of the business," she said coldly.

"I'm afraid for you, Aurelie."

"I've nothing to fear."

"Yes, you have," he said quickly. "This man has sworn to destroy you."

"Then let me go."

"Are you strong enough?"

"I've all the strength I need to escape from this prison in which you keep me and never to see you again," she said bitterly.

He shrugged his shoulders with an air of discouragement.

"Don't say that," he said. "I could not live without you. I have suffered too much during your absence. I would rather endure anything—anything rather than be separated from you. My whole life depends on your regard, on you."

She drew herself up, trembling with indignation, and cried: "I forbid you to speak to me like that. You swore to me that I should never hear a word of that kind again—abominable words!"

She sank back in her chair, exhausted by the effort. He moved away from her and threw himself into an arm-chair, his head between his hands, his shoulders shaken by his sobs, like a vanquished man for whom existence is an intolerable burden.

After a long silence he began again in a dull voice: "We're still worse enemies than we were before you went away. You have come back quite different. What did you do, Aurelie—not at Sainte-Marie—but during the first three weeks during which I was hunting for you like a mad-man, before I thought of the convent? That wretched fellow William—you did not love him that I know. Nevertheless, you followed him. Why? And what became of the two of you? What has become of him? I have an intuition that very serious things happened. I see that you are worried to death. In your delirium you talked like one who had been flying without stopping; and you kept seeing blood-corpses."

She shuddered. "No, no!" she cried. "It is not true. You misunderstood me."

"I did not understand you," he replied, shaking his head. "Look, at this very moment your eyes are terrified. One would think that your nightmare was still going on."

He came nearer to her and said slowly: "You need a long rest, my poor child, and that is what I want to suggest to you. This morning I asked for leave and we will go away. I swear to you that I will not say a single word that might offend you. What is more, I will not say a word about that secret which you ought to have confided to me, since it belongs as much to me as to you. I will not even try to read it in the depths of your eyes in which it hides itself and in which I have so often tried, by force I confess, to find the key to this insoluble problem. I will leave your eyes alone, Aurelie. I will never look at you again. That is my definite promise. But come with me, poor child, you rack me with pity. You are waiting for I do not know what, and it is only misfortune which can respond to your appeal. Come with me."

She kept silence with a stubborn obstinacy. The quarrel between them was past mending; it was impossible to utter a word which would not inflict a wound, or be an outrage. The odious passion of Bregeac separated them more than all that had happened and than the profound reasons which had always set them in opposition.

"Will you?" he said at last.

She said firmly: "I will not. I cannot stand your presence any longer. I can no longer live in the same house with you. I shall go away at the first opportunity."

"And not alone—any more than the first time," he sneered. "It's William, I suppose."

"I've got rid of William."

"Some one else then, some one for whom you are waiting, I'm convinced of it. Your eyes are always looking for him—your ears are always listening for him. Yes: at this very moment!"

The front door had been opened and shut.

"What did I tell you?" cried Bregeac with an evil laugh. "One would really think that you were hoping that some one was going to come. No, Aurelie; no one will come, neither William, nor any one else. It is Valentine whom I sent to the Ministry to fetch my courrier, for I shall not go there again."

They heard the sound of the servant's footsteps on the stairs to the first floor and then on the landing. He entered.

"Did you do as I told you, Valentine?"

"Yes, sir."

"There were letters—letters to be signed?"

"No, sir."

"That's odd. But my courrier?"

"He had just been transferred to M. Marescal."

"But what right? Did Marescal dare?—Was Marescal there?" cried Bregeac in a tone of sudden anxiety.

"No, sir. He came and went away at once."

"Came away? At half-past two? Then it must be some important affair."

"Yes, sir."

"Did you try to find out what it was?"

"Yes; but they did not know anything at the office."

"Was he alone?"

"No: he went with Labonce, Tony, and Sauvinoux."

"With Labonce and Tony?" cried Bregeac. "Well, in that case it's a matter of an arrest! Why wasn't I informed of it? What can be happening?"

Valentine went away. Bregeac once more began to walk up and down the room.

He said thoughtfully: "Tony, Marescal's right-hand man,—Labonce, one of his favorites—and without informing me."

He fell silent for a minute or two and paced up and down. Aurelie watched him anxiously. Then he went to one of the windows, opened one of the shutters a few inches, and looked out.

"But they're there at—the end of the street! They're keeping watch!"

"Who?"

"Both of them, Marescal's assistants—Tony and Labonce."

"Well?" she said in a faint voice.

"Those are the two he always employs in important matters. It was with them he was working this morning."

"And they're there?" said Aurelie.

"They're there. I've seen them."

"And is Marescal coming?"

"Of course he is. You heard what Valentine said," said Bregeac impatiently.

"He's c-c-coming—he's c-c-coming," she stammered.

"What's the matter?" asked Bregeac, astonished that she should be so disturbed.

"Nothing," she said, again in control of herself. "One gets frightened in spite of one's self. But there's no real reason."

Bregeac reflected. He too was hard put to it to keep his nerves under control. Then he said: "Of course there's no reason. One generally gets excited for perfectly puerile reasons. I'll go and question them and I'm sure that everything will be cleared up. Quite sure. For after all it looks rather as if they were watching the house opposite than us."

Aurelie raised her head sharply and said quickly: "What house?"

"I told you about the business—the man they arrested this morning, just before noon. If you'd only seen Marescal when he left his office at eleven. I met him as he left it. He was wearing an expression of immense satisfaction and simply ferocious hate. That's what bothers me. One can only feel such hate as that in one's life for some one person. And it is I whom he hates like that, or rather the two of us. So I thought it was we who were threatened."

Aurelie rose to her feet, paler than ever.

"What's that you say? An arrest in the house opposite?" she cried.

"Yes; a man of the name of Limézy, who pretends to be an explorer—a Baron de Limézy. I had news of the arrest at one o'clock at the Ministry. They had just brought him to Headquarters."

She did not know Ralph's name, but she was certain that Bregeac was talking of no one else, and asked in a trembling voice: "What has he done? Who is he? This Baron de Limézy?"

"According to Marescal he is the murderer of the express. The third confederate whom they were seeking."

She was on the point of falling. She wore a distracted air and groped giddily in the empty air to find something to hold on to.

"What's the matter, Aurelie? What connection has this business—"

"We are lost," she groaned.

"What do you mean?"

"You cannot understand."

"Explain yourself. Do you know this man?" he cried on a rising note.

"Yes, yes. He rescued me. He saved me from Marescal and from William and from that man Jodot who used to come here. He would have saved us again to-day."

He stared at her, confounded, and said: "Was it him you were waiting for?"

"Yes," she said. "He promised to be on the spot. I was quite easy in mind. I have seen him do such things—fool Marescal."

"Well?" said Bregeac.

"Well," she replied in the same distracted tone. "It would perhaps be better to get into hiding—you as well as I. There are stories to your disadvantage—stories of years ago."

"You're mad!" cried Bregeac, aghast. "There's nothing of the kind! For my part, I fear nothing!"

In spite of his denials, he went out of the room, dragging Aurelie with him on to the landing. It was she who at the last moment resisted.

"But no. What use would it be? We shall be saved—he will come—he will escape. Why not wait for him?"

"One does not escape from Headquarters," snarled Bregeac.

"You think not? Oh, how horrible all this is!"

She did not know what to do. Terrible ideas whirled through her mind, weakened by her illness—fear of Marescal and of immediate arrest—and the police who were going to seize her and twist her wrists.

The terror of her step-father decided her. Carried away by the fury of the storm, she ran to her room and reappeared at once with a suit-case in her hand. Bregeac was also ready. They had the air of two criminals who had nothing else to look at except a desperate flight. They went down the staircase and crossed the hall.

At that very moment the bell rang.

"Too late," whispered Bregeac.

"No," she said, encouraged by a sudden hope. "Perhaps he has come. He has come and is going to take me away."

She thought of her friend and of the convent terrace. He had sworn never to abandon her and that at the very last minute even he would be able to save her. Obstacles? Were there any obstacles for him? Was he not master of men and of events?

The bell rang again.

The old servant came out of the dining-room.

"Open," said Bregeac to him, in a low voice.

They heard whisperings and the shuffling of feet on the other side of the door. Some one knocked.

"Open the door," said Bregeac again.

On the doorstep stood Marescal with three men. She leaned against the bannisters of the staircase and groaned in such a low voice that Bregeac alone heard it:

"Heavens! It is not him!"

Confronted with his subordinate, Bregeac drew himself to his full height.

"What do you want, Monsieur? I have forbidden you the house," he said sternly.

"I am here on an official matter, Monsieur le Directeur. By order of the Minister," he said with a snarl.

"An order which concerns me?"

"Which concerns you and mademoiselle too," said Marescal.

"And which compels you to secure the help of three men?"

Marescal laughed and said: "Goodness, no. That was a mere accident. They were taking a walk this way, we fell into conversation, and they came along with me. There's nothing to be put out about."

He entered and caught sight of the two suit-cases.

"Ah, a short journey. What? A minute later and my trouble would have been wasted."

"Monsieur Marescal," said Bregeac firmly, "if you have a mission to perform–a communication to make to me, make it at once and here."

"Don't let's have a scandal, Bregeac. And don't let's have any nonsense. No one knows anything so far, not even my men. Let's talk things over in your study," said Marescal in threatening accents.

"No one knows anything about what, Monsieur?" said Bregeac.

"About what is happening; and it's serious enough. If your step-daughter has not told you about it, perhaps she will admit that an explanation without witnesses would be preferable. What do you think, Mademoiselle?" said Marescal in a jeering tone.

Pale as death, still holding on to the bannisters, Aurelie seemed on the point of fainting.

Bregeac slipped an arm round her and held her up.

"Come on up," he said, helping her up the stairs.

She let him do so. Marescal told his men to enter.

"Don't stir out of the hall, any of you, and don't let any one come in, or go out," he said. He turned to Valentine and added: "Go into the kitchen and stay there."

Valentine went.

"If there's any trouble upstairs, I'll whistle," he said to his men. "And Sauvinoux will come to the rescue. Do you understand?"

"We understand," said Labonce.

"Don't make any mistake."

"We shan't make any mistake, chief. You know that we're not novices. And that we'll stand by you to a man," said Sauvinoux.

"Even against Bregeac?"

"Rather."

"Right. Give me the bottle, Tony."

He took the bottle, or rather the cardboard case which held it, and went briskly up the stairs, assured that his orders would be obeyed, and entered the study out of which he had been so ignominiously turned six months before, with the air of a master. What a victory for him! And with what an insolence did he make his triumph plain! He walked round the study, with his thumbs in the armholes of his waistcoat, looking at the photographs which hung upon the wall, photographs of Aurelie, as a baby, a little girl, and a young girl.

Bregeac snapped: "Try to behave yourself, Marescal."

At once Marescal put him in his place.

"It's no use, Bregeac; shut up!" he said. "Your weakness is that you don't know the weapons I hold against Mademoiselle, and consequently against you. Perhaps, when you do know them, you'll realize that it's your duty to do as you're told."

Facing one another, drawn to their full height, the two enemies tried to stare one another down. Their hate for one another, springing from opposing ambitions, warring instincts, and above all from a rivalry in love that all these other factors made more bitter, was equal. Beside them Aurelie waited, sitting upright on her chair.

The curious thing was, and it struck Marescal, that she seemed to have recovered herself. Still feeble, with drawn face, she no longer wore, as at the beginning of the attack, her air of a helpless, exhausted quarry. She maintained that rigid attitude which he had observed her assume on the bench at Sainte-Marie. Her eyes, open wide, wet with tears which trickled down her pale cheeks, were fixed on something invisible to either of them. Of what was she thinking? Sometimes from the very bottom of the abyss one rises again. Did she think that he, Marescal, could be moved to pity? Had she a plan of defense which would allow her to escape the penalty of the law?

He banged his fist down on the table and cried: "We'll see about that!"

Leaving the girl out of it for the moment, he gave all his attention to Bregeac. He stepped right up to him, thrusting his face forward, so that his chief had to recoil a step, and said to him: "It won't take me long to deal with you. The facts and only the facts! Some of them are known to you, Bregeac, as they are known to everybody; but to the majority of them there is no witness but me, or rather they have been discovered by me alone. Do not try to deny them; I am giving them to you exactly as they are, in all their simplicity. Here they are in the form of an indictment. On the 26th of April last—"

Bregeac quivered, and said quickly: "The twenty-sixth of April was the day on which we met on the Boulevard Haussmann."

"Yes; and it was the day on which your step-daughter left you," said Marescal, and he added sharply: "It was also the day on which three persons were murdered on the Marseilles express."

"What? What connection is there between the two facts?" asked Bregeac in astonished accents.

"Don't be impatient," said Marescal pompously. "You will get each fact in its place, in its chronological order." He paused to cough. Then went on: "On April the twenty-sixth, car number five, in the express, was occupied by only four persons. In the last compartment were an English girl of the name of Miss Bakersfield—a crook she was—and Baron de Limézy, a pretended explorer. In the last compartment were two men, the brothers Loubeaux, residing at Neuilly-sur-Seine.

"In the car behind, the fourth car, besides several persons who played no part in the affair and knew nothing about it, were, firstly, a Commissary of the Secret Service, secondly, a young man and a young girl, alone in a compartment, in which they had covered the light and pulled down the curtains, as if they were going to sleep, and consequently passed unnoticed by everybody, even by the Commissary. I was that Commissary, on the track of Miss Bakersfield. The young man was William Ancivel, a stock-jobber and burglar, a frequent guest at this house, who was flying secretly with his companion."

"You lie! You lie!" cried Bregeac indignantly. "Aurelie is above suspicion!"

"I did not say that his companion was Mademoiselle," Marescal retorted.

Bregeac scowled at him.

Marescal went on coldly: "As far as La Roche nothing happened. For another half hour nothing happened. Then came the abrupt and violent drama. The young man and girl emerge from the darkness and pass from the fourth car to the fifth. They are disguised by long gray blouses, caps, and masks. In the last compartment of the fifth car Baron de Limézy is waiting for them. The three of them murder and rob Miss Bakersfield. Then Baron de Limézy is tied up by his confederates, who hurry to the end of the car and murder and rob the two brothers. When they come back down the car they meet the conductor. There is a fight; and they escape. The conductor finds Baron de Limézy trussed up as one of their victims and pretending he has been robbed, also. That's the first act. The second is their flight up the embankment and through the woods. But the conductor has given the alarm. I learn what has happened; I take the necessary measures. The result is that the two fugitives are surrounded. One of them escapes. The other is arrested and shut up. I am informed of it. I go to examine him in the dark corner into which he has shrunk. It is a woman."

"A woman?" said Bregeac in incredulous accents.

"Let me finish," said Marescal. "Thanks to the pseudo-Baron, in trusting whom I made a mistake, this woman gets away and rejoins William Ancivel. I find traces of them at Monte Carlo. Then I lose track of them again. I hunt for it in vain till the day on which it occurs to me to return to Paris and to learn whether your investigations, Bregeac, have not been more fortunate than mine and whether you have discovered your step-daughter's hiding-place. That was how I was able to reach the convent of Sainte-Marie several hours before you did and to make my way to a certain terrace on which Mademoiselle was listening to a tale of love. Only the lover has changed: instead of William Ancivel it is Baron de Limézy, that is to say, their confederate."

Bregeac was listening to these monstrous accusations with a growing fear. It all seemed to him so inevitably true; it explained so exactly his own intuitions and agreed so closely with the half confidences Aurelie had just made to him with regard to her unknown savior. He did not even try to protest. At intervals he looked at her, always to find her sitting, motionless and dumb, in her rigid attitude. Marescal's words did not appear to penetrate to her understanding, one would have said that she was listening to noises outside rather than to his words. Was it that she still hoped for an impossible intervention?

"And then?" said Bregeac impatiently, as Marescal paused.

"Then," replied the Commissary, "thanks to him, she succeeded once more in escaping. But to-day I swear to you I can laugh at all that, since—to-day I have my revenge."

He paused to gloat over Aurelie, who seemed wholly unaware of his existence.

"And what a revenge, Bregeac!" he went on. "Do you remember that six months ago you dismissed me as if I had been a valet—one might almost say you kicked me out? And now I hold her—this child—in the hollow of my hand; and all is over."

He turned his hand as if he were turning a key in a lock, and that so exact gesture showed so clearly and definitely his terrible resolution with regard to Aurelie that Bregeac exclaimed: "No, no. It isn't true, Marescal! It can't be true! You are not going to hand this child over to the police."

"Down there at Sainte-Marie I offered her peace," said Marescal in harsh accents. "She repulsed me. All the worse for her! To-day is too late!"

Bregeac approached him with his hands stretched out in a gesture of supplication and began an incoherent prayer. He cut it short.

"It's useless!" he cried. "All the worse for her! All the worse for you! She wouldn't have me—she shall have nobody. And it's mere justice. To pay her debt for the crime she has committed is to pay me for the harm she has done me. She must be punished; and I avenge myself in punishing her. All the worse for her!"

He emphasized his phrases by stamping his foot or banging on the table. Then giving way to the natural grossness of his nature he turned on Aurelie and cried: "Look at her, Bregeac! Is she thinking for a moment of asking my forgiveness? If you bow your head, does she show any humiliation? And do you know the reason of this dumbness, of this sustained and intractable hardness? It's because she still hopes, Bregeac. Yes, she hopes; I'm certain of it. She hopes that the man who has saved her three times from my claws, will save her a fourth."

Aurelie never stirred. He snatched up the receiver of the telephone and rang up the Prefecture of Police.

"Hullo! Is that the Prefecture? Put me on to Monsieur Phillipe—it's M. Marescal speaking."

He turned to the young girl and held the second receiver to her ear. Aurelie did not stir.

Some one answered at the other end of the line:

"Is that you, Marescal?"

"Yes. Listen. There is a person here to whom I wish to afford complete certainty. Answer my questions exactly."

"Right."

"Where were you at noon to-day?"

"At Headquarters as you asked me to be. I received the person whom Labonce and Tony brought from you."

"Where did we arrest him?"

"In his lodgings in the Rue de Courcelles in the house exactly opposite Bregeac's."

"Was he charged?"

"Before me."

"Under what name?"

"Baron de Limézy."

"And what did they charge him with?"

"With being the leader of the train robbers in the express case."

"Have you seen him since this morning?"

"Yes. Just now, when they were taking his measurements. They're taking them still."

"Thanks, Phillipe, that's what I wanted to know. Good-by."

He hung up the receivers and cried: "Well, my pretty Aurelie, you know where your savior is! In prison! Jailed!"

"I knew it," she said.

He burst out laughing.

"She knew it! And she went on expecting him just the same! That's really funny. He has the whole of the police and the weight of the law on the top of him—he's a rag, a tatter, a straw in the wind, a soap-bubble, and she's expecting him! The walls of his prison are going to fall down! The warders are going to offer him a car! He's here! He's going to come down the chimney or through the ceiling!"

Beside himself, he shook the young girl impassive and heedless of him, by the shoulder.

"There's nothing to be done, Aurelie! There's no more hope! Your savior's done for! The Baron's under lock and key! And in an hour it will be your turn, pretty one! Cropped hair! Saint Lazare! The court! I've wept often enough for your beautiful eyes, you little crook; and it is to them——"

The words were cut short on his tongue. Absorbed in Aurelie, he had forgotten Bregeac; and Bregeac gripped him by the throat from behind with two frenzied hands. The action had been involuntary. Marescal had gripped the girl's shoulder; he came at him in a fury of revolt at such an outrage. Marescal staggered before his onset and the two men rolled on the floor. There was a furious fight. Both of them were beside themselves with rage, a rage aggravated by their fierce rivalry. Marescal was the more vigorous and stronger, but Bregeac was sustained by such a savage jealousy that the issue remained long in doubt.

Aurelie gazed on them with horrified eyes; but she did not stir. Both of them were her enemies, equally detestable.

At last Marescal, who had freed himself from the strangling grip of Bregeac's murderous hands, was able to make an effort to get at the revolver in his hip pocket. But Bregeac, seeing what he would be at, so twisted his right arm that it was paralyzed. But with his left hand Marescal got hold of his whistle which was hanging on a chain in his breast pocket and blew a shrill call on it. Bregeac tried once more with all his might to get his adversary by the throat. The door was flung open; a man came bounding into the room, and flung himself on to the struggling figures. Almost on the instant Marescal found himself free and Bregeac was looking down the barrel of a revolver about ten inches from his eyes.

"Bravo Sauvinoux!" cried Marescal. "I shan't forget that little bit of help in a hurry, my lad!"

His rage was still so furious that he was cowardly enough to spit in Bregeac's face.

"You cad! You blackguard! Did you think you were going to dispose of me as easily as that?" he shouted. "Your resignation, and at once! The Minister demands it—I have it in my pocket! You've only to sign it!"

He produced a paper from his pocket.

"Your resignation—and Aurelie's confession. I've written it out ready. Sign it, Aurelie. Come, read it. 'I confess that I took part in the crime on the express, on the 26th of last April. That I fired at the brothers Loubeaux. I confess that—' In fact it's a resumé of the whole story. You needn't bother to read it. Sign! Don't waste any more time!"

He dipped a pen into the ink-pot and tried to force it between her fingers.

Slowly she pushed the hand of the Commissary aside, took the pen and signed, as Marescal had willed her to sign, without taking the trouble to read it. The handwriting was steady. Her hand did not tremble.

"Ah," he said with a deep sigh of relief. "That's done. I did not think that I could get it nearly so quickly. It's a good thing, Aurelie, that you understood the situation. And now you, Bregeac."

Bregeac shook his head and refused.

"What!" cried Marescal. "You refuse. Do you fancy that you can keep your post? Perhaps you think that you will be promoted. What? Promoted as the step-father of a criminal? That's good, that is. And you would continue to give me orders, you, Bregeac? You're a funny chap. Do you suppose that this scandal won't be enough to clear you out, that to-morrow, when people read in the papers of the arrest of this child, you won't be obliged to resign?"

Bregeac's fingers closed upon the pen held out to him. He read the letter of resignation and hesitated.

Aurelie said to him: "Sign, Monsieur."

He signed.

"There we are!" said Marescal, pocketing the two papers—the confession and the resignation. "My chief is down and out; his post is empty; and it has been promised to me. And the girl will be in prison which little by little cures me of the love which was gnawing my heart."

He said this with a cold cynicism, that bared the bottom of his vile soul.

Then, with a cruel laugh, he turned on Bregeac and went on: "But we haven't finished yet, Bregeac. When I play a game, I play it to the end."

Bregeac smiled bitterly: "You're going still further? What's the use of it?" he said.

"I'm going further," said Marescal, glowering at him. "With regard to this child's crimes, we've come to the end of them. Everything is settled. But are we to stop there?" He thrust forward his face and glared into Bregeac's eyes. "What do you say about it?" He paused, then went on: "You know what I mean. If you hadn't known, and known that it was true, you wouldn't have signed, and you wouldn't have let me take this tone I have with you. Your resignation is a confession. And if I am able to take this tone, Bregeac, it is because you are afraid!"

"I'm afraid of nothing!" protested Bregeac. "I am bearing the burden of this unfortunate child's crimes—crimes she must have committed in a moment of madness."

"And the burden of what you have done yourself, Bregeac."

"Besides that, there is nothing."

"Besides that, there is the past," said Marescal slowly and with gloomy severity. "We'll say no more of the crime of to-day. But what about the crime of bygone days, Bregeac?"

"The crime of bygone days? What crime? What do you mean?"

Marescal banged on the table, his final argument, which perhaps emphasized an explosion of anger.

"Explanations? It's I who am asking for explanations. What does that recent expedition of yours to the bank of the Seine mean? On Sunday morning? And your watch near the empty villa? And your pursuit of the man with the sack? Am I to refresh your memory and remind you that that villa belonged to the men your step-daughter murdered, and that the man you watched was an individual of the name of Jodot—I'm searching for him high and low, by the way—the partner of the brothers Loubeaux? Jodot whom I used to meet in this very house. Goodness, how it all hangs together! How clear the connection grows between all these events!"

Bregeac shrugged his shoulders and muttered: "Absurdities! Imbecile hypotheses!"

"Hypotheses: yes—fancies to which I did not pay very much attention when I used to come here formerly—till I scented, like the keen sleuth I am, all the embarrassment, the reticence, the confused apprehension that colored your actions and your words. But hypotheses which have for some time and little by little been confirmed—which we are going to turn into certainties, Bregeac—yes: you and I together, Bregeac—without your being able to get out of it—of which I'm going to produce the irrefutable proof—and you a complete confession, without knowing it—here—immediately."

He took up the cardboard case which he had brought with him and set it on the mantelpiece, and opened it. It contained one of those straw sheaths used to prevent bottles from breaking. There was a bottle in it. Marescal took it out and set it on the table in front of Bregeac.

"There, comrade Bregeac. You recognize it, don't you? It's the bottle you stole the other day from Jodot, which I took from you and which a third person stole from me before your eyes. That third person? It was Baron Limézy and no one else. I found it in his lodgings a little while ago. What? Do you understand, darling? This is a real treasure, this bottle is. Look at it, Bregeac. Look at its label and the formula on it—of some mineral water—Eau de Jouvence. Here it is. Limézy has corked and sealed it with red sealing-wax. Look at it carefully. Do you see that little piece of rolled-up paper at the bottom of it. It's certain that you wanted to get it from Jodot—a confession, to a dead certainty. A most compromising specimen of your handwriting. My poor Bregeac!"

It was his hour of triumph. As he knocked off the sealing-wax and uncorked the bottle he threw out phrases and interjections at haphazard.

"Marescal famous all the world over!... Arrest of the express murderers!... Bregeac's past!... What surprises at the inquiry and at the assizes!... Sauvinoux, you have handcuffs for the girl?... Call Labonce and Tony.... Victory! Complete Victory!"

He turned the bottle upside down. The paper fell out of it. He picked it up, unfolded it, and carried away by this whirl of windy words, like a runner whom his dash carries beyond his goal, without pausing to grasp the meaning, he read out:

"Marescal is a blockhead!"

CHAPTER X
WORDS AS GOOD AS ACTIONS

There was a stupefied silence while this incredible sentence went on ringing through the air. Marescal almost doubled up like a man who has received a blow in the stomach. Bregeac, still threatened by Sauvinoux's revolver, appeared almost as much amazed.

Suddenly a laugh rang out, a nervous laugh there was no repressing, but nevertheless struck a note of gayety in the gloomy atmosphere of the room. It was Aurelie, provoked by the immense expression of discomfiture on the face of the Commissary to this excess of truly untimely hilarity. The fact that the comic sentence had been pronounced loudly by the very man who was the object of its ridicule, brought the tears to her eyes: "Marescal is a blockhead!"

Marescal gazed at her with a sudden inquietude. How did it come about that the girl had this excess of gayety in the terrible situation in which she found herself, actually panting in the grip of her enemy.

"Was the situation no longer the same?" he asked himself. "In what way had it changed?"

And doubtless he perceived a connection between this unexpected laugh and the strangely calm attitude of the girl since the beginning of the struggle. What then was she hoping? Was it possible that in the midst of events which should have brought her to her knees, she still stood on firm ground, the solidity of which appeared to her unshakeable.

Things took on a truly disagreeable aspect; he began to suspect a cleverly laid trap. There was danger in the house. From what side did it threaten? How could he admit that an attack could take place when he had taken every possible precaution?

"If Bregeac moves, all the worse for him—a bullet through his head," he said to Sauvinoux.

He went to the door and opened it. He could hear the murmur of the voices of Tony and Labonce.

He leaned over the bannisters and called out: "Is everything right down there, Tony? Has any one come in?"

"No one, Chief. Did you have a row upstairs?" said Tony.

"No—no—Besides, Sauvinoux is with me," said Marescal.

More and more uneasy in mind, he returned quickly to the study. Bregeac, Sauvinoux, and the girl had not stirred. Only,—only—an unheard of, incredible, unimaginable, fantastic phenomenon, which paralyzed his legs and held him unable to stir in the frame of the doorway, met his eye: Sauvinoux had an unlighted cigarette between his lips and was looking at him in the manner of one asking for a light.

A nightmarish vision, in such violent opposition to reality that Marescal at first refused to admit to himself its obvious meaning. Sauvinoux, owing to some aberration for which he would be punished, wished to smoke and was asking for a light—that was all. Why look any further? But little by little the face of Sauvinoux was lighted up by a mocking smile in which there was so much mischief and impertinent *bonhommie* that Marescal tried vainly to shut his eyes to it. It could not be that Sauvinoux, his subordinate Sauvinoux, was little by little becoming in spirit a new creature who was no longer Sauvinoux, no longer a policeman, but on the contrary was crossing over to the camp of the enemy. Sauvinoux? it was——

In the ordinary course of his profession Marescal would have put up a longer fight against such a monstrous fact. But the most fantastic happenings seemed to him quite natural when it was a matter of the man whom he called "the man of the express." Though he refused to utter, even in the depths of his heart, the irrevocable admission and submit to the truly hateful reality, how could he escape the evidence of his eyes? How could he fail to realize that Sauvinoux, the admirable assistant whom the Minister had recommended to him a week before, was no other than that infernal personage whom he had arrested that morning and *who was at the moment actually at the*

Police Headquarters in the office set aside for Bertillon measurement.

"Tony!" howled the Commissary, dashing out of the room a second time. "Tony! Labonce! Come up at once, dammit!"

He had shouted at the top of his voice; he was dancing about and banging the bannisters, for all the world like a cat on hot bricks.

His men came running upstairs.

He stuttered: "Sauvinoux! D-D-Do you know who he is? It's the b-b-beggar we–we–arrested this m-m-morning–escaped! Disguised!"

Tony and Labonce stared at him, aghast: the chief had gone off his head!

He pushed them into the study and drew his revolver.

"Hands up, you crook! Hands up! Cover him too, Labonce!" he howled.

The good Sauvinoux had propped up a small hand mirror on the top of the desk, and he did not stir. He began to strip off, slowly, his disguise. He had even set the revolver with which he had been threatening Bregeac down on the desk beside him.

Marescal sprang forward, snatched up the weapon, and sprang back, with both revolvers leveled.

"Hands up, or I fire! D'you hear, you crook!" he howled again.

The crook took no more notice of him. Under the leveled revolvers a few feet away from him, he removed the hair which formed mutton-chop whiskers on his cheeks, and gave his eyebrows an unwonted thickness.

"I'll fire! I'll fire! D'you hear, you scoundrel? I'll count three and fire! One–two–three!"

"You're going to make a fool of yourself, Rudolph," murmured Sauvinoux.

Rudolph made a fool of himself. He had lost his head. He let fly with both weapons, at random, at the pier-glass, the walls, the pictures, like a murderer drunk with the smell of blood who plunges his knife again and again into the corpse of his panting victim. Bregeac crouched before the storm of bullets. Aurelie did not risk a movement. Since her savior did not try to save her, since he let it happen, it must be that there was nothing to fear. Her confidence in him was so complete that she almost smiled. With his handkerchief and some Vaseline Sauvinoux removed the grease-paint from his face. Little by little Ralph appeared.

Twelve reports had banged out. The room was full of smoke; mirrors were smashed; there were holes in the walls, broken picture-frames, ruined pictures. It looked as if it had been taken by storm.

Marescal stood dazed; a sudden shame at his fit of madness overwhelmed him. He pulled himself together and said faintly to his men:

"Wait on the staircase. Come the moment I call."

"Look here, Chief: since Sauvinoux is no longer Sauvinoux, hadn't we better arrest whoever he is," Labonce suggested. "I've disliked him ever since you engaged him last week. Shall we? The three of us can collar him all right."

"Do as I tell you," said Marescal.

Doubtless three to one did not seem to him good enough odds.

He shut the door on them.

Sauvinoux finished his transformation, straightened his waistcoat and his tie; and another man faced them. The measly-looking policeman of a minute or two before had become a debonair fellow, sure of himself, well dressed, elegant, even young, in whom Marescal beheld once more his habitual prosecutor.

"How do you do, Mademoiselle? Allow me to introduce myself—Baron Limézy, explorer—and for the last week a detective. You recognized me at once, I think. Yes? I guessed it down in the hall. Maintain your silence by all means, but still laugh. How good it was to hear your laugh just now! What a reward for my efforts!"

He bowed to Bregeac and said: "How do you do, sir?"

Then he turned to Marescal and said cheerfully: "And how are you, old chap? Of course you didn't recognize me—you wouldn't. You're still asking yourself how I managed to take Sauvinoux's place. For you still believe in the existence of Sauvinoux. Heavens! that there should be a man who believes in the existence of Sauvinoux and that he held the rank of chief turnip in the police world! But, my good Rudolph, Sauvinoux never did exist. Sauvinoux's a myth. He's a non-existent personage who was warmly recommended to the foreign minister, and the foreign minister's wife had him appointed your collaborator in the express case. And that's how it came about that I've been in your service for the last ten days, that is to say, that I have guided you in the way you should go, that I pointed out to you the flat of Baron de Limézy, that I had myself arrested by myself this morning, and that I found, where I had hidden it, the marvelous bottle which proclaims the incontestable truth that Marescal is a blockhead."

One would have thought that the Commissary would have sprung at Ralph's throat; but he kept control of himself. And Ralph went on in the tone of mockery which gave Aurelie a feeling of complete security and lashed Marescal like a whip: "You're looking devilishly uncomfortable, Rudolph. Why are you itching so? Are you annoyed because I'm here and not in a cell, and you're asking yourself how I was able at one and the same time to go to prison as Limézy and lunch with you as Sauvinoux? What an infant it is! What a fine sleuth! But, my good Rudolph, it's simplicity itself! Having myself arranged the invasion of my domicile! I substituted for Baron de Limézy an obliging and well-paid gentleman, who had the very slightest resemblance to that Baron, but was instructed to endure without immediate protest all the misfortunes which might befall him to-day. Conducted by my old servant, you rushed like a bull at this gentleman, whose head I instantly covered with a handkerchief; and off he goes to Headquarters. The result: rid of the formidable Limézy, absolutely reassured, you came to arrest Mademoiselle, a thing you would never have done, had I been free. *Now, it was necessary that what has taken place should take place.* You understand, Rudolph? It was necessary. This little interview between the four of us was necessary. It was necessary that matters should be brought to a point at which there was no turning back. They have been brought to that point, haven't they? Once more we all breathe easily. What a lot of nightmares we have been freed from! How pleasant it is, even for you, to think that in ten minutes from now Mademoiselle and I will be bidding you good-by."

In spite of this biting mockery, Marescal had recovered his coolness. He wished to seem as calm as his opponent, and with a careless movement he took the receiver from the telephone.

"Hello. The Prefecture of Police, please.... Is that the Prefecture?... Put me on to Monsieur Philippe?... Is that you Philippe?... What? The mistake has already been discovered.... Yes: I know about it—and more.... Listen.... Bring two police cyclists with you—big ones—with you quickly—here—to Bregeac's. You understand? There's not a moment to lose!"

He put back the receiver and said to Ralph: "You revealed yourself a trifle too soon, my young friend," he said, jeering in his turn. "The attack has failed—and you know the counter-attack. On the landing Labonce and Tony. Here Marescal and Bregeac, for he has nothing to gain by backing you up. That's the first line, if the fancy takes you to save Aurelie. And in another twenty minutes three specialists from Headquarters. Is that enough for you?"

Ralph was absorbed in sticking matches into a groove in the table. He stuck in seven one after another close together and one, by itself, at a little distance from them.

"Seven to one," he said. "The odds are a trifle short. What you really want is—may I?"

With a timid air he stretched out his hand towards the receiver.

Marescal let him take it up, but watched him closely.

"Hello!" said Ralph. "... Elysées 2233, please.... Hello. Is that the President of the Republic?... Please, Monsieur le President, send at once to Monsieur Marescal a battalion of Horse Marines."

Furious, Marescal snatched the receiver out of his hand.

"Stop fooling!" he cried. "I suppose you haven't come here just to play the joker. What is your object?"

Ralph looked uncommonly disappointed. "So you've no sense of humor, have you?" he said mournfully. "But there's always time for a little joke."

"Speak, will you!" snapped the Commissary.

"I beg you to explain," said Aurelie in an imploring tone.

He smiled at her and said: "You're afraid of the big policemen, Mademoiselle, and you don't want any of their politeness. You're right. We will explain." Then in a more serious tone he went on: "I will explain, since you ask me, Marescal. To speak is as good as to act, sometimes, and nothing equals the solid reality of certain words. If I am master of the situation, I am master of it for reasons still secret, but which I must now reveal, if I wish to give my victory unshakeable foundations—and convince you."

"Of what?"

"Of the absolute innocence of this young lady," said Ralph firmly.

"Indeed?" sneered Marescal. "She is not a murderess?"

"No."

"And perhaps you're not a murderer either?"

"No."

"Then who did commit the murders?"

"Some one else."

"It's a lie!"

"It's the truth. From the beginning to the end of this business, Marescal, you've been mistaken. When I saved this young lady at Beaucourt Station I did not know her. I had only seen her having tea at the confectioner's on the Boulevard Haussmann and then talking to you on the pavement. It was only at Sainte-Marie that we had a few talks. Now, during those interviews she always avoided any allusion to the murders on the express; and I never questioned her about them. The truth has been established, without her having anything to do with it, thanks to my strenuous efforts, and thanks above all to my conviction, instinctive but as weighty as actual reasoning, that, with a face of that innocence, she was no criminal."

Marescal shrugged his shoulders with an incredulous air, but did not protest. In spite of everything he was curious to know how this strange person interpreted the facts of the case.

He looked at his watch and smiled. Philippe and the big policemen from Headquarters were drawing near.

Bregeac listened without understanding and stared at Ralph. Aurelie's anxious eyes never quitted his face.

He began, employing, without being aware of it, the words used by Marescal.

"On the twenty-sixth of last April car number five of the Marseilles express was occupied by only four persons. An English woman, of the name of Miss Bakersfield—"

He stopped short suddenly, reflected for some seconds, and began again firmly: "No: that is not the way in which to set out the facts. It is necessary to go further back, to the very source of those facts and to unfold the whole affair, or rather what one might call the two periods in the affair. I ignore certain details in it; but what I do know, along with what one can suppose with practical certainty, is enough to make it clear and connect the facts together without a break." He paused, then went on more slowly: "About eighteen years ago—I repeat the number Marescal—eighteen years—that is the first period in the story—eighteen years ago at Cherbourg four young men used to meet one another at different cafés with a certain regularity, one of the name of Bregeac, secretary at the Commissariat Maritime, one of the name of Jacques Ancivel, one of the name of Loubeaux, and a fellow of the name of Jodot. The relations between the four were not very intimate and they did not last long, since the last three of them came to loggerheads with the law and the official position of the first, that is to say of Bregeac, did not allow him to frequent their society any longer. Moreover, Bregeac married and went to live at Paris.

"He had married a widow, the mother of a little girl called Aurelie d'Asteux. His wife's father, Etienne d'Asteux, was an old eccentric who lived in the country, an inventor, an inquirer always on the lookout for new facts and who, several times, had just missed acquiring a great fortune or discovering a great secret which gives you a great fortune. Now, some time before the marriage of his daughter with Bregeac, he appeared to have discovered one of those miraculous secrets. At least he lays claim to having done so in the letters he wrote to his daughter; and to prove it to her, he made her come, with the little Aurelie, to visit him. The journey was kept secret but unfortunately Bregeac learned about it, not much later, as Mademoiselle thinks, but almost immediately. He questioned his wife about it. Keeping silent about the essential facts, as she had sworn to her father to do, and refusing to tell him the place they had been to, she made certain admissions which led Bregeac to believe that Etienne d'Asteux had buried a treasure somewhere. Where? And why not reap the benefit of it now?

"Their home life became painful. Bregeac grew more irritated every day. He writes importunate letters to Etienne d'Asteux, questions the child, who does not answer, persecutes his wife, threatens her, in a word lives in a state of growing excitement.

"Then, one on the top of the other, two events bring his exasperation to its height. His wife dies of pleurisy and he learns that his father-in-law, attacked by a serious illness, is doomed to an early death. Bregeac falls into a panic. What will become of the secret, if Etienne d'Asteux does not speak? What will become of the treasure if Etienne d'Asteux leaves it to his grand-daughter Aurelie, on the condition of her coming into possession of it on attaining her majority, as he talked of doing in one of his letters? In either case Bregeac would get nothing. All these riches, which he presumed to be fabulous, would pass him by. It was necessary, at any cost, by any means, to learn the secret.

"These means a fatal chance put in his way. In handling a case of robbery and hunting down the thieves he lay hands on his three old comrades of Cherbourg, Jodot, Loubeaux, and Ancivel. The temptation was too great for him. He succumbs to it and tells them the story. They come to an agreement on the spot: for the three rogues it means immediate liberty. They will go straight to the Provençal village, in which the old man is in his dying agony, and tear from him, by force if necessary, the information they must have.

"The plot failed. The old man, assaulted in the middle of the night by the three blackguards, summoned to answer their questions and tortured, dies without speaking a word. The three murderers take to flight. Bregeac has on his conscience a crime from which he has reaped no benefit."

Ralph paused and looked at Bregeac. Bregeac said nothing. Was he refusing to defend himself against improbable accusations? Was he confessing the truth of them? You would have said that all this was of no importance to him and that the recalling of the past, terrible as it might be, could not increase his present distress.

Aurelie had listened without displaying any more than he the impression the story made on her. But Marescal was recovering little by little his coolness, astonished certainly that Limézy revealed before him facts of such gravity and handed over to him, bound hand and foot, his old enemy Bregeac. And once more he looked at his watch.

Ralph went on: "The crime then was useless, but the results of it were to make themselves severely felt, in spite of the fact that justice had never known anything about it. In the first place one of his accomplices, Jacques Ancivel, in his terror fled for America. Before going, he confided everything to his wife. She came to Bregeac and compelled him, under penalty of immediate denunciation, to sign a paper in which he took upon himself all the responsibility for the crime against Etienne d'Asteux and declared the innocence of the three guilty men. Bregeac was frightened and stupidly signed the paper. Handed over to Jodot, the paper was enclosed by him and Loubeaux in a bottle which they found under the bolster of Etienne d'Asteux and which they had kept at every risk. From that time they had Bregeac in their power and could blackmail him whenever they wanted to.

"They had him in their power; but they are intelligent rogues and they prefer, rather than to exhaust him by blackmail in a small way, to let him rise in the administration. They have only one idea in their minds, the discovery of that treasure of which Bregeac had had the imprudence to speak to them. Bregeac still knows nothing about it. No one knows anything about it, except the little girl who has seen the country in which it is, and who in the mysterious depths of her mind, keeps obstinately the silence imposed upon her. It is necessary then to wait and watch. When she leaves the convent to which Bregeac has sent her, they will act.

"Well, she comes out of the convent, and on the very next day, two years ago, Bregeac receives a letter in which Jodot and Loubeaux inform him that they are entirely at his service to hunt for the treasure. That he must make the girl speak and pass the information on to them. If he does not—

"This letter is a sudden clap of thunder to Bregeac. Twelve years had passed; he hoped that the affair was definitely buried. He had even ceased to be interested in it. It recalled to him a crime which horrified him, and a period of his life that he remembered only with anguish. And lo! All these shameful things rise up out of the darkness! And with them his old comrades rise again. They harass him. What is he to do?

"The question he asks himself is one of those which do not even bear discussion. Whether he wants to or not, he must obey: that is to say he must torment his step-daughter into speaking. He decided to do so, urged on by the need to know the secret and grow rich, which once more invades his spirit. From that moment not a day passes without questionings, quarrels, and threats. There is a perpetual hunt through the thoughts and memories of the unfortunate girl. On this closed door, behind which, when quite a child, she has shut a little group of images and impressions, they knock more and more loudly. She wants to live: they do not allow it. She wants to amuse herself, and she does sometimes amuse herself, goes to the houses of a few friends, plays in private theatricals, sings. But, on her return home it is an unceasing martyrdom.

"A martyrdom to which is presently added a really odious circumstance, one I dread to recall: Bregeac's love. Don't let us speak of it. About that you know as much as I do, Marescal, since from the moment you saw Aurelie d'Asteux there sprang up between you and Bregeac the ferocious hatred of two rivals in love.

"In that way it came about, little by little, that flight appeared to the victim as the only possible way of escape. She was encouraged to fly by a person whom Bregeac had to put up with, in spite of himself, William, the son of the last of his Cherbourg friends. Ancivel's widow had been keeping him in reserve. He plays his part, in the shade up to this point, very cleverly, without awaking distrust. Guided by his mother, and knowing that Aurelie d'Asteux, on the day on which she shall love, will have full freedom to confide the secret to the fiancé she has chosen, he dreams of bringing her to love himself. He offers his help. He will escort her to the South whither, exactly at the right moment, his business calls him.

"The twenty-sixth of April comes.

"Observe carefully, Marescal, the situation of the actors in the drama at this date and the exact position of things. First of all there is Mademoiselle who is escaping from her prison. Happy at the thought of the liberty she is so soon to enjoy, she consents, on the last day, to have tea with her step-father at a confectioner's on the Boulevard Haussmann. Bregeac is late. She has tea with some street urchins she has picked up, and comes out of the confectioner's. Just outside she chances on you. There is a scene. Bregeac takes her back home. She escapes and at the railway station joins William Ancivel.

"William has at the moment two affairs on hand: he is going to make Aurelie his; but at the same time he is going to commit a burglary at Nice, under the direction of the notorious Miss Bakersfield, of whose gang he is a member. It was in this way that the unfortunate English girl found herself caught up in a drama in which she did not herself play a part of any kind.

"Finally we have Jodot and the two brothers Loubeaux. These three have acted so cleverly that William and his mother do not know that they have reappeared and are competing with them. The three rogues have followed all William's maneuvers; they know everything that is going on and being planned in Bregeac's house; and they are on the spot on the twenty-sixth of April. Their plan is laid: they will carry off

Aurelie and compel her to speak by any means to hand. That's clear, isn't it?"

He paused and looked round at their attentive faces.

Then he went on: "And now this is the real distribution of these persons on the express. Car number five: in the back compartment Miss Bakersfield and Baron de Limézy; in the front compartment Aurelie and William Ancivel. You quite understand, Marescal, *in the front compartment*, Aurelie and William, and not the two brothers Loubeaux, as one has hitherto believed. The two brothers as well as Jodot are elsewhere. They are in car number four, your car, Marescal, well hidden in the darkness of the covered lamp and drawn curtains. Do you understand?"

"Yes," said Marescal in a low voice.

"That's a good thing!" said Ralph. "Well, the train starts. Two hours pass. It stops at La Roche station. It starts again. The moment has come. The three men from car number four, that is to say Jodot and the brothers Loubeaux come out of their dark compartment. They are masked, dressed in gray blouses, and wear caps. They slip into car number five. At once they see in the first compartment, two sleeping figures, a man and a lady with fair hair. Jodot and one of the brothers fall upon them while the other brother keeps watch. The Baron is knocked on the head and bound. The Englishwoman defends herself. Jodot grips her by the throat and only then learns the mistake they have made: it is not Aurelie, but another woman with fair hair. They leave the Baron bound and the girl dying and go out of the corridor to the last compartment, where William and Aurelie really are. But here everything changes. William has heard a noise. He is on his guard. He has his revolver and brings the business to an end with a couple of shots. The two brothers fall, and Jodot flies.

"We are in full agreement, aren't we, Marescal? Your mistake, my mistake at the beginning, the mistake of the magistrates, everybody's mistake is to have judged the facts in accordance with their appearance and in accordance with this rule, which is quite reasonable: when there is a murder, the dead are the victims and the people who fly the murderers. One never thought that the exact opposite might happen, that the assailants might be killed and the assailed, safe and sound, might take to flight. And how should William not have thought of flight on the instant? If William waits, William is done for. William the burglar cannot allow justice to meddle in his affairs. The smallest enquiry and the underside of his equivocal existence will rise into the full light of day. Was he going to resign himself to that? It would be too foolish. When the train is slowing down the remedy is at hand. He does not hesitate; he hustles his companion and shows her the scandal that the business will set going—a scandal for her and a scandal for Bregeac. Helpless, in an immense confusion of mind, terrified by what she has seen and the presence of these two corpses, she does as he bids her. William dresses her in the blood-stained blouse and mask and cap of the younger Loubeaux. He dresses himself in the disguise of the elder Loubeaux, carries away their suit-cases to leave no trace behind him. They hurry down the corridor, upset the conductor, and jump from the train.

"An hour later, after a terrible flight through the wood, Aurelie was arrested, imprisoned, found herself in the hands of her implacable enemy, Marescal, and was lost.

"But for a *coup de théâtre. I* enter the scene!"

Nothing, neither the gravity of the circumstances, nor the dolorous attitude of the young girl who is weeping at the memory of that accursed night—nothing could have prevented Ralph from playing the part of an actor who enters on the scene.

He rose, went to the door, and came back, with the magnificent air of an actor whose entry must produce an overwhelming effect.

"Then I enter on the scene," he repeated, smiling with an air of satisfaction. "It was time. I am sure, Marescal, that you also are pleased to see, in the midst of these rogues and imbeciles, an honest man who at once takes up the right attitude, without knowing anything, and simply because Mademoiselle has beautiful green eyes, comes forward as the champion of persecuted innocence. Here at last is a firm will, a penetrating insight, a helping hand, a generous heart—Baron de Limézy! As soon as he arrives, things begin to clear up. The facts line up, like good children, in their true and proper order; and the drama ends in laughter and good temper."

He walked a few steps up and down the room, and bent over the weeping girl.

"Why do you go on crying, Mademoiselle, now that this nightmare is at an end, and even Marescal himself bows before an innocence he clearly sees? Do not weep, Mademoiselle. Always I enter on the scene at the decisive moment. It's a habit of mine, and I never miss my entry. You saw it yourself that horrible night: Marescal shut you up; I set you free. Two days later, at Nice, it was Jodot. I rescue you. At Monte Carlo, at Sainte-Marie, it is Marescal again. I rescue you. And was I not here just now? Then what are you afraid of? All is over, and we can go quietly away before the big policemen arrive and the Horse Marines surround the house. Isn't that so, Rudolph? You don't put any obstacle in the way, and Mademoiselle is free? Isn't it a fact that you're ravished by this dénouement which satisfies your sense of justice and your genial soul? You are coming, Mademoiselle?"

She rose timidly, feeling strongly that the battle was not won. In fact, on the threshold of the door, Marescal, pitiless, barred their way. Bregeac ranged himself beside him. The two men made common cause against their triumphant rival.

CHAPTER XI
BLOOD

Ralph stepped up to them, and without paying any attention to Bregeac said quietly to Marescal: "Life seems very complicated because we only see it in scraps, and those by unexpected lights. It is so with this express case. It's as entangled as a newspaper serial. The facts spring up at random, stupidly, like fireworks which will not go off in the order in which you arrange them. But when a lucid mind sets those facts in their places, all things become reasonable, simple, in perfect accord with one another, as natural as a page of history. It is that page of history that I've just read to you, Marescal. You know now the whole business; you know that Aurelie d'Asteux is innocent. Let her go."

Marescal shrugged his shoulders and growled: "No."

"Don't get obstinate, Marescal. You can see that I am not fooling or joking any longer. I simply ask you to recognize your mistake."

"My mistake?"

"Certainly, since she did not commit murder, since she was not a confederate, but a victim."

Marescal said in sneering accents: "If she did not commit the murder, why did she fly? In the case of William, I can admit reasons for flight. But in her case, what did she gain by flying? And why hasn't she said anything about it since—except a few words at the beginning of the affair when she kept wailing to the policeman: 'I wish to speak to the magistrate, I wish to tell him the story.' Apart from that, silence."

"That's a good point, Marescal," Ralph admitted. "It's a point well worth raising. This silence has often bothered me also, this stubborn silence which she has always kept, even with me, who was helping her, and who would have found a confession of the greatest use in my enquiries. But her lips remained closed. And it is here only, in this house, that I have solved this problem. I hope that she will forgive me for having searched her drawers when she was ill. It was necessary. Read these words, Marescal, which are among the instructions which her dying mother, and who had no illusions about Bregeac, left her: 'Aurelie, whatever happens and whatever the conduct of your step-father may be, never accuse him. Defend him, even if you have to suffer at his hands, even if he is guilty: I have borne his name.' "

"But she did not know about Bregeac's crime," protested Marescal. "And even if she had known of it, she could not have guessed that it had anything to do with the crimes on the express. Bregeac therefore could not have come into the matter."

"She did know of it."

"Who from?"

"From Jodot."

"What proof is there of it?"

"The statement which William's widowed mother made to me. I hunted her up in Paris, where she lives, and I paid her handsomely for a written statement of all that she knows about the past and the present. Her son told her that in the compartment of the express, face to face with Mademoiselle, above the two dead brothers, with his mask torn off and covered by William's revolver, Jodot shook his fist at her and said with an oath:

" 'If you breathe a word of this business, Aurelie, and give the police my name and I am arrested, I will inform them of the crime committed years ago. It was Bregeac who murdered your grandfather d'Asteux!'

"It was this threat, repeated later at Nice which overwhelmed Aurelie d'Asteux and made her keep silence. Have I spoken the exact truth, Mademoiselle?"

"The exact truth," she murmured.

"Then you see, Marescal, your objection falls to the ground. The silence of the victim, this silence which left you still suspicious, is on the contrary a proof in her favor. For the second time I ask you to let her go."

"No!" said Marescal stamping his foot.

"Why not?"

Of a sudden Marescal's rage burst forth and he shouted: "Because I wish to avenge myself! I want the scandal! I want everybody to know that whole business, her flight with William, her arrest, Bregeac's crime! I want her to be dishonored and shamed. She has rejected me. Let her pay! And let Bregeac pay too! You've been stupid enough to give me the damning details I had missed. I hold Bregeac and the young woman more firmly than I thought—and Jodot and the Ancivels and the whole band! Not one of them shall escape me; and Aurelie is one of the gang!"

He was raving with rage, and came to a stop for sheer lack of breath, and leaned back against the door. In the silence that followed they heard Tony and Labonce talking on the landing.

Ralph picked up from the table a scrap of paper taken from the bottle, a scrap on which was written: "Marescal is a blockhead." He unfolded it with a careless air and handed it to Marescal.

"Take it, old chap, have it framed, and hang it up at the foot of your bed," he said in the kindest accents, smiling amiably.

"Yes, yes: go on fooling!" snarled Marescal. "Go on fooling as much as you like. It doesn't alter the fact that I've got you too! You showed me the truth at the very beginning! That business of the cigarette! 'Could you oblige me with a light.' I'll oblige you with a light all right! A light that will last you the rest of your life—in prison! Yes, in prison from which you came, and to which you're going back straight away. In prison, I repeat—in prison! If you think that during my struggle with you I have not pierced your disguise; if you think that I do not know who you are and that I haven't already all the necessary proofs to strip the mask off you, you're wrong. Look at him, Aurelie, look at your sweetheart; and if you wish to know who he is, think for a moment of the king of crooks, of the most gentlemanly of burglars, of the master of masters, and say to yourself that Baron de Limézy, pseudo-nobleman and pseudo-explorer is no other man than—"

The front door bell rang loudly and cut him short. It was Philippe and his two big policemen. It could be no one else.

Marescal rubbed his hands and took a long breath.

"I think you're well in the soup, Lupin. What do you think?"

Ralph looked at Aurelie. The name of Lupin appeared to have made no impression upon her. With an expression of anguish she was listening to the sounds below.

"Poor lady with the green eyes, your faith is not yet perfect," said Ralph. "How on earth can a gentleman of the name of Philippe torment you?"

He opened the window, and speaking to some one on the pavement below, he said: "It's the gentleman named Philippe from the Prefecture, isn't it? Just a word with you, my friend, apart from your three big policemen, for they are three, hang it all! Don't you recognize me? Baron de Limézy. Hurry up! Marescal is waiting for you."

He shut the window.

"They're all here, Marescal," he said. "Four downstairs and three up here for I don't count Bregeac, who seems to have lost interest in the business. That makes seven three-headed giants to make only one mouthful of me. I am horror-stricken, and so is the young lady with the green eyes."

Aurelie forced herself to smile; she even muttered two or three words they could not catch.

Marescal was waiting on the landing. The front door was opened; hurrying steps came up the stairs. At once Marescal had to hand, eager to pull the quarry down, like a pack of hounds ready to be let loose, six men. He gave them their orders in a low voice, then entered, smiling all over his face.

"You don't want a useless fight, do you, Baron?" he said cheerfully.

"No fight, Marquess. The idea of killing all seven of you, like the seven wives of Bluebeard, is positively hateful to me," said Ralph.

"Then you'll follow me?"

"To the end of the world!" said Ralph with enthusiasm.

"Unconditionally, you understand?"

"Oh, no, there's one condition: you've got to buy me a meal," said Ralph.

"Right. Dry bread, dog-biscuit, and water," said Marescal.

"No," said Ralph.

"Well, what is your bill of fare?" said Marescal.

"The same as yours, Rudolph. Meringues Chantilly babas au rhum, and Alicante wine."

"What do you mean?" asked Marescal on a sudden high note of acute anxiety and surprise.

"My meaning is perfectly simple. You invite me to tea. I accept with pleasure. Haven't you an appointment at five?"

"An appointment!" cried Marescal almost in a squeak.

"Yes. You haven't forgotten it? At your place—not your house—your bachelor's flat—Rue Duplan—a little flat looking on the street. Isn't it there that you meet every afternoon and stuff with meringues dipped in Alicante, the wife of your——"

"Be quiet!" said Marescal in a strangled whisper.

He was as white as a sheet. All his self-confidence had vanished. He looked as if he would never joke again.

"Why do you want me to keep silent?" asked Ralph innocently. "Is the invitation off? Aren't you going to introduce me to—"

"Silence, damn you!" hissed Marescal.

He went back on to the landing, shut the door behind him, and took Philippe aside.

"Just a few minutes, Philippe. There are some details to straighten out before we make an end of it. Take your men downstairs so that they mayn't hear anything."

He came back into the room, rather shakily, went to Ralph and with his face almost touching Ralph's face, said in a voice too low for Bregeac and Aurelie to hear it: "What do you mean? What are you getting at?"

"Nothing at all."

"Then what are you talking about? How do you know?"

"The address of your flat, and the name of your pretty friend? Goodness, all I have to do in your case was what I did in the case of Bregeac and Jodot and his colleagues, make discreet inquiries about your private life, which enquiries brought me to a mysterious ground-floor flat, very prettily furnished where you entertain charming ladies. Dim lights, incense, flowers, sweet wines, divans as deep as tombs—Marescal's Folly. What?"

"And what ab-b-bout it?" stammered Marescal. "Haven't I the right to do as I like? What connection is there between that and my arresting you."

"There wouldn't be any connection at all, if you hadn't been guilty of the further folly of choosing this little abode of love as a safe place to hide those ladies' letters."

“It’s a lie!” snapped Marescal.

“If I were lying, you wouldn’t be as white as a sheet,” said Ralph.

“The details?” said Marescal savagely.

“In a cupboard there’s a secret drawer. In this drawer is a casket. In this casket some charming letters from women, tied up in packets with colored ribands. Letters that compromise two dozen ladies and actresses whose passion for the handsome Marescal is expressed without the slightest restraint. Shall I name a few? The wife of the Procureur B., Mademoiselle X. of the Comédie Française–and above all, above all, the worthy spouse, a little mature, but still presentable of—”

“Shut up, you dog!”

“The dog,” said Ralph amiably, “is a man who takes advantage of his physique to obtain protection and promotion.”

With a hang-dog air and bowed head, Marescal walked up and down the room. Then he stopped before Ralph and said in the same low voice:

“How much?”

“How much what?”

“What do you want for the letters?”

“Thirty shekels, like Judas.”

“Stop your fooling! How much?”

“Thirty millions.”

Marescal trembled with impatience and rage.

Ralph laughed and said: “You’ll make yourself ill, Rudolph. I’m a good fellow, and I like you–you’re so sympathetic. I’m not asking a cent for your comico-amorous literature. I value it too highly. There’s months and months’ amusement in it. But I demand—”

"What?"

"That you throw down your weapons, Marescal. Absolute peace for Aurelie and Bregeac, and even for Jodot and the Ancivels. I'm going to deal with them myself. Since the whole of this case from the police point of view is in your hands, and there is no actual proof, no real evidence, let it drop. It will be pigeon-holed."

"And you'll give me back the letters?"

"No. They're a pledge; and I keep them. If you do not play fair, I publish some of them in all their simple crudeness. All the worse for you—all the worse for your pretty friends."

The drops of sweat stood out on Marescal's forehead.

"I've been betrayed," he snarled.

"Very likely," Ralph agreed.

"Betrayed by *her*. For some time I've had a feeling that she was spying on me. It's thanks to her that you've been able to manage this business exactly as you liked. She recommended you to her husband and had you placed with me."

"What do you expect?" said Ralph cheerfully. "All's fair in war. If you employ such discreditable means in your fighting, could I act otherwise, when it was a matter of defending Aurelie against your abominable hatred? And then you've been too simple, Rudolph. How could you suppose that a man like me would go to sleep for a month and wait on events and your good pleasure? You saw me act at Beaucourt, at Monte Carlo, and Sainte-Marie, and you saw me get away with the bottle and the paper? Why didn't you take precautions?"

He shook him affectionately by the shoulder.

"Come, Marescal, don't bow before the storm," he went on. "You lose the game—be it so. But you have Bregeac's resignation in your pocket, and since you stand well at Court, and his post has been promised you, it's a great step forward. The good days will come again, Marescal, be sure of it. One condition however: don't trust women. Don't use them to rise in your profession, and don't use your profession to succeed with them. Be a lover, if it's your fancy, and be a detective, if you like the job; but don't be either a lover-detective, or a detective-lover. In conclusion, a word of advice: if ever you meet Arsène Lupin on your path, slip away by a by-path. For a detective, it's the beginning of wisdom. I have spoken. Give your orders and–good-by."

Marescal chafed at the bit. He turned and twisted in his fingers the points of his beard. Should he yield? Was he going to throw himself on his enemy and summon his giants? A storm in a skull, thought Ralph. Poor Rudolph, what use was it to struggle on?

Rudolph did not struggle long. He was too clearsighted not to see that any resistance would make the situation worse. He obeyed therefore with the air of a man who admits that he has to obey. He summoned Philippe and talked to him. Philippe went away with the policemen and the detectives. The front door opened and shut. Marescal had lost the battle.

Ralph turned to Aurelie.

"Everything is in order, Mademoiselle, and we have only to start. Your suit-case is down in the hall, isn't it?"

She murmured as if she were awaking from a nightmare: "It is possible? No more prison? How did you get—"

"Oh," he said quickly. "One gets everything one wants from Monsieur Marescal, by the exercise of a little tact and reason. He's a good fellow. Shake hands with him, Mademoiselle."

Aurelie did not shake hands with him: she shrank away. Besides, Marescal had turned his back on her, and stood with his two elbows on the mantelpiece, his face buried in his hands. She showed a slight hesitation as she passed Bregeac. But he seemed wholly indifferent to her and was wearing a strange air which Ralph was to remember almost immediately.

"One word," said Ralph, stopping in the doorway. "I undertake, in the presence of Marescal and your step-father, to conduct you to a quiet retreat, where you will not see me at all for a month. In a month I shall come to ask you how you intend to arrange your life. Do you agree?"

"Yes," she said.

"Then let us go."

They went. But he had to put his arm round her on the staircase to support her; she was so shaken.

"My car is near here," he said. "Do you think you'll be strong enough to travel all night?"

"Yes," she said. "It's such a joy for me to be free!" She paused and added in a low voice: "And such anguish!"

Just as they were leaving the house a muffled report came from an upper story. Ralph quivered; but Aurelie, in her feebleness, did not seem to have heard it.

"I've forgotten something. There's my car, down the street. There's an old lady inside it, the old lady of whom I have already spoken to you, my old nurse. Will you go to her? I must just run upstairs and tell Marescal something. I'll be with you in a couple of minutes."

She turned down the street; he ran quickly upstairs.

In his study Bregeac was lying on a sofa in his death agony. A revolver, fallen from his nerveless hand, lay on the floor beside him. Marescal was bending over him. The blood poured from his mouth; a last shudder shook him; he did not move again.

"I ought to have foreseen it," murmured Ralph. "His downfall—the loss of Aurelie. Poor devil! He has paid his debts."

He said to Marescal: "Telephone for a doctor and get this business hushed up. Hemorrhage, is what it is. Don't let there be any question of suicide. At any cost Aurelie must not hear about it at present. She is not strong enough. You can say that she's ill in the country, staying at the house of a friend."

Marescal grasped his wrist and said: "Answer me. Who are you? You're Lupin, aren't you?"

"Splendid!" said Ralph. "Professional curiosity always comes to the top."

He faced Marescal, then turned his profile to him and then his three-quarter face, and said with a laugh: "You've seen it, duffer!"

He ran downstairs quickly and caught Aurelie up; the old lady was helping her into the back of a comfortable limousine.

But, having, in accordance with his custom of always taking precautions, cast a look up and down the street, he said to Victoire: "You haven't seen any one prowling about the car?"

"No one," she declared.

"Are you sure? A rather stout man, accompanied by a man with his arm in a sling?" he persisted.

"Yes, of course I have! They were walking up and down on the pavement lower down the street."

He started off at a run and overtook, in the little passage which runs round the church of Saint Philippe du Roule, two men, one of whom carried his arm in a sling.

He tapped them both on the shoulder and said cheerfully: "Well, well, well, so you know one another, you two? How goes it, Jodot? And you, William Ancivel?"

They turned. Jodot, dressed like a prosperous tradesman, thick-chested and with the hairy face of a vicious dog, showed no astonishment.

"Ah, it's you, is it? The gentleman of Nice?" he said. "I said that it was you who was with the little girl just now."

"And it's also the gentleman of Toulouse," said Ralph to William. And he went on: "What have you been messing about here for, brave boys? You were watching Bregeac's house. What?"

"For the last two hours," said Jodot arrogantly. "The arrival of Marescal and his detectives and the police, the departure of Aurelie, we've seen everything."

"Well?" said Ralph.

"Well, I suppose that you know all about the business, that you've been fishing in troubled waters, and that Aurelie slips away with you, while Bregeac fights it out with Marescal. Resignation without a doubt—probably arrest as well."

"Bregeac has just killed himself," said Ralph.

Jodot started: "What?" he said sharply. "Bregeac? Bregeac dead!"

Ralph gazed at them curiously for a moment; then he said: "Listen to me, both of you. I've forbidden you to meddle with this business. You, Jodot, murdered Etienne d'Asteux, you murdered Miss Bakersfield and were the cause of the death of the brothers Loubeaux, your friends, associates and confederates. Am I to hand you over to Marescal? And you, William, you'd better know that your mother has sold me all her secrets for a big sum, and on condition that you were left alone. That promise covers the past. But, if you start afresh, it does not hold any longer. Am I to break your other arm and hand you over to Marescal?"

William, panic-stricken, was ready to give in. But Jodot held out.

"In a word, you're to have the treasure," he growled. "Nothing could be plainer."

Ralph shrugged his shoulders and said: "You believe then in that treasure, do you?"

"I believe in it as you do," growled Jodot. "I've been working on it for nearly twenty years; and I'm going to get away with it in spite of all your maneuvers."

"Get away with it! You've got to find out first of all where it is and what it is," said Ralph sharply.

"I know nothing and neither do you, no more than Bregeac. But the girl knows. And that's why——"

"Would you like to go shares in it," said Ralph laughing.

"It isn't worth while. I shall manage to get my share of it, on my own, and a good share too. And all the worse for those who get in my way! I've more trumps in my hand than you think. Good evening. You've had your warning," growled Jodot.

Ralph watched them walk away. The incident annoyed him. What the devil was this ill-omened bird of prey up to?

"Rubbish!" he murmured. "If he wishes to run after the car for two hundred and fifty miles, I shall be delighted to act as pace-maker."

The next day, at noon, Aurelie awoke in an airy room from which she saw, across gardens and meadows, the somber and majestic cathedral of Clermont-Ferrand. An old boarding-house, situated on a hill, and transformed into a sanatorium, afforded her a most discreet retreat and one well fitted to re-establish definitely her health.

There she passed peaceful weeks, speaking to no one but Ralph's old nurse, walking in the park, dreaming for hours at a time, her eyes fixed on the town or on the mountains of the Puy-de-Dome of which the hills of Royat form the first strongholds.

Not once did Ralph come to see her. She found in her room flowers and fruit which his nurse brought her, books and magazines. Ralph kept out of sight in the little lanes which wound between the vineyards on the ridges hard by. He watched her from a distance and poured forth to her, in his heart, long speeches, teeming with the passion that grew more intense every day.

He gathered from her movements and her supple carriage that life was welling up in her, like an almost dried-up spring into which fresh water flows again. A dusk was falling over the hours of terror, the sinister faces, the corpses and the crimes and over and above forgetfulness there was the expansion of a tranquil happiness, serious and unconscious, sheltered from the past and even from the future.

"You are happy, lady with the green eyes," he murmured. "Happiness is a state of mind which allows one to live in the present. While suffering nourishes itself on painful memories and hopes by which it is not duped, happiness mingles itself with all the little things of everyday life and transforms them into elements of serenity and joy. Yes, you are happy. When you pluck the flowers or stretch yourself out on your lounge chair, you do it with an air of contentment."

On the twentieth day came a letter from him inviting her to go for a motor drive one morning the following week. He had important things to discuss with her.

Without hesitating, she wrote to accept the invitation.

On the appointed morning she walked along the little rocky lanes which brought her down to the high road where Ralph was waiting.

When she caught sight of him, she stopped short in a sudden, disquieted confusion—like a woman who asks herself at a solemn moment whither she is directing her steps and whither circumstances are taking her. But he came to her quickly and signed to her to be silent. It was for him to say the words that must be said.

"I did not doubt that you would come," he said. "You knew that we must see one another again because this tragic business is not yet at an end and certain parts of the problem still await solution. Which they are, is of little importance to you. You have given me a commission to arrange everything, to solve everything and to do everything. You will simply obey me. You will let yourself be guided by my hand, and whatever happens, you will no longer be afraid. That is over, the fear which overwhelms and presents visions of hell. Isn't that so? You will smile beforehand at the things that happen, and welcome them as friends."

He held out his hand. She allowed him to press hers. She would have liked to speak and tell him that she was grateful, that she trusted him. But she must have understood the vanity of such words, for she was silent.

They started and passed through the old village of Royat, with its hot baths.

The hands of the church clock pointed to half-past eight. It was a Saturday, the fifteenth of August. The mountains rose under the sunniest of skies.

They did not exchange a word. But Ralph never ceased pouring out the tenderest protestations to her, in his heart.

"Well, so you detest me no longer, lady with the green eyes, you have forgotten my offense at our first meeting. And I, I have so much respect for you that I do not wish to remember it. Come: smile a little since you have now fallen into the habit of regarding me as your good genius. One smiles at one's good genius."

She did not smile. But he felt that she was friendly and very close to him.

The car traveled for barely an hour. They came round the Puy-de-Dome and took a fairly narrow road which ran southwards, with zigzag ascents, and descents through the middle of green valleys and dark forests.

Then the road grew narrower and ran through a deserted, arid region and became steep. It was paved with enormous slabs of lava of different sizes, with large cracks between them.

"An old Roman causeway," said Ralph. "There is not an old corner of France in which one does not find some relic of this kind, some road of Cæsar."

She did not answer. Of a sudden she appeared to have grown absent-minded and dreamy.

The old Roman causeway was now little more than a goat path. The ascent of it was difficult. At the top of it was a small plateau in the middle of which stood an almost abandoned village. Aurelie read the name of it on a fingerpost: Juvains. Then came a wood, and then, of a sudden, a grassy plain of pleasing aspect. Then once more the Roman causeway, which climbed upwards, quite straight, between grassy embankments. At the top of this ladder they stopped. Aurelie had drawn more and more into herself. Ralph did not cease to watch her closely.

When they had mounted a series of boulders which rose one above the other like a staircase, they came to a circular stretch of country, which delighted the eye with the fresh greenness of its turf. It was shut in by a high wall of rough stone, the mortar in which had not been destroyed by the bad weather of years. It stretched, right and left, to a distance. A large door in it faced them. Ralph had the key of it. He opened it. The ground continued to rise. When they had reached the crest of the slope, they saw before them a lake set in a glassy smoothness, in the hollow of a circle of rocks which rose evenly above it.

For the first time Aurelie asked a question; and it revealed the manner in which her mind had been working.

"May I ask whether, in bringing me here rather than somewhere else, you had a motive? Or was it just chance?" she said.

"The view is indeed rather gloomy," said Ralph without answering her directly. "But all the same it displays a ruggedness and wild melancholy which are not without character. They tell me that tourists never make excursions to it. However, one can go for a row on the lake, as you see."

He took her towards an old boat moored to a stake by a chain. She stepped into the stern and sat down without a word.

He took the oars and they moved gently over the surface.

The water, slate-colored, did not reflect the blue of the sky but rather the somber hue of invisible clouds. From the end of the oars fell shining drops which looked to be as heavy as mercury; and it seemed astonishing that the boat could make its way through this, so to speak, metallic flood. Aurelie dipped her hand into it, but had to draw it out at once, so cold and unpleasant was the water.

"Oh!" she said and sighed.

"What is it? What's the matter?" asked Ralph.

"Nothing–or at least–I don't know."

"You're troubled–moved."

"Moved, yes–I'm conscious of impressions which surprise and trouble me. It seems to me—"

She paused.

"It seems to you?" he said.

"I can't quite tell you. It seems to me that I'm another creature–and that it isn't you who are here. Do you understand?"

"I understand," he said smiling.

She murmured: “Don’t explain it to me. What I feel is rather painful, and yet for nothing in the world would I miss feeling it.”

The circle of cliffs, on the summit of which the great wall here and there appeared, ran at a radius of five or six hundred yards. Suddenly there appeared in the middle of it a hollow in which began a narrow channel, hidden by high walls from the rays of the sun. The boat entered it. The rocks were blacker and gloomier. Aurelie gazed at them with amazement, for they were of strange shapes: crouching lions, massive chimneys, colossal statues, gigantic gargoyles.

Of a sudden, when they reached the middle of this fantastic corridor, they were, as it were, smitten by a blast of murmurs, faint and indistinct, which came, by the road they had themselves taken, from the regions they had left little more than an hour before.

They were the chiming of church bells, of smaller bells, clear notes of bell-metal, delicate and joyous notes, all a trembling of heavenly music, under which droned the big bell of the cathedral.

Aurelie turned faint. She understood now the meaning of her distress. The voices of the past, that mysterious past which she had done everything not to forget, echoed within and around her. They came echoing back from the cliffs in which granite was mingled with the lava of ancient volcanoes. They sprang from rock to rock, from statue to gargoyle, moved over the hard surface of the water, mounted to the blue strip of Heaven, fell again like spray to the bottom of the gulf, and went in rolling echoes towards the other end of the passage where shone the light of day.

Overcome, trembling with memories, she strove to struggle against so many emotions and braced herself not to succumb to them. But she was no longer strong enough. The past weighed her down like a bending branch, and she bent her head, murmuring with a sob:

“Who are you? Who are you?”

She was astounded by this inconceivable miracle. Having never revealed the secret that had been instructed to her; guarding jealously, since her childhood, the treasure of remembrances over which her memory watched so dutifully, which she was not to hand over, according to her mother's command, to any one but the man she should love, she felt herself wholly feeble before this strange being who read the very depths of her soul.

"Then I haven't made a mistake? It is really here, is it not?" said Ralph, infinitely touched by the girl's charming abandon.

"It is really here," murmured Aurelie. "During the whole drive the things that met my eye seemed to me things I had already seen—the road—the trees—the paved causeway which rose between two embankments—and then this lake, these rocks, the color and the coldness of this water—and above all the sound of these bells! They are the same as long ago—they have come to our ears at the very spot at which they came to my mother, my mother's father, and the little girl I then was. As to-day we came out of the shadow to enter the other part of the lake under as bright a sun."

She had raised her eyes and was gazing ahead. In truth, another lake, smaller, but on a more grandiose scale, opened before them, ringed by steeper cliffs and of an aspect of a yet more savage and more striking solitude.

One by one the memories awoke in her. She told Ralph of them quietly, as confidences one makes to a friend. She called up before his mind a little girl, happy, care-free, amused by the spectacle of the shapes and colors which she was again contemplating to-day, with her eyes shining with tears.

"It is as if you took me on a journey through your life," said Ralph, in tones shaken by emotion. "And I take as much pleasure in seeing the scene on that long distant day as you in recalling it."

She went on: "My mother was sitting where you are, and her father was facing her. I was holding my mother's hand. Look, that tree all by itself, in that hollow in the cliff, it was there—and also those great red stains on that rock over there—and see how the cliffs narrow just as they did then. But there is no more of the channel—it's the end of the lake. This other lake stretches in a curve like a half moon. We're going to come to a quite small beach at the end of it. Look, there it is—with a waterfall on the left springing out of the cliff. There is another to the right of it. You'll see the sand in a minute; it sparkles like mica. And there is a big grotto—yes, I'm sure of it—and at the entrance of this grotto——"

"At the entrance of this grotto?"

"There was a man waiting for us, a queer-looking man with a long, gray beard and wearing a maroon blouse. We saw him from here, standing upright, very tall. Aren't we going to see him now?"

"I thought that we should see him," said Ralph. "And I'm very much astonished that we don't. It's nearly noon; and our appointment was at noon."

CHAPTER XII
THE WATER THAT ROSE

They disembarked on the little beach, on which grains of sand shone like mica. The cliff on the right and the cliff on the left in coming together formed an acute angle, the lower part of which was hollowed out into a small grotto, protected in front by a slate roof.

Under this roof stood a small table, covered with a cloth on which were plates, a junket, and fruit. On a visiting card on one of the plates were written these words:

"The Marquess de Talencay, the friend of your grandfather Etienne d'Asteux, greets you, Aurelie. He will be with you presently and begs to offer his excuses for being unable to meet you until later in the day."

"He was expecting me, then?" said Aurelie.

"Yes," said Ralph. "We had a long talk, he and I, four days ago, and I was to bring you here at noon to-day."

She looked round her. A painter's easel was leaning against the wall of the grotto, under a large shelf heaped with drawing materials, measures, and boxes of colors. There was on it also a pile of old clothes. Hanging across the grotto was a hammock. At the back of the grotto two large stones formed a fireplace and a pipe rose into a crevice in the cliff like the flue of a chimney.

"Does he live here?" asked Aurelie.

"Often, especially in the summer. For the rest of the year he lives at the village of Juvains, where I found him. But he comes here every day. Like your dead grandfather, he is an old eccentric, very cultivated, very artistic, though he does paint very bad pictures. He lives alone, a little after the manner of a hermit, hunts, cuts down and saws up his trees, watches over his shepherds, and feeds all the poor of the countryside, which belongs to him for six miles round. And he's been waiting for you for fifteen years, Aurelie."

"Or at least waiting for me to be of age."

"Yes; by reason of an agreement with his friend d'Asteux. I questioned him about it. But he did not wish to discuss it with any one but you. I had to tell him the whole story of your life and what had happened during the last few months. Then, as I promised to bring you, he lent me the key of the door in the wall. He is immensely delighted that he is going to see you."

"Then why isn't he here?"

The absence of the Marquess de Talencay surprised Ralph greatly, though he had no reason for attaching much importance to it. But, since he did not wish to make the girl anxious, he gave full play to his wit and humor during this first meal they took together, in such curious circumstances and at so odd a place. Always careful not to ruffle her by a display of too great tenderness, he was conscious that she felt quite safe with him. She must be quite aware that this was no longer the enemy from whom she had fled, but a friend who only wished her well. So many times already had he saved her. So many times had she been surprised at having hope only in him, at seeing her own life dependent wholly on this unknown, and her happiness rise or decline according to his will.

She murmured: "I should love to thank you; but I do not know how. I owe too much to pay the debt."

He said to her: "Smile, lady with the green eyes, and look at me."

She looked at him and smiled.

"You've paid the debt," he said.

At a quarter to three the music of the bells began again and the big bell of the cathedral came droning round the angle of the cliffs.

"It really is quite natural; and the phenomenon is well known all through the district," Ralph explained. "When the wind blows from the north-east, that is to say from Clermont-Ferrand, the acoustic qualities of the country cause a strong current of air to carry all these sounds by a compulsory route which winds among the mountains and ends at the surface of the lake. It is inevitable; it is mathematical. The bells of all the churches of Clermont-Ferrand and the big bell of its cathedral cannot do anything else but come and ring here as they are doing at the moment."

She shook her head.

"No," she said. "It is not so. Your explanation does not satisfy me."

"Have you another?"

"The true one."

"What is it?"

"I firmly believe that it is you who bring the sound of these bells here to revive all my impressions as a child."

"I'm omnipotent, then?"

"You're omnipotent," she said in a tone of profound conviction.

"And I'm omniscient also," said Ralph. "Here, at this very hour, fifteen years ago, you slept."

"What do you mean?"

"That your eyes are heavy with sleep since your life of fifteen years ago is being lived again."

She did not try to oppose his wish and stretched herself out in the hammock.

Ralph kept watch for a while at the mouth of the grotto. Then, having looked at his watch, his face clouded with annoyance. A quarter past three—and the Marquess de Talencay had not come.

"But after all—after all—it isn't of any importance," he said to himself.

But it was of importance; and well he knew it. There are situations in which everything is of importance.

He went back into the grotto and gazed at the girl, who was sleeping under his protection, and wished once more to apostrophize her and thank her for her trust in him. But he could not. A growing anxiety was invading him.

He crossed the little beach and discovered that the boat, the bow of which he had drawn up on to the beach, was now floating two or three yards from the edge of it. He had to draw it in with a pole, and then he made a second discovery, which was that the boat, which, during their passage across the lake, had contained two or three inches of water, now contained twenty or thirty.

He succeeded in turning it upside down on the beach.

"Goodness! What a miracle it was we didn't go to the bottom!" he thought to himself.

It was not a matter of an ordinary crack, easy to stop up, but of a whole plank rotted, of a plank also which had been recently inserted in the bottom of the boat and only fastened by four nails.

Who had done this? At first Ralph thought of the Marquess de Talencay. But with what object would the old gentleman have acted in this manner? What reason was there for thinking that d'Asteux's friend desired to bring about a catastrophe at the very moment at which the young girl was brought to him?

Then another question presented itself: by what road was Talencay coming to the place now that he had no boat at his service? From what quarter would he arrive? Was there a way by land which came down to this beach?

He started to look for it. There was no possible way of getting out on the left: there were the obstacles of the two waterfalls in addition to the obstacles of the cliff. But on the right, just above where the cliff dipped into the lake and formed the beach, twenty steps had been cut in the rock and from the top of them along the front of the cliff rose a path, or rather a ledge so narrow, that, here and there, it was necessary to hold on to projections from the cliff to get along it.

Ralph climbed the steps and made his way up it. Here and there an iron hasp had been driven into the surface of the cliff by which one prevented one's self falling into space. And so he was able to reach, with considerable difficulty, the plateau above, to find that the path ran round the second lake and turned towards the passage between the two. A grassy plain, studded with boulders, stretched around him. Two shepherds were moving off it, driving their flocks towards the high wall. Nowhere did he see the tall figure of the Marquess de Talencay.

He returned to the beach after an hour's exploration, to make the disagreeable discovery that, during that hour, the water had risen and covered the bottom steps in the cliff. He had to jump to the beach.

"It's queer," he murmured with an anxious air.

Aurelie must have heard him, for she came quickly out of the cave to him. Then she stopped, astonished.

"What's the matter?" asked Ralph.

"The water," she said. "How high it is. It was much lower when I went to sleep, wasn't it? I'm sure it was."

"You're right."

"How do you explain it?"

"It's a quite natural phenomenon, like those bells," he said quickly. Then in reassuring accents, he added: "The lake is subject to the law of the tides, which, as you know, produces an ebb and flow."

"But when is it going to stop rising?"

"In an hour or two."

"That's to say that the water will fill half the grotto?"

"Yes. It certainly does flow into the grotto, as this black line on the wall, which is evidently the high-water mark, proves."

He had lowered his voice a little. Above the black line to which he had pointed, there was another just under the ceiling of the grotto. What did that one mean? Was he to understand that at certain periods the water would reach the ceiling? But owing to what exceptional phenomena, to what immense cataclysm?

"But no," he said to himself, pulling himself together. "A supposition of that kind is absurd. A cataclysm? That only happens once in a thousand years. An oscillation of the ebb and flow? Fantasies in which I don't believe. It can only be mere chance, a passing incident."

That might be so. But what was it that produced this passing incident? In spite of himself he felt a vague dread. He thought of the inexplicable absence of Talencay. He thought of the connection which might exist between this absence and the dull menace of the danger he did not yet fully grasp. He thought of the scuttled boat.

"What's the matter?" Aurelie asked. "You seem absent-minded."

"The fact is, I'm beginning to believe that we are wasting our time here," he said. "Since your grandfather's friend is not coming, we had better go to him. The interview can take place quite as well at his house at Juvains."

"But how are we to go? The boat seems useless."

"There is a road to the right, very difficult for a woman, but all the same practicable,—only you will have to let yourself be carried."

"Why shouldn't I walk too?"

"What point is there in your getting wet? It's just as well that I should be the only one to get into the water."

He made this suggestion without any afterthought. But he saw that she was blushing. The idea of being carried by him, as she had been carried along the Beaucourt Road, must be hateful to her.

They were silent, both of them embarrassed.

Then the girl, who was standing on the edge of the lake, bent down and plunged her hand into it.

"No—no—I couldn't stand this icy water; I really couldn't," she said.

She went back into the grotto, and he followed her.

A quarter of an hour passed; and to Ralph it seemed a long quarter of an hour indeed.

At last he said: "We ought to be going. The situation is becoming dangerous."

She followed him out of the grotto. But at the moment she mounted his back, there came the whine of a bullet and the shower of splinters from the face of the cliff. The report of the rifle rang.

She dropped from his back. A second bullet whined and struck the cliff. He picked her up, carried her into the grotto, sat her down, and sprang out of it as if he were dashing to the assault.

"Ralph! Ralph! I forbid you! They'll kill you!" she cried, following him.

He caught her up again, and forced her back into the grotto. But this time she did not let go of him, but clung to and held him back.

"Stay here—please!" she cried.

"No, no: you're wrong. I must act!"

"I won't have it! I won't have it!" she cried.

She held him with trembling hands; and she, who had been so frightened of being carried by him a few moments before, held him clasped to her, with a grip there was no loosening.

"Don't be frightened," he said quickly.

"I'm not frightened," she said. "But we must remain together. The same danger threatens us. Let's stick to one another."

"I won't leave you," said Ralph. "You're right." He put his head out of the door to take a look round. A third bullet shattered one of the tiles of the roof.

So they were besieged, compelled to stay where they were. Two marksmen armed with long-range rifles prevented any attempt to get away. Ralph had time to learn the position of these marksmen, from two little clouds of smoke which were rising at a distance. Posted a little way from one another on the cliff on the right, they were about two hundred and fifty yards away. From that point they commanded the whole length of the lake and the little corner of the beach that still remained above the water and nearly all of the interior of the grotto. All of it, except a recess on the right, in which they were huddled, and the very back of it where were the two stones which served as a fireplace, which was hidden by the slope of the roof, was open to their fire.

By a violent effort Ralph forced himself to laugh.

"This is funny," he said.

His laughter seemed so spontaneous that it quieted Aurelie.

He went on: "Here we are blockaded. At the slightest movement, a bullet. And the line of fire is such that we're obliged to hide ourselves in a mousehole. You must admit that it is jolly well planned."

"Who by?"

"I thought at first by the old Marquess. But it isn't him. It can't be him."

"Then what has become of him?"

"He's shut up somewhere. There's no doubt about it. He must have fallen into some trap which was laid for him by the very people who are blockading us."

“That’s to say?”

“Two formidable enemies from whom we need not expect any pity. Jodot and William Ancivel.”

He was thus brutally frank on this point, to turn Aurelie’s attention from the real danger which threatened them. For Jodot and William and their rifles counted very little in his eyes compared with the rising invasion of this stealthy water which the two crooks had made their formidable ally.

“And why this ambush?” she asked.

“The treasure,” said Ralph. “That’s the only possible explanation. I reduced Marescal to impotence; but I did not forget that one day or other we should have to deal with Jodot and William. They have got ahead of me. Having learned my plans by some means or other, they have attacked your grandfather’s friend, imprisoned him, robbed him of the papers he was going to communicate to you, and have been ready for us since the morning. If they did not shoot us down when we were coming through the passage between the two lakes, it was because shepherds were moving about the plateau. It was evident that we should wait for Talencay here, on the strength of the visiting card, and the few words that one of the two confederates scribbled on it. And it’s here that they’ve set their ambush. Scarcely had we passed through the passage before big flood-gates were closed, and the surface of the lake, swollen by the two waterfalls, began to rise without its being possible for us to notice it for four or five hours. But by then the shepherds would have returned to the village, and the lake become the most lonely and admirable of rifle ranges. The boat being scuttled, the bullets prevent any sortie of the besieged; and it is impossible for them to take flight. That’s how Ralph de Limézy has let himself be caught like a common Marescal.”

He said this in the chaffing tone of a man who is the first to laugh at a trick that has been played him. Aurelie almost wanted to laugh.

He lit a cigarette and held out the burning match. Two reports from the plateau; then immediately a third and a fourth. But the bullets missed.

The flood, however, was rising quickly. The beach was quite covered and little waves were now flowing over its flat surface and lapping against the entrance of the grotto.

"We shall be more comfortable on the two stones of the fireplace," said Ralph.

They sprang across the grotto, and reached them without drawing fire. Ralph lifted the girl into the hammock, which, hanging high, was hidden by the tiled roof. Then he made a dash at the table, caught up in a napkin all that was left of their lunch, leaped back and set it on the shelf, beside the drawing materials. Two rifles rang out.

"Too late!" he said. "We've nothing more to fear. A little patience and we shall go quietly away. My idea is to rest and have a meal; and by that time it will be dark. As soon as it is dark I will carry you on my shoulder to the path up the cliff. The strong point of our adversaries is that the daylight enables them to blockade us. Darkness means safety."

"Yes, but the water will be rising," said Aurelie. "And it will be an hour before it's dark enough to start."

"Well, what of it? Instead of getting my feet wet, I shall get wet to the waist," said Ralph.

It sounded very simple. But he was quite aware of the flaws in his plan. In the first place, the sun had scarcely disappeared behind the summit of the mountains; and that meant another hour and a half or two hours of daylight. Moreover, the enemy would draw nearer, little by little, and post themselves at the top of the path; and how was he, hampered by the girl, to force a passage?

Aurelie was doubtful, asking herself what she was to believe. In spite of herself, her eyes were fixed on marks in the wall, which enabled her to follow the rising of the water. But Ralph's coolness was uncommonly impressive.

"You will save us, I'm sure of it," she murmured.

"Presently," he said airily. "You trust me?"

"Yes: I trust you. You told me one day—do you remember? When you were reading the lines on my hand—that I was to beware of danger from water? Your prediction is being accomplished; and yet, I am not at all afraid, for you can do anything. You work miracles."

"Miracles?" said Ralph, still maintaining his efforts to reassure her by speaking lightly. "No: not miracles. I merely reason, and then act as the occasion demands. Because I never questioned you about your childish memories, and nevertheless brought you here to the very scene you saw so long ago, you think me a kind of sorcerer. You're wrong. It was all a matter of reasoning and thought. Yet I had no more precise information than the rest of them. Jodot and his confederates knew the bottle as well as I did, and like me read the formula inscribed under the name of Eau de Jouvence. What information did they get from it? None. But I made inquiries, and I saw that nearly the whole of the formula was a reproduction, with the exception of one line of the analysis of the springs of Royat, one of the principal hot bath establishments of Auvergne. I looked at the map of Auvergne and on it I find the village and lake of Juvains—Juvains, an obvious contraction of the Latin word Juventia, which means Jouvence. I knew where I was. After an hour's gossip at Juvains I learned that old M. de Talencay, the Marquess of Carabas of this part of the world, must be at the very heart of the business, and approached him as your envoy. When he told me that you had formerly come here on the Sunday and Monday of the Assumption, that is to say the fourteenth and fifteenth of August, I fixed our visit for the same day. As it happens, the wind was blowing from the north-east, as on your earlier visit. So we had the escort of the bells. And that's all the miracle there was about it, young lady with the green eyes."

But words were not enough to distract her attention any longer.

A moment later she murmured: "The water is rising—it's rising. It's covered the two stones and is wetting your shoes."

He stepped down into the water, raised one of the stones, and set it on the other. Thus elevated, he rested his elbow against the rope of the hammock, and with untroubled mien began to talk again, for he feared the effect of silence on the girl.

But all the while he was talking about their safety, his underthought had been busy with other trains of reasoning and other reflections about the implacable reality, the growing menace of which he was watching with a growing fear. What was taking place? How was he to handle the situation? Owing to the action of Jodot and William, the surface of the water was rising. So be it. But the two ruffians were evidently taking advantage of a state of things already existing and which had existed for centuries. Must he not then suppose that those who made possible this raising of the surface for reasons now hidden from him—but certainly not for the purpose of blockading and drowning people in the grotto—must have made it equally possible to let the surface sink back to its normal level? The closing of the flood-gates implied the existence of invisible machinery which would, when the lake was too full, let the water out. But where was he to look for this machinery?

Ralph was not one of those who await death with idle hands. He considered carefully the plans of getting to grips with his enemies, or of swimming to the flood-gates. But if a bullet hit him, or if the icy coldness of the water gave him cramp, what would become of Aurelie?

Careful as he was to hide his anxiety from Aurelie, she could not longer fail to understand certain inflections of his voice and pauses in his task when he was tongue-tied by the fear which was torturing her.

"Please—please—answer me," she said. "I would much rather know the truth. There is no longer any hope, is there?"

"What! But it's getting dark."

"But not quickly enough. And when the night does come we shall be none the more able to get away."

"Why not?"

"I don't know. But I have a feeling that it is all over with us; and that you know it."

He said firmly: "No—no. The danger is great. But it's a long way off as yet. We shall escape it, if we keep cool. Everything rests on that. Thought and understanding. When I understand everything, I'm sure that there will be time to act. Only——"

"Only?"

"You must help me. To understand everything I need your memories, all your memories."

His voice had grown serious; he went on with restrained fervor: "I know you promised your mother to keep them secret from every one except the man you should come to love. But death is an even stronger reason for speaking than love. And if you do not love me, I love you as your mother would have wished that you should be loved. Forgive me for telling you this in spite of the vow I made to you; but there are times at which one can keep silent no longer. I love you—I love you and I wish to save you—I love you. I cannot allow you to keep silent, for it would be a crime against yourself. Answer my questions. Perhaps a few words will be enough to enlighten me."

"Question me," she murmured.

"What passed during your last visit after your coming here with your mother? What scenes did you see? Where did your grandfather and his friend take you?"

"Nowhere," she said confidently. "I'm sure of having slept here, in a hammock, as I have done to-day. The others were talking. The two men were smoking. These are things which I had forgotten and which

I now recall. I remember the smell of the tobacco and the noise of the uncorking of a bottle. And then—then—I was quite awake, and we had a meal. Outside, the sun was shining—"

"The sun?"

"Yes, it must have been the next day."

"The next day? You're sure? Everything lies in this detail," he said quickly.

"Yes: I'm certain. I awoke here the next day, and, outside, the sun was shining. I see myself still here, yet it is somewhere else. I see the rocks, though they're no longer in the same place."

"How? They're no longer in the same place?" he said in bewildered accents.

"No: the water was no longer washing the foot of them."

"The water was no longer washing the foot of the cliffs and yet you came out of this grotto?" he said.

"I came out of this grotto. Yes: my grandfather led the way; my mother followed, holding me by the hand. It was slippery under our feet. Around us were odd-looking houses—ruins. And then came the chiming of the bells—the same bells we heard to-day."

"It is so—it certainly is so," murmured Ralph. "Everything is in accordance with my supposition. There is no possible doubt about it."

A heavy silence fell on them. The water was lapping against the walls with a sinister sound. The table, the easel, the books, and the chairs were floating about.

He had to sit on the end of the hammock crouched down under the granite ceiling.

Outside, the dusk was mingling with the fading light. Of what use would the darkness be to him, however thick it might be? In what quarter was he to act? He cudgelled his brains desperately, trying to force them to discover the solution. Aurelie was half sitting up, and he guessed that her eyes were kind and affectionate. She took hold of one of his hands, bent down, and kissed it.

"Heavens!" he cried. "What are you doing?"

She murmured: "I love you."

Her green eyes were shining in the dusk. He heard the beating of her heart. Never had he experienced so profound a joy.

She put her arms round his neck and said in the tenderest accents:

"I love you. That is my great and only secret, Ralph. The other does not interest me. But this secret is all my life—all my soul! I have loved you from the beginning, without knowing you, even before I saw your face. I loved you in the darkness, and it was because of that that I detested you. Yes: I was ashamed. It was your lips that took me, on the road to Beaucourt. They stirred in me something I had never known and which frightened me. So much pleasure, so much happiness, on that horrible night—from a man I did not know! To the very depths of my being, I felt the delightful and revolting feeling that I belonged to you, and that you had only to will it to make me your slave. If I fled from you, it was because of that, Ralph—not because I hated you, but because I loved you too dearly and was afraid of you. I was troubled and confused. I wished at any cost never to see you again and yet I only thought of seeing you again. If I was able to endure the horror of that night and all the abominable tortures which followed it, it was because of you—because of you from whom I fled who always came again at the hour of danger. I hated you for it with all my heart; and every time I felt myself yet more yours. Ralph, Ralph, clasp me tightly, Ralph, I love you."

He clasped her to him with a dolorous passion. In his heart he had never doubted the existence of this love. It had been revealed to him by the ardor of a first kiss; and at every one of their meetings, it had displayed itself in a fear of which he had divined the profound cause.

But he was afraid even of the happiness he was feeling. The tender words of the young girl, the caress of her fresh breath intoxicated him. The dauntless will to fight was weakening in him.

She had divined this lassitude in the depths of his being, and drew him yet closer to her.

"Let us resign ourselves, Ralph," she said. "Let us accept the inevitable. I do not fear death with you. But I want it to surprise me in your arms—my mouth on your mouth, Ralph. Life can never give us greater happiness."

Her two arms enlaced him like a collar from which he could no longer free himself. Little by little her lips drew nearer and nearer to his.

He resisted, however. To kiss those lips which offered themselves to him, was to accept defeat and, as she said, resign himself to the inevitable. But he would not. All his nature rose in revolt against such cowardice.

But Aurelie implored him, stammering the words which weaken and disarm.

"I love you—do not refuse that which should be—I love you—I love you."

Their lips met. He enjoyed the intoxication of a kiss in which there was all the ardor of life and the terrible pleasure of death. Darkness seemed to envelop them more quickly, now that they abandoned themselves to the delicious torpor of the embrace. The water was rising.

It was a passing weakness; and Ralph tore himself out of it violently. The thought that this charming creature, whom he had saved so many times, was about to endure the terrible torture of the water that forces its way into you and smothers you and kills you, shook him with horror.

"No, no!" he cried. "This shall not be! Death for you? No! I will find a way to prevent such a monstrous thing!"

She wished to hold him back. She grasped his wrists and implored him in lamentable accents:

"I implore you! I implore you! What are you going to do?"

"Save you! and save myself!"

"It is too late."

"Too late? But the night has come! I no longer see your dear eyes; I no longer see your lips. Why should I not act?"

"But in what way?"

"How do I know! The essential thing is to act! Moreover I do know certain facts. There must necessarily be means of neutralizing, at a given moment, the action of the closed flood-gates. There must be sluices which let the water flow swiftly away. I must find them!"

Aurelie did not listen to him. She groaned: "I implore you not to leave me alone in this dreadful darkness! I'm afraid, Ralph."

"No: since you are not afraid to die, you're not afraid to live—to live two hours. Not more. The water cannot reach you for two hours. And I shall be here—I swear to you, Aurelie, that I shall be here, whatever happens, to tell you that you are saved—or to die with you!"

Little by little, pitilessly, he freed himself from her desperate arms. Then he bent over her and said passionately:

"Trust me, my beloved. You know that I have never failed in my efforts. The moment I have succeeded, I will let you know by a signal—I'll whistle twice. But even when you feel the water chilling you, believe blindly in me!"

Nerveless, she fell back.

"Go," she said. "Go since you wish to."

"And you will not be frightened?"

"No: since you do not wish it."

He took off his coat and waistcoat and shoes, glanced at the illuminated figures of his watch, fastened it round his neck, and slipped out of the hammock.

Outside, darkness. He had no weapon, no clue.

It was eight o'clock.

CHAPTER XIII
IN THE DARKNESS

Ralph's first impression was terrible. A starless night, crushing, implacable, a night of thick fog, weighed stilly and heavily on the invisible lake and the indistinct cliffs. His eyes were of no more use to him than the eyes of the blind. His ears heard only silence. The noise of the waterfalls was no longer heard: the fog absorbed them. And in this bottomless gulf it was necessary to see, to hear, to move, and to reach the goal. Sluices? Not for a moment did he think of them. It would have been folly to play the fatal game of hunting for them. No; his objective was the two ruffians. And they were in hiding. Fearing doubtless the direct attack on an adversary such as he, they were keeping prudently under cover, with every sense alert. Where to find them?

The icy water in which he was standing, breast-high, chilled him to the marrow so painfully that he did not think it possible to swim to the flood-gates. Moreover how would he be able to open them without knowing where the machinery was?

He stumbled along the edge of the cliff, reached the submerged steps, and mounted to the path which hugged the face of the cliff.

The ascent of it was very difficult. Suddenly he stopped. At a distance, through the fog, a faint light was shining.

Where? It was impossible to be sure. Was it on the lake? Was it on the top of the cliffs? In any case it faced him, that is to say it was shining from the vicinity of the passage, from the very spot, that is, from which the two ruffians had fired. It looked as if they must be camping on it. And that light could not be seen from the grotto, which showed that they were taking precautions and was a further proof of their being there.

He hesitated. Should he follow the path by land with all its windings, over the peaks and down into the ravines, climb up rocks, descend into hollows, in which he would lose sight of the precious light? The thought of Aurelie, imprisoned in the heart of that awful granite sepulchre, made up his mind for him. Quickly he came tumbling down the path he had mounted and sprang from the steps into the lake.

He thought that he was going to suffocate. The torturing iciness of the water was unbearable. Though the distance was not more than two hundred to two hundred and fifty yards, he was on the point of giving it up—so far beyond human strength did it seem. But the thought of Aurelie never left him. He saw her under that pitiless ceiling. The water was pursuing its ferocious course, which nothing could stop or slacken. Aurelie was listening to its diabolical chuckling and feeling its icy chill.

He redoubled his efforts. The light guided him like a beneficent star, and he stared at it with burning eyes, as if he were afraid that it would suddenly vanish under the formidable assault of all the powers of darkness. But on the other hand was it not a sign that William and Jodot were on the watch, and that, turned downwards towards the lake, it enabled them to watch the path from which the attack would come?

As he came nearer to it, he felt a certain relief, due evidently to his using his muscles. He moved forward with long, silent strokes. The star grew larger, doubled in size by the mist.

He turned aside, out of the field of light. As far as he could judge, the two ruffians had posted themselves on the top of a promontory which jutted out at the entrance of the passage. His foot struck a reef of rocks, then a beach of small pebbles; he crawled out of the water on to it.

From above his head, but a little to the right, came the murmur of voices.

How far was he from Jodot and William? What was the cliff he had to scale like—a sheer wall, or sloping enough to climb? He could not tell. He must trust to luck.

He stripped and rubbed his chilled limbs and body with handfuls of gravel. Then he wrung out his sopping shirt and trousers and put them on again. His warmed body quickly warmed them, and feeling fit again, he attacked the cliff.

It was neither a sheer fall, nor a slope. It was composed of huge steps, a cyclopean staircase. He could climb them, leaping up, catching the edge of each step, but with what an immense effort! Loose pebbles slipped from under his gripping fingers; plants he grasped were unrooted. Again and again he fell, only to leap again. But the voices above were growing louder.

In the light of day he would never have attempted such a climb. But the unceasing "Tick-tack! Tick-tack!" of his watch drove him on with an irresistible impulsion. Every second that struck on his ear, was a moment in Aurelie's waning life. He *must* succeed!

He succeeded. Of a sudden no other cyclopean step barred his way; he was on level turf; and a light was shining through the darkness.

A few yards from him the surface of the plateau dipped into a hollow, in the middle of which stood a small ruined hut; from a branch of the tree which towered above it hung a lantern.

On the opposite edge of the hollow, two men lay at full length on their bellies on the turf with their backs to him. Their rifles and revolvers lay within reach. Between them stood an electric lamp, the light of which had been his beacon.

He looked at his watch and shivered. It had taken him fifty minutes, much longer than he had thought to reach the top of the cliff.

"I have half an hour at the most to stop the water rising," he said to himself. "If I haven't torn from Jodot the secret of the sluices in half an hour, all that is left for me is to return to Aurelie and die with her, as I promised."

He crawled, hidden by the long grass, towards the hut. Forty feet away from him Jodot and William were talking. In perfect security, loudly enough for him to distinguish their voices, but not loudly enough for him to hear what they were saying. What was he to do?

He had come without any definite plan; he meant to act as the circumstances demanded. Having no weapon, he decided that to start a hand to hand struggle of which when all was said and done, he might get the worst, was too dangerous. Besides, if he did get the best of it, would he be able by threats to make such a tough opponent as Jodot speak, to confess himself beaten and hand over the information which he had obtained with such difficulty?

He continued to crawl forward therefore, with infinite precaution and very slowly, in the hope of catching a sentence that would enlighten him. So slowly did he move that he could not himself hear the rustling of his body through the grass. He advanced six feet, then ten, and so reached a point from which he could hear distinctly what they were saying.

"For goodness sake, don't make yourself ill, thinking about it," growled Jodot. "When we last went down to the flood-gates, the surface of the lake had risen to the fifth mark which is level with the ceiling of the grotto; and since they couldn't get away, their hash is settled. It's as certain as that two and two make four."

"All the same you ought to have posted yourself nearer the grotto and kept watch on them from there," grumbled William.

"And why not you, my lad?"

"Me! With my arm still stiff! It's just about as much as I can do to fire my rifle."

"And then you're afraid of the beggar," sneered Jodot.

"And so are you," retorted William.

"I don't say I'm not. I preferred to use my rifle and the dodge of flooding the grotto, since we'd got old Talencay's papers."

"I wish you wouldn't talk about him," snapped William.

He spoke in a shaky voice and Jodot chuckled.

"Cowardly dog!" he sneered again.

"Just you bear in mind that when I came back from hospital my mother said: 'All right. You know where this devilish fellow, this poisonous Limézy has hidden Aurelie, and you declare that if you watch him he'll lead you to the treasure. Very good; my son will lend you a helping hand. But no crimes—no blood.' What?"

"And there wasn't a drop of blood," said Jodot in jesting accents.

"Oh, you know what I mean and what happened to the poor beggar. When there's a dead man, there's a crime. It's just the same in the case of Limézy and Aurelie. Are you going to say there hasn't been a crime?"

"And what about it? Were we to let this business drop? Do you think that a beggar like Limézy would have made way for you for love of your beautiful eyes? You know the cursed blighter too well. He broke your arm. He would have ended by breaking your neck. It was him, or us; and we had to choose."

"But Aurelie?"

"The two of them were one. There was no way of getting at the one without getting at the other."

"The unfortunate girl——"

"Well, do you want the treasure, or don't you? You're not going to get it by just smoking your pipe—not a treasure like this."

"All the same——"

"Have you, or haven't you seen the Marquess's will?" exclaimed Jodot impatiently. "Aurelie inherits the whole of the Juvains estate. What did you think of doing then? Marry her perhaps? It takes two people to make a marriage, my lad; and I've an idea that that fine fellow, William, wouldn't have been one of them."

"Well?"

"Well, this is what is going to happen, my lad. To-morrow the lake of Juvains will be neither higher nor lower than usual. The day after and no sooner, since the Marquess has forbidden them to come on to the plateau, the shepherds will return. They will find the Marquess killed by a fall into a ravine; and nobody will suspect that any one lent him a helping hand to lose his balance. Then no heir is found since he has no relations, and no will, since I've got it. Consequently the estate becomes the property of the republic. Six months later it is sold. We buy it."

"And where do we get the money?" said William doubtfully.

"We shall easily find it in six months," said Jodot in sinister accents. "Besides, what's the estate worth to any one who does not know the secret?"

"And suppose a prosecution is started?"

"Who's going to be prosecuted?"

"Ourselves."

"What for?"

"This business of Limézy and Aurelie."

"Limézy? Aurelie? Drowned, vanished, impossible to find!"

"They'll be found in the grotto."

"They will not. We'll go round to-morrow morning, tie a couple of big stones to their legs and drop them in the lake."

"And Limézy's car?"

"We'll drive away in it as soon as we've sunk the bodies; and no one will ever know that they came here. Every one will think that the girl has been carried off from the sanatorium by her lover and that they're traveling about the country. That's my plan. What do you think of it?"

"Excellent, you old blackguard," said a voice close to them. "But there's one great drawback to it."

They turned their heads with a start of terror. A man was squatting on the turf in oriental fashion a few feet away on their left

"A great drawback," the man repeated. "All this fine plan depends on deeds done. But what happens if the lady and gentleman of the grotto took it into their heads to clear out?"

Their hands moved stealthily towards their rifles and revolvers. They were no longer there.

"Weapons? What for?" said the man in mocking accents. "A sopping shirt and trousers, that's all I've got. Weapons? Between brave fellows like us?"

Jodot and William did not stir. For Jodot, it was the man of Nice who had re-appeared; for William it was the man of Toulouse. Above all it was the formidable enemy of whom, they believed, they had got rid, and whose corpse—

"Faith, yes!" he said, affecting utter carelessness: "Alive. The fifth mark is not on a level with the ceiling of the grotto. Besides, if you imagine that one gets the better of me by little dodges of that kind—alive, my good Jodot! And Aurelie too. She's well hidden, a long way from the grotto, and not even damp. So we can talk at our ease. But it won't take long—five minutes at the most, and not a second longer. What do you say?"

Jodot was silent, stupefied and terrorstricken. Ralph looked at his watch, and calmly and carelessly, without a sign that his heart was constricted by an indescribable anguish, he went on:

"That's where you stand. Your plan is useless. As long as Aurelie is not dead she inherits; and there's no sale of the estate. If you murder her, and there is a sale, I am still here and I buy it. You must kill me too; and it can't be done–invulnerable, you know. So you're sold. There's only one way out of it."

He paused; Jodot bent forward. There was a way out of it, then?

"Yes: there's one way out of it," said Ralph again. "–to come to an understanding with me. Would you like to?"

Jodot did not answer. He was crouching ten feet away from Ralph; and his blazing eyes were fixed on him in a feverish glare.

"You don't answer. But I see that your eyes are blazing like a wild beast's. Do you think I make you an offer because I need you? I never need any one. But for the last fifteen or eighteen years you have been pursuing an object and were on the point of attaining it, which gives you certain rights, rights which you made up your mind to defend by any and every means, murder included. These rights I'm willing to buy from you, for I don't want to be bothered and I don't want Aurelie bothered either. One day or other you'd find a way of doing us a bad turn; and I don't want it. How much do you want?"

Jodot appeared to relax a little; he growled: "What's your offer?"

"It's this," said Ralph. "As you know, it isn't a matter of a treasure of which every one can take his share, but a business proposition which will take a lot of developing and the profits—–"

"Will be considerable," said Jodot.

"I agree. And my offer is based on that fact–five thousand francs a month."

The ruffian started, dazzled by such a figure.

"For both of us?" he gasped.

"Five thousand for you–two thousand for William."

William could not contain himself; he almost shouted: "I accept!"

"And you, Jodot?"

"Perhaps. I must have a guarantee—and something in advance."

"How will a quarter's advance suit you? I'll meet you at three to-morrow, in Jande Square at Clermont-Ferrand, and give you a cheque."

"Yes: that's all very well," said the distrustful Jodot. "But I've got no assurance that to-morrow Baron de Limézy won't have me arrested."

"That won't happen because they'd arrest me at the same time."

"You?"

"Rather! And it would be a more important capture than you suppose."

"Who are you?"

"Arsène Lupin."

The name had an immense effect on Jodot. He understood now why all his plans had come to grief and the sway this man exercised over him.

Ralph went on: "Arsène Lupin, wanted by all the police in the world for more than five hundred robberies, found guilty more than a hundred times. We were born to understand one another. I hold you. But you hold me; and you accept my terms, I am sure. I could have knocked you on the head just now. But no: I would sooner come to an agreement with you. Besides, I shall employ you if I get the chance. You have your faults; but you have great qualities. For example, the way you traced me to Clermont-Ferrand was a real exploit, for I don't yet understand how you did it. You have my word, then; and the word of Lupin is as good as gold. Is it settled?"

Jodot consulted with William in a low voice and replied: "Yes: we agree. What is it you want?"

"Me? I don't want anything, old chap," said Ralph carelessly. "I'm a man who is seeking for peace and pays the necessary price for it. We become partners: that's the real truth. If you wish to invest anything in the partnership after to-day, it's just as you like. You have documents."

"Lots of them. The instructions of the Marquis with regard to the lake."

"That's clear enough, since you were able to shut the flood-gates. Are they fully detailed instructions?"

"Yes: five sheets of small writing."

"And have you them here?"

"Yes; and I have the will too—in favor of Aurelie."

"Hand them over."

"To-morrow—in return for the checks," said Jodot firmly.

"Right: to-morrow, in return for the checks. Shall we shake hands on it? That will be the signing of the agreement; and I'll be getting away."

They shook hands.

"Good-by," said Ralph.

The interview was at an end; but the real battle was yet to be fought—with a few words. Everything that had been said so far and all these promises were so many trifles to put Jodot off the real scent. The essential thing was to get the sluices going. Would Jodot speak? Would Jodot guess the real situation, the real reason of Ralph's crafty negotiations?

Never before in his life had Ralph been so anxious. But he said carelessly enough: "I should like very much to see the thing working before I go away. I suppose you couldn't open the sluices that let the water run away before me?"

"It's necessary, according to the instructions of the Marquess, for the sluices to be open seven or eight hours before they've done their work," said Jodot.

"Never mind: open them at once. To-morrow morning we shall see, you from here, Aurelie, and I from over there, the whole bag of tricks, that is to say the treasure. The machinery is quite close too, isn't it? Just beneath us? Near the flood-gates?"

"Yes."

"Is there a direct path to it?"

"Yes."

"And you understand the working of it?"

"It's easy. The instructions show you how quite clearly."

"Let's go down," Ralph suggested. "I'll give you a helping hand."

Jodot rose and took the electric lamp. He had not smelled the trap. William followed him. As they passed they saw the rifles which Ralph had drawn towards him at the beginning, and pushed a little further away. Jodot slung one of them from his shoulder, William the other.

Ralph took the lantern hanging from the bough and followed on the heels of the two ruffians.

"This time I'm bringing it off," he said to himself with a lightness of spirit which must have shown in his face. "A few more convulsions perhaps. But the main battle is won."

They went down the cliff. At the edge of the lake Jodot moved along a sandy and gravelly beach at the foot of the cliff, went round a rock which hid a fairly deep cave at the mouth of which a boat was moored, dropped on his knees, removed some big stones, and uncovered four levers in a line at the end of four chains which ran into earthenware pipes.

"Here it is, quite close to the machinery of the flood-gates," he said. "The chains raise the slabs which close the sluices at the bottom of the lake."

He pulled up one of the levers. Ralph pulled up another and felt quite plainly that the chain grew taut and raised the slab that closed the sluice. The other two levers seemed to work no less successfully. There came from some distance away the sound of a sudden ebullition in the waters of the lake.

The hand of Ralph's watch pointed to twenty past nine. Aurelie was saved.

"Lend me your rifle," said Ralph. "Or, rather, fire it yourself—a couple of shots."

"Whatever for?" said Jodot in some surprise.

"It's a signal."

"A signal."

"Yes. I left Aurelie in the cave, which was nearly full of water, and you can imagine how frightened she must be. When I left her I promised to let her know by firing a rifle twice that she had nothing to fear."

Jodot was stupefied. The audacity of Ralph, this frank admission of the danger which Aurelie was still running, astounded him and at the same time increased in his eyes the prestige of his late adversary. Not for a second did he think of taking advantage of the situation. The two reports of the rifle rang out among the rocks and cliffs.

"Hang it all! You are a leader, you are," said Jodot. "You're one to obey without asking any questions. Here are the documents of the Marquess, and here's his will."

"That shows real sense," said Ralph as he took the documents. "I shall make something out of you. Not an honest man—never in this world at least—but a pretty fair crook. You don't want this boat, do you?"

"Rather not."

"I shall find it useful to return to Aurelie in. And just another word of advice: don't show yourselves any more in this district. If I were you I should make a point of getting to Clermont-Ferrand before morning. Good-by, comrades."

He stepped into the boat; Jodot cast off the chain.

"What splendid fellows!" said Ralph to himself, as he rowed vigorously towards the grotto. "The moment one appeals to their noble hearts, to their natural generosity, there's no stopping them. Certainly, comrades, you shall have your checks! But I do not guarantee that there's still a balance in my favor in my Limézy account. But you shall have them all the same, signed with my proper signature as I promised."

He made nothing of the two hundred and fifty yards after an expedition so fruitful of results. He was at the grotto in a few minutes. He went straight into it, with the lantern in the bow.

"Victory!" he exclaimed. "You heard my signal? Victory!"

A cheerful light filled the small retreat in which they had so nearly met their death. The hammock stretched from wall to wall. Aurelie was sleeping peacefully in it. Trusting to the promise of her friend, convinced that nothing was impossible to him, freed from her anguish at her danger and from the jaws of that death she had so desired, she had succumbed to her weariness. Perhaps, too, she had heard the noise of the two reports. In any case the noise he made did not awaken her.

When she opened her eyes next morning she saw surprising things in the grotto in which the light of day mingled with the light of the lantern. The water had flowed away. In the bottom of a boat resting against the wall, Ralph, dressed in a shepherd's overcoat and linen trousers which he must have taken from the heap of clothes of the old Marquess on the shelf, was sleeping as deeply as she had slept herself.

For a long while she gazed at him with loving eyes, in which there also shone a restrained curiosity. Who was this extraordinary being, whose will opposed the decrees of destiny and whose acts assumed the very appearance of miracles? She had heard, without any distress—what did it matter to her?—Marescal's accusation and the name of Arsène Lupin the Commissary had snarled at him. Was she to believe that Ralph was no other than Arsène Lupin?

"Who are you? You whom I love more than my life?" she thought. "Who are you? You who unceasingly save me as if it were your only mission? Who are you?"

"The blue bird."

Ralph awoke, and the unspoken question of Aurelie was so clear that he answered without hesitation:

"The blue bird charged with the task of bringing happiness to good and trusting little girls, to defend them against ogres and wicked fairies, and to conduct them to their kingdom."

"Have I then a kingdom, dearest?"

"Yes. At the age of six you made a progress through it. To-day it belongs to you by the will of the old Marquess."

"Quick, Ralph! Quick! Let me see it—or rather let me see it again."

"First of all let's have some food," he said. "I'm dying of hunger. Besides, the visit to your kingdom will not last long, and it must not last long. That which has been hidden for centuries must not be revealed definitely in the light of day till you shall be mistress of your kingdom."

As was her custom, she asked no questions about the way in which he had acted. What had become of Jodot and William? Had he any news of the Marquess of Talencay? She preferred to know nothing and let him guide her.

A minute later they came out of the grotto together, and Aurelie, once more overwhelmed by emotion, rested her head against Ralph's arm and murmured:

"That's really it, Ralph! That is just what I saw so long ago—on the second day—with my mother."

CHAPTER XIV
THE SPRING OF JOUVENCE

Strange spectacle! Below them in a deep arena from which the water had retired, over all the ground in the circle of cliffs were the ruins of monuments and temples, still standing, but with truncated columns, dislocated steps, scattered arches, roofless, without pediments or cornices, a forest decapitated by lightning, but a forest the dead trees of which held still all the nobility and all the beauty of ardent life. Through the whole of it ran the Roman road, a triumphal road, bordered with broken statues, framed by symmetrical temples, it passed between the pillars of demolished arches and came up the bank to the grotto in which they offered their sacrifices.

All of it was still dripping, shining, covered in places by a cloak of ooze; and fragments of marble or gold sparkled in the sun. On the right and on the left wound two long silver ribands. They were the waterfalls which had once more found the bed of their stone canals and poured their waters along them.

"The forum," said Ralph, who was a trifle pale and whose voice betrayed the emotion with which the sight filled him. "The forum—almost of the same dimensions and the same shape. The papers of the old Marquess contain a plan and explanations of it which I studied last night. The town of Juvains was under the big lake, under this one were the hot baths and the temples consecrated to the Gods of Health and Strength, all ranged round the temple of Youth, of which you see the circular colonnade."

With an arm round Aurelie's waist, to help her over the slippery ground, he led her down the sacred way. The great slabs were slippery under their feet. Moss and water plants and small pebbles covered their surface. Here and there among the pebbles were pieces of money. Ralph picked up two of them: they were stamped with the effigy of Constantine.

They stopped before a small temple dedicated to Youth. What remained of it was delightful; and there was enough to enable the imagination to reconstruct an admirably proportioned rotunda, raised upon several steps. Under it was the basin of a fountain, held up by four plump and sturdy children, from the middle of which must have risen the statue of Youth. Only two of them were still to be seen, charming, gracious, dipping their feet in the basin, from which in days gone by four of them hurled jets of water into the air.

Large pipes of lead, doubtless hidden when the city flourished, appeared to come from a spot in the cliff, where was the spring which supplied the fountain. To the end of one of them a tap had been recently soldered. Ralph turned it. A jet of water darted out of it, a trifle muddy.

"L'Eau de Jouvence," said Ralph. "This is the water that was in the bottle they took from the death-bed of your grandfather. The analysis of it was written on the label of that bottle."

For two hours they strolled about this fabulous city. Aurelie felt again the sensations she had felt on her first visit, latent in the depths of her being, and suddenly revived. She had seen that group of funeral urns, and this mutilated Goddess and that street with broken pavement and this arcade that made her tremble with melancholy joy.

She said softly: "My beloved, it is to you that I owe all this happiness. But for you I should feel nothing but misery. While I am with you everything is beautiful and delightful. I love you."

At ten o'clock the bells of Clermont-Ferrand were chiming for High Mass. Aurelie and Ralph came to the mouth of the passage. The two cascades poured into it, running on the right and left of the triumphal way, and vanished down four open sluices.

The amazing visit came to an end. As Ralph said once more, that which had been hidden during the ages must not yet appear in the light of day. No one must see it before the hour at which Aurelie should have been acknowledged its mistress.

Therefore he closed the sluices which let the water run out and slowly turned the winch of the flood-gates and little by little opened them.

Forthwith the water began to accumulate in the confined area; the big lake pouring in in a broad sheet of water, the two cascades rearing above their stone beds.

Then they ascended the cliff by the path down which Ralph had come the night before with the two crooks, and stopping half way, they saw the water rising quickly in the little lake, flowing round the bases of the temple and rising quickly towards the magic spring.

"Yes: magic," said Ralph. "That was the word the old Marquess used. In addition to the constituents of the springs at Royat it contains, according to him, principles of energy and strength, principles springing from an astonishing radio-activity of an almost incredible power. Rich Romans of the third and fourth centuries came to rejuvenate themselves at this spring; and it was thee last proconsul of the province of Gaul who, after the death of Theodosius and the fall of the Empire, decided to hide it from the eyes of the invading barbarians and protect against their enterprises the marvels of Juvains. Among many others a secret inscription bears witness to it:

"By the will of Fabius Aralla, Proconsul, in order to protect them from the Scythians and the Borussi, the waters of the lake have covered the Gods whom I loved and the temples in which I worshiped them."

"Fifteen centuries since that day! Fifteen centuries during which these masterpieces in stone and marble have been worn away. Fifteen centuries which might have been followed by a hundred more in which the destruction of these memorials of a glorious past would have been completed. If your grandfather, exploring the abandoned estate of his friend Talencay, had not by chance discovered the machinery of the flood-gates. Forthwith the two friends searched and groped and studied and cudgelled their brains. They repaired the machinery. They set machinery of the old massive wooden gates, which in days gone by kept the little lake at the level which submerged the tops of the buildings, working again. They repaired the machinery which worked the sluices.

"That's the whole story, Aurelie, and this is the city you visited when you were six years old. Your grandfather died; the Marquess never left his estate at Juvains again; he consecrated himself body and soul to the recovery of the invisible city. With the help of two of his shepherds he excavated, dug, cleaned, consolidated, and restored the work of the past; and that is the gift he offers you, a wonderful gift, which not only brings you incalculable wealth from the exploitation of a spring more precious than all those of Royat and Vichy, but also gives you a collection of works of art and monuments such as exists nowhere else."

Ralph's enthusiasm knew no bounds. It was sustained for more than an hour during which he expressed all the exaltation with which this affair of the drowned city filled him. Hand in hand they watched the rising water and the sinking columns and statues.

Aurelie, however, kept silent. At last, astonished to feel that they were no longer enjoying a complete communion of thought, he asked her the reason of it.

She did not answer at once; but presently she said:

"You don't know yet what has become of the Marquess of Talencay, do you?"

"No," said Ralph, not wishing to spoil the girl's happiness. "I expect that he remained at home, in the village, out of sorts perhaps—always supposing that he has not forgotten the appointment."

It was a poor excuse; and Aurelie did not appear satisfied by it. He guessed that, after all the emotion she had felt and all the anguish from which he had freed her, she was thinking of the things which still remained obscure and that she was still troubled by not understanding them.

"Let's be going," she said.

They climbed up to the ruined hut where the two crooks had encamped the night before. Ralph proposed to go from it to the high wall through which the shepherds had driven their flocks.

As they came round a rock near it she drew Ralph's attention to a good-sized bundle. A canvas sack resting on the edge of the cliff.

"It looks as if it moved," she said.

Ralph glanced at it, told her to stay where she was, and ran to it. An idea had suddenly struck him.

On reaching the edge of the cliff he seized the sack and thrust his hand into it. Out of it he drew the head and then the body of a child. At once he recognized Jodot's little confederate, the boy whom the crook carried with him like a ferret and set hunting in cellars and through gratings and palings.

The child was half asleep. Ralph, furious, suddenly solved the problem which had so puzzled him.

He shook the child and said: "You little blighter! You followed us from the Rue de Courcelles! What? Jodot managed to hide you on the luggage rack of my car. And you traveled like that to Clermont-Ferrand, and sent him a post-card from there! Confess it! Or I'll spank you!"

The child did not quite understand what was happening to him; and his vicious, street-urchin's, pale face filled with fear.

He muttered: "Yes. Tonton made me."

"Tonton?"

"Yes: Uncle Jodot."

"And where's your uncle now?"

"We went away last night, all three of us, and then came back."

"And then?"

"Then they went down below, when the water had gone, and hunted everywhere and gathered things."

"Before me?" cried Ralph.

"Yes: before you and the young lady. When you came out of the grotto they hid themselves behind a wall down there, further off than the grotto. I saw everything from here, where Tonton told me to wait for him."

"And now where are they both?"

"I don't know. It was hot, and I went to sleep. I awoke for a little while, and they were fighting."

"Fighting?" said the astonished Ralph.

"Yes, for something they'd found, something that shone like gold. I saw that they fell–Tonton gave William a jab with his knife–and then I don't know what happened exactly–I went to sleep again perhaps. But it looked to me as if the wall fell and buried both of them."

"What–what? What are you t-t-telling me?" stammered the horrified Ralph. "Answer–where did this happen? At what time?"

"When the bells began to ring–quite at the end. Look–there."

The child bent over the cliff and looked astounded. "Oh!" he said. "The water's come back!"

He thought for a moment then began to cry, and wailed: "Then–then–if the water has come back–they weren't able to get away. So Tonton—"

Ralph cut him short, saying: "Be quiet!"

Aurelie stood before them with troubled face; she had heard it.

Jodot and William, wounded, insensible, unable to stir or to call out, had been covered by the flood and smothered and drowned. The stones of the fallen wall lay upon their bodies.

"It's terrible," she stammered. "What a punishment for those two men!"

The sobs of the child grew louder. Ralph gave him some money and a visiting card.

"Here: here's a hundred francs. Go and take the train to Paris and go to this address. You'll be taken care of."

The return journey was made in silence and at the entrance of the sanatorium Aurelie's good-by was very grave.

"Let us separate for some days," she said. "I will write to you."

Ralph protested. "Separate? Those who love one another do not separate!"

"Those who love one another have nothing to fear from separation. Life always brings them together again," she replied.

He yielded, sadly, for he felt that she was leaving him.

A week later, in truth, he received this short letter:

My friend,

I am overwhelmed. I have learnt by chance of the death of my step-father Bregeac! Suicide, was it not? I know also that they found the Marquess de Talencay at the bottom of a ravine, into which he had fallen they say, by accident. A crime, was it not? Murder? And then the terrible death of Jodot and William. And then so many deaths! Miss Bakersfield, and the two brothers, and, long ago, my grandfather.

I am going away, Ralph. Do not try to learn where I am going. I do not know yet, myself. I must think things over, consider my life, come to a decision.

I love you, my friend. Wait and forgive me.

Ralph did not wait. The distress of mind shown by this letter, the suffering she was enduring, his own suffering and anxiety, everything drove him to action and urged him to seek for her.

His enquiries proved vain. He thought that she had taken refuge at Sainte-Marie; he did not find her there. He made inquiries in every quarter. He organized his friends to help him find her. His efforts were useless. In despair, fearing that some new enemy was tormenting her, he passed two really painful months. Then one day he received a telegram. She begged him to come to Brussels next day, and fixed a meeting-place in Cambre wood.

Ralph's joy was boundless when he saw her arrive, smiling, at peace, wearing an air of infinite tenderness, her face clear of all painful memories.

She held out her hand and said: "You forgive me, Ralph?"

They walked along, side by side, for a little way, as near to one another as if they had never parted.

Then she said: "You told me, Ralph, that I had two opposing destinies which struggle with one another and hurt me. One is a destiny of good fortune and gayety which is in accord with my true nature. The other is a destiny of violence, death, mourning, and catastrophe, a whole array of hostile forces which have persecuted me since I was a child and strove to drag me into a gulf into which I should have fallen ten times, if, ten times, you had not saved me. So after the two days at Juvains, and in spite of our love, Ralph, I was so cowardly that I had a horror of life. All that affair, which you considered marvelous and fairy-like, for me took on an aspect of darkness and hell. And isn't this right, Ralph? Think of all I have endured! And think of all I have seen! 'There is your kingdom', you said. I don't want it, Ralph. Between the past and me I only want one bond. If I have hidden myself away for some weeks it is because I had a confused feeling that I must escape from the grip of an affair of which I am the only survivor. After years, after centuries, it came to an end in me; and it is I who have the task of restoring to the light of day that which is hidden and benefiting by all its rarity and magnificence. I refuse. If I am the heir of its wealth and its splendors, I am also the heir of crimes and punishments of which I could not bear the weight."

"So that the will of the Marquess?" said Ralph, drawing the document from his pocket and handing it to her.

She seized the will and tore it into fragments, which fluttered away in the wind.

"I tell you again, Ralph. It is at an end. I shall not take the affair up again. I am too frightened lest it should bring about, once more, other crimes and other punishments. I am not a heroine."

"What are you, then?"

"A woman who loves, Ralph—a woman who loves and who has remade her life—remade it for love and nothing but love."

"Lady with the green eyes," he said. "It's a very serious thing to take a pledge like that!"

"Serious for me, but not for you. Be sure that if I offer you my life, I want no more of yours than you can give me. You will maintain around you this mystery which pleases you. You will never have to defend it against me. I take you just as you are; and you are the noblest and most fascinating thing I have ever met. I only ask one thing of you—to love me as long as you can."

"For ever, Aurelie."

"No, Ralph: you are not the man to love for ever, nor even, alas! for very long. But however short a time it lasts, I shall have known such happiness that I shall have no right to complain. And I shall not complain. Till this evening. Come to the Theater Royal, you will find a box waiting for you there."

They parted.

That evening Ralph went to the Theater Royal. They were playing "La Vie de Bohême" with a young singer newly engaged in the part of *Mimi*, Lucie Gautier.

Lucie Gautier was Aurelie.

Ralph understood. The independent life of an artist allows one to disregard certain conventions. Aurelie was free.

When the play came to an end—amid what ovation! He made his way to the dressing-room of the triumphant girl. The pretty fair head bent towards him. Their lips met.

So ended the strange and dreadful affair of Juvains, which, for fifteen years, was the cause of so many crimes and such anguish. Ralph endeavored to snatch the small confederate of Jodot from his evil ways. He handed him over to the care of the widow Ancivel. But William's mother, whom he had informed of the manner of her son's death, took to drink. The child, corrupted too early, could not rise from the depths. They were obliged to shut him up in a reformatory. He escaped from it, found the widow, and both of them went to the United States.

As for Marescal, having learned his lesson, but still obsessed with his lady-killing ideas, he rose in rank. One day he asked for an interview with M. Lenormand, the famous head of the detective police. At the end of the interview M. Lenormand came a little nearer to his inferior, and said to him, with a cigarette in his mouth: "Could you oblige me with a light?" and that in a tone which made Marescal tremble. He had instantly recognized Lupin.

He recognized him again under other disguises, always mocking and with a winking eye. And every time he received point blank that terrible, bitter, biting, unexpected little sentence and so funny by reason of the effect it produced on him.

"Could you oblige me with a light?"

Ralph bought the estate of Juvains. But out of deference to the girl with the green eyes, he would not divulge the marvelous secret. The lake of Juvains and the Fountain of Jouvence may be reckoned among the number of the accumulated marvels and fabulous treasures that France will inherit from Arsène Lupin.